THE SEA RUNNERS

ALSO BY IVAN DOIG

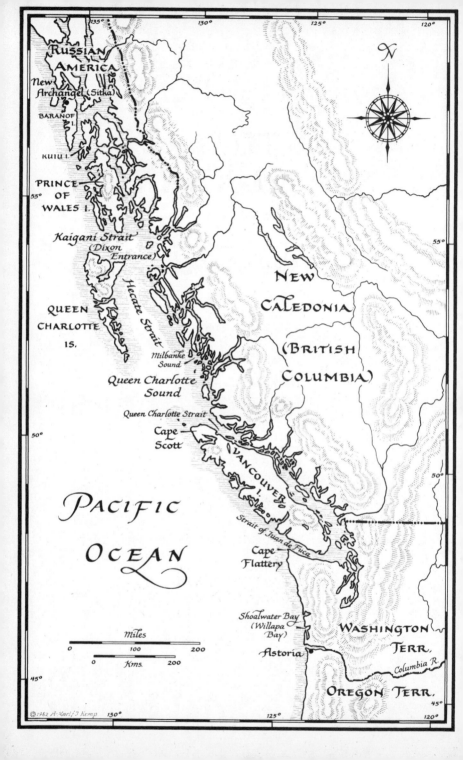

THE
SEA RUNNERS

Ivan Doig

A HARVEST BOOK
HARCOURT, INC.
Orlando Austin New York
San Diego Toronto London

Requests for permission to make copies of any part of
the work should be mailed to the following address:
Permissions Department, Harcourt, Inc.,
6277 Sea Harbor Drive, Orlando, Florida 32887-6777.

www.HarcourtBooks.com

First published by Atheneum in 1982

Library of Congress Cataloging-in-Publication Data
Doig, Ivan
The sea runners/Ivan Doig.—1st Harvest ed.
p. cm.
"A Harvest book."
1. Indentured servants—Fiction. 2. Escapes—Fiction.
3. Alaska—Fiction. I. Title.
PS3554.O415S4 2006
813'.54—dc22 2005037024
ISBN-13: 978-0-15-603102-8 ISBN-10: 0-15-603102-7

Printed in the United States of America

First Harvest edition 2006
DOC 10 9 8 7

The old ocean at the land's foot, the vast
Gray extension beyond the long white violence . .
And the gray air haunted with hawks:
This place is the noblest thing I have ever seen.
Robinson Jeffers, *The Place for No Story*

THE SEA RUNNERS

A HIGH-NOSED cedar canoe, nimble as a sea-bird, atop a tumbling white ridge of ocean.

Carried nearer and nearer by the water's determined sweep, the craft sleds across the curling crest of wave and begins to glide the surf toward the dark frame of this scene, a shore of black spruce forest. On a modern chart of the long, crumbled coastline south from the Gulf of Alaska toward the Strait of Juan de Fuca this particular landfall is written in as Arisankhana Island. None of the four voyagers bobbing to its shore here in a winter dusk of the year 1853, however, knows anything of this name, nor would it matter to their prospect if any did.

Now the canoemen as they alight. Karlsson and Melander and Wennberg and Braaf. More days than they wish to count they have been together in the slender canoe, dodging from one of this coast's constant humps of forest-and-rock to the next. Each man of them afraid a number of times in these days; brave almost as often. Here at Arisankhana they land wetly, heft their slim but laden craft across the gravel beach into hiding within the salal and salmonberry.

"Hope to Christ"—the broad man, Wennberg, this —"this's drier than last night's."

"Oh, aye, and God send you wine and figs too, Wennberg?"

"Ought've left him, Melander." The one named Braaf, here. "Ought've left him cooped in New Archangel."

The slender one of them, called Karlsson, stays silent.

They turn away to the abrupt timber. As the trees sieve them from sight, another white wave replaces the rolling hill of water by which the four were borne to this shore where they are selecting their night's shelter, and where one of them is to die.

Their escape from New Archangel was of Melander's making. In any day's comings and goings at that far-north assemblage of hewn logs and Russian tenacity, Melander you would have spied early. Toplofty

man with lanks of arms and high hips, so that he
seemed to be all long sections and hinges. His line of
jaw ran on as well, and so too his forehead; in the extent of Melander only the bright blue eyes and stub
nose and short mouth neighbored closely, a sudden
alert center of face amid the jaw-and-forehead expanse
as if peering in wily surprise out of the hole of a tree
trunk.

"A strong right arm is the lever of life, these Russians say. You'd think by chance the Castle crowd
might once put the lever to something other than hoist-
ing a glass of champagne, aye?" Early on, too, you
would have come to know the jointed talk of the man,
this Melander habit of interrupting himself to affirm
whether he dared go on with so mesmerizing a line of
conversation. All such reluctance to dazzle further notwithstanding, thirty-one times out of thirty Melander
could be counted on for continuation. "But no, lie
around up there like seals they all do, yip-yipping
down at the rest of us. . . . Luck for them that we
were born, else they'd starve to death figuring out right
boot from left foot. . . . To be Russian is to be a
toothache to the world, aye?"

Born on the isle of Gotland and thinking of himself
as a Swede, Melander actually numbered in the land-
less nationality, that of the sea. Beyond memory his
people on Gotland were fisherfolk, generation upon
generation automatically capable with their reaping
nets as if having happened into the world with hands
shaped only for that task. So it came as a startling
flex of independence when Melander, himself begin-

ning to resemble a sizable height of pine spar, went off
from his village of Slite to tall-masted vessels. Aboard
ship he proved rapidly apt, the type of sea roamer of
whom it was appraised that each drop of his blood was
black Stockholm tar and his every hair a rope yarn.
Ten or so years of sailing the Baltic and the North Sea
bettered his position almost voyage by voyage, and then
—"Had I been born with brass on my corners, you'd
one day be calling me Admiral," Melander half-joked
to his deckhands the day he was made first mate.

Just such a billet, second in command of a schooner
bearing twenty fresh seven-year men from Stockholm
in the spring of 1851, was the one that shunted Melander to Alaska. Russian America, that world-topping
wilderness yet was known as, its wholesale purchase by
the United States—and consequent rechristening of
New Archangel to what the coast's natives knew this
vital speck of site as, Sitka—waiting a decade and
a half into the future.

Although he had no farthest thought of new endeavor at the onset of that voyage, a pair of outlooks
swerved Melander into staying on at New Archangel.
The first loomed square ahead—the eleven-month expanse of return voyage in the company of the schooner's
captain, a fidgety little circle-faced Finn who was
veteran in the Baltic trade but had proved to be quite
literally out of his depth on the ocean. The other lay
sidewise to Mister First Mate Melander's scrutiny,
berthed there against a backdrop of Alaskan forest the
spring morning when he reached final exasperation

with his dim captain: The Russian-American Company's steamship, the *Emperor Nicholas I.*

In a time and place earlier, Melander would have been the fellow you wanted to set a spire on a cathedral; in a later, to oversee a fleet of mail planes. But on an April day in 1851 at one of the rim ends of the known world, what sat at hand was this squatty wonder of self-propulsion. This, and a proclaimed shortage of gifted seamen in these northern Pacific waters which the fur-trading Russians historically had navigated, pre-*Nicholas* and pre-Melander, like men lurching across ice.

"If the wind were clever enough," Melander observed to the baffled Finnish skipper upon taking leave of him, "it ought to snuff out these steamsnorters before they get a start, aye?"

Melander maybe under different policy would have gone on to earn his way up the ranks of the Russian-American Company at New Archangel like a lithe boy up a schooner's rigging; become a valued promyshlennik, harvester of pelts, for the tsar's Alaskan enterprise in the manner, say, of occasional young Scotsmen of promise who, along the adjoining fur frontier of northmost North America, were let to fashion themselves into field captains of the Hudson's Bay Company by learning to lead brigades of trappers and traders, keep the native tribes cowed or in collaboration, deliver a reliable profit season upon season to London; and, not incidentally, to hold those far spans of map not only in the name of their corporate employers but for the British crown, which underlay the company's

charter terms like an ornate watermark. Simpson, Mc-
Loughlin, Douglas, Campbell, Rae, others: Caledonians
who whittled system into the wilderness, names known
even yet as this continent's northern roster of men of
enterprise and empire. But maybe is only maybe, and
the facts enough are that on the broad map of mid-
nineteenth-century empires Alaska lies apart from the
Hudson's Bay span of Canadian dominion. ("It was
but natural," the magistrate of America's frontier history, H. H. Bancroft, would aver, "in the gigantic
robbery of half a world, that Russia should have a
share; and had she been quicker about it, the belt might
as well have been continued to Greenland and Ice-
land.") That, indeed, this colossal crude crown of
northwestmost wilderness is tipped sharply, as if in
deliberate spurn, away from London to the direction of
Siberia and St. Petersburg. That within the tsar's
particular system of empire-by-proxy, Swedes and
other outlanders who signed on with the Russian-
American Company's fur-gathering enterprise did so
as indentured laborers, seven-year men. And that the
name Melander thus is not to be discovered anywhere
among the frontier baronage.

For as will happen, Melander after pledging to the
Russian-American Company did find his life altered by
the alluring new nautical machinery, right enough.
But not in the direction hoped. Only seldom the Russians fired up the *Nicholas,* whose boilers proved to re-
quire approximately two days of woodchopping for
each day of voyage—a visiting Hudson's Bay officer
once amended the vessel's name to *Old Nick,* on the

ground that it consumed fuel at the rate you might expect of Hell—and on the occasions when its paddle-wheels were set into ponderous thwacking motion, positions aboard were snatched by bored officers of the small Russian navy contingent stationed at New Archangel. Melander's service aboard the *Nicholas* occurred only whenever the Russian governor, Rosenberg, took his official retinue on an outing to the hot springs at Ozherskoi, an outpost south a dozen miles down Sitka Sound. In Melander's first Alaskan year this happened precisely twice, and his sea-time-under-steam totaled six days.

The rest of his workspan? A Russian overseer conferred assignment on Melander as promptly as the supply schooner vanished over the horizon on the voyage back to Stockholm and Kronstadt. "Friend sailor," the overseer began, "we are going to give you a chance to dry out your bones a bit," and Melander knew that what followed was not going to be good. Because of his ability of handling men and, from time on the Baltic, his tongue's capability with a bit of Russian—and his Gotland knowledge of fish—henceforth Melander was in charge of the crew that salted catches of salmon and herring for New Archangel's winter larder.

Seven-year men. "The Russians' hornless oxen," as Melander more than once grumbled it.

"Deacon Step-and-a-Half is at it again."

Melander peered with interest along the cardplayers and conversationalists in the workmen's barracks to

see where the gibe had flown from. A fresh turn of
tongue was all too rare in New Archangel. Melander
himself had just tried out his latest declaration to no
one in particular: "A seven-year man is a bladeless
knife without a handle." That had attracted him the
anonymous dart, not nearly the first to bounce off his
seaman's hide.

These shipmates—Melander corrected himself: barrackmates—were an everysided lot. Finns and Swedes
under this roof, about all they could count in common were their term of indentureship and the convic-
tion that they were sounder souls than the Russian
work force in the several neighboring dwellings. The
Scandinavians after all had been pulled here. Most of
the Russian laborers simply were shoved; stuffed
aboard ship at Okhotsk on the coast of Siberia and
pitched across the North Pacific to the tsar's Alaskan
fur field. Be it said, these Siberian vagabonds had not
been encouraged onward to Russian America for habits
such as nudging ducks into puddles. Thugs, thieves,
hopeless sots, no few murderers, the flotsam of any vast
frontier, jostled among them. ("Where," an appalled
governor of New Archangel once wrote home to a
grandee of the Russian-American Company, "do you
get such men?") But so did debtors, escaped serfs,
those whose only instinct was to drift. Melander, by
now no admirer of anything Russian, saved his con-
tempt for the New Archangel officialdom. These others,
the Okhotskans, simply had made humankind's usual
blunder, forgot to get themselves highborn.

As for this crew in evening dawdle all around him,

they nested here idle as— Abruptly Melander stood up, a process like staves suddenly framing themselves together into a very large scarecrow. Amid a card game several bunks away a shipwright from Karlskrona flicked a nervous glimpse his way.

Grinning at so easy a giveaway, Melander awarded a mocking nod to his derider and in galumphing strides went from the barracks. Outside held another sort of confinement, but at least airier than in. Melander as ever glanced up, the way he might have checked a top-gallant sail, at the peak that thrust over all their lives at New Archangel, ungainly Verstovia. Its summit a triangle of rough rock atop a vaster triangle of forested slope, Verstovia presided up there broad and becrowned, the first presence each morning, the last at every dusk. And farther, snowier crags attended Verstovia on both sides. A threefold Jericho, this place New Archangel, walled first by the stockade, next by these tremendous mountains, and last, the distances to anywhere else of the world.

Odd, the deceit of distance. How it was that men would brave the miles to a new place, the very total of those miles seeming to promise a higher life than the old, and then find the work dull, the wage never quite totting up to what it should, the food worse than ever— the longing to be elsewhere now pivoted straight around. Yes, that was the way for a seven-year man, distance played these tricks as if a spyglass had spun end-for-end in his hands.

Melander moved off toward the central street of the settlement and encountered one of the company clerks, no doubt on his way to the governor's hill garden. Many of the Castle Russians strolled such a constitutional at evening, any custom of home being paced through more devoutly here than in Muscovy itself. Melander considered that the man was wasting footsteps. More than beds of pansies and fuchsias were required to sweeten the soul of any Russian. Nonetheless—

"Drostia," the lanky Swede offered with a civil nod and was greeted in turn. Perhaps a Melander could not rise at New Archangel, but at least he could invest some care to stay level.

This was one of the lengthening evenings of summer of 1852, the moment of year when darkness seemed not to care to come and New Archangel's dusk took advantage to dawdle on and on. Before the season turned, eventide would stretch until close onto midnight. The long light copied Swedish summer. Which meant that while this slow vesper of the Alaskan day was the time Melander liked best, it also cast all the remindful shadows of what he had become absented from. His birthland. The sea. And his chosen livelihood. Triple tines of exile. Much to be prodded by.

Only because the route afforded the most distance for his restless boots, Melander roved on west through the narrow shoreline crescent of settlement. Past log building after log building, bakery, joinery, warehouses, officers' quarters, smithy; if bulk of timbering were the standard of civilization, New Archangel could have preened grand as Stockholm. Sea drifter he was, Melander had never got used to this hefty clamped-

into-the-wilderness feel of the port town. "Log barns
and sawdust heads," the style of Russian America was
summed by Melander.

In about four hundred paces from his barracks departure Melander's traipse necessarily ended, the high
timbered stockade with its closed sally port here stop-
pering New Archangel until morning.

Melander still needed motion. And so changed course
to the north. Rapidly passed the gate watchman yawn-
ing within his hut. Climbed the short knoll where the
first of the stockade's blockhouses overlooked the gate.
In long pulls clambered up the ladder to the catwalk
beside the blockhouse. Here met the quizzing glance of
the Russian sentry and muttered: "The damned Finns
are singing in the barracks again. They sound like death
arguing with the devil."

The sentry nodded in pitying savvy and returned
to his watching slot within the timbered tower. Melander was left solitary, scanning out beyond Sitka Sound
and its dark-treed islands schooled like furry whales
to the threadline of horizon that is the Pacific.

A time of studying seaward. The ports of all the
planet were out there. Danzig and Copenhagen, Kronstadt, Trondheim, Rotterdam, London . . . Men and
women are hard ore, we do not go to slag in a mere few
seasons of forge: Melander aland was yet Melander,
First Mate.

A raven flapped past, pulled a glance from the tall
man. These black birds ruled the roofs of New Archangel and their metallic comment up there somehow
struck an odd humility into a person.

13

Finally, as if at last reassured that the water portion of the world still hung in place, Melander dropped his gaze. Now was peering directly down at the edge of shore subjacent to the outside end of the stockade.

Here his looking held for a good while.

Eventually, the tall man murmured something. Something so softly said that the sentry nearby in the blockhouse mistook the sound for another mutter against twittering Finns.

It was not that, though. This:

"Maybe not bladeless."

Do such things have a single first moment? If so, just here Melander begins to depart from a further half-dozen years of the salting of fish.

"Take our swig outside the stockade, whyn't we? The farther you can ever get from these Russians, the better anything tastes. Aye?"

Tin mugs of tea in hand, Melander and Karlsson passed the sentry at the opened gateway of the stockade and sauntered to the edge of the native village which extended in a single-file march of dwellings far along the shoreline. In front of the two Swedes now stretched Japonski, biggest of the islands schooled thick in Sitka Sound. The channel across to Japonski was just four hundred yards or so, but one of the quirks of New Archangel's spot in the world was that this moatlike side of water somehow emphasized isolation more than the open spans of the bay.

This Karlsson was a part-time bear milker. That is

to say, ordinarily he worked as an axman in the timber-felling crew, but also had sufficiently skilled himself as a woodsman that he was sent with the hunting party which occasionally forayed out to help provision New Archangel—to milk the bears, as it was jested. The sort with nothing much he cared to put to voice and of whom even less was remarked, Karlsson. It is told that at a Scandinavian free-for-all, Danes will be the ones dancing and laughing, Norwegians endeavoring to start a fight, Finns passing bottles, and Swedes standing along the wall waiting to be introduced. Melander constituted a towering exception to this slander, but Karlsson, narrow bland face like that of a village parson, would have been there among the wall props.

"They say it'll be rice kasha for noon again. A true Russian feast they're setting us these days, anything you want so long as it's gruel, aye?"

"Seems so," answered Karlsson.

Sociability was nothing that Melander sought out of Karlsson. A time, he had noticed Karlsson canoeing in across Sitka Sound here, back from a day's hunting. Karlsson's thrifty strokes went beyond steady. Tireless, in a neat-handed, workaday fashion. The regularity of a small millwheel, Melander had been put in mind of as he watched Karlsson paddle.

What brought down Melander's decision in favor of Karlsson, however, was a feather of instant remembered from shipboard. Karlsson had been borne to Alaska on the same schooner as Melander, and Melander recalled that just before sailing when others of the indentured group, the torsion of their journey-to-come tremendous in them at the moment, were talking large of the bright success ahead, what adventure the frontier life would furnish and how swiftly and with what staggering profit their seven years of contract with the Russians would pass, Karlsson had listened, given a small mirthless smile and a single shake of his head, and moved off along the deck by himself. Whatever directed Karlsson to Alaska, it had not been a false northern sun over his future.

"I don't see why that water doesn't pucker them blue. They must have skins like seals with the hair off."

As Melander and Karlsson stood and sipped, a dozen natives had emerged from one of the nearest longhouses, men and women together and all naked, and waded casually into the channel to bathe.

Karlsson's reply this time was a shrug.

One further impression of the slender man's interesting constancy also was stored away in Melander. The observation that Karlsson visited more often to the women in the native village than did any of the merchants of wind who perpetually bragged in the barracks about their lust. Or as Melander mused it to himself, the mermaids had hold of Karlsson's towrope but he didn't go around yipping the news.

Melander swept the bay and channel east to west with an arm, as if in salute to the day. He purposely had chosen this rainless morning of late June, gentle gray-silver overcast cupping the day's light to lend clarity down to the spruce islands of the harbor and the sudden spearing mountains behind the settlement, the usual morning wind off the bay lazed to a breeze, to approach Karlsson before work call. His thought was that if Karlsson would entertain escape on this most silken of New Archangel days, he truly was ready.

Melander's words, however, began where his motion ended. "Those canoes are longer than they look, aye?" In a row on the beach the natives' cedar shells lay; the line of lithe craft, like sea creatures dozing side by side on the sand, which his gaze had been drawn to when he stood atop the stockade. "We could step into one here and step out at Stockholm."

Karlsson's face, all at once not nearly so bland, suggested the standard skepticism toward talk of un-cooping oneself from New Archangel. Because of the isolation so far into the North Pacific and because muskeg and sinkholes and an alpine forest so thick it seemed to be thatched began just beyond the stockade wall, the matter of escape always narrowed instantly to the same worn point. Where, except up to the sweet blue meadows of heaven, was there to go?

"The world has a lot of wheres," vouched Melander now. "We need just four of them."

He drained his mug in a final gulp, folded himself down to rest one knee on the dirt, and with a stick began to trace.

A first south-pointing stab of shoreline, like a broad knife blade. "This one, we've got"—Baranof Island, on the oceanward side of which they squatted now.

A speckle of isles, then another large landform, south-pointing too, like the sheath Baranof had been pulled from. "The Queen Charlottes."

Another brief broken isle-chain of coast, then a long blunt slant, almost sideways to the other coastal chunks. "Vancouver's Island."

At last, fourth and biggest solidity in this geographical flagstone of Melander's, the American coastline descending to the Columbia River. The place where the dirt lines of coast and the river met, Melander Xed large. "Astoria," Melander said this mark was.

Map lesson done, Melander recited to the close-tongued Karlsson the main frame of his plan. That if they selected their time well and escaped by night they could work a canoe south along the coast. That there at its southern extent, down beyond the Russian territory and that of the Hudson's Bay Company, the place called Astoria was operated by the Americans as an entry port. From there ships would come and go, ships to the docks of Europe. To, at last, Stockholm.

Six weeks' canoe journey, Melander estimated, to Astoria. If they caught luck, could manage to sail part of the voyage, a month.

"You talk us in royal style from here to there, Melander. But this God-forgotten coast, in a canoe . . ."

Karlsson fell silent again, looking off around the island-speckled bay and up into the timbered mountains. Verstovia's skirt forest showed every branch distinct today, almost every bristle; vast green lacework, it seemed.

Melander knew he was going to have a wait. There always was about this Karlsson a calm just short of chill. He was a Smålander, and that ilk were known to have in them whatever stone God had left over after He filled their fields with it. "One word, good as two"— this was the anthem of Smålanders. Right now the lean man was appraising the horizon of Alaska as if someone had offered him the whole tumbled country for forty riksdaler.

Then again, Melander noticed Karlsson's glance come back twice and linger in the vicinity of the bathing native women.

On such a New Archangel day sound carried like light, and from the blacksmith shop within the stockade began to chorus the measured clamor of hammer against anvil.

As if roused by the clangor, Karlsson turned to the taller man.

"Two of us are not enough strength for that much paddling."

"No," Melander agreed. "Our other man is Braaf."

"Braaf? That puppy?"

Melander tendered his new coconspirator a serious smile in replica of Karlsson's own aboard the schooner in Stockholm harbor.

"We need a thief," Melander explained.

That is the way they became two. Disquieted shipman, musing woodsman, now plotters both. Against them, and not yet knowing it, although habitually guardful as governing apparatuses have to be, stood New Archangel and its system of life. The system of all empires, when the matter comes to be pondered. For empires exist on the principle of constellations in the night sky—pattern imposed across unimaginable expanse—and the New Archangels of the planet at the time, whether named Singapore or Santa Fe or Dakar or Astoria or Luanda or Sydney, were their specific scintillations of outline. Far pinspots representing vastly more than they themselves were.

That voyage which deposited Melander and Karlsson into their indentured situation illustrates that here in the middle of the nineteenth century, this work of putting out the lines of star web across the planet had to be done with the slow white wakes of sailing ships. But done it was. Sea-lanes were extended and along them the imperial energies resolutely pulsed back and forth, capital to colony and colony to capital. Africa, Asia: the lines of route from Europe were converging and tensing one another into place for decades to come. North America: the gray-gowned wee queen of England reigned over Ojibwas and Athapaskans and Bella Coolas, the United States was taking unto itself the western vastness between the Mississippi and the Pacific, the tsar's merchants of Irkutsk and St. Petersburg were being provided fortunes by bales of Alaskan furs.

Such maritime tracework seemed, in short, to be succeeding astoundingly. Yet . . . yet all this atlas of order rested on the fact that it requires acceptance, a faith of seeing and saying, "Ah yes, here is our Great Dipper, hung onto its nail in heaven," to make constellations real. So that what the makers of any imperial

configuration always needed be most wary of was minds
—such as Melander's, such as Karlsson's, such as the
one Melander was calculating upon next to ally with
their two—which happened not to be of stellar allegiance.

Braaf would have given fingers from either hand to
be gone from New Archangel. He had after all the
thief's outlook that in this many-cornered world of
opportunity, an occasion would surely arrive when
he could pilfer them back.

Put it simply, stealing was in Braaf like blood and
breath. He was a Stockholm street boy, son of a water-
front prostitute and the captain of a Baltic fishing
ketch, and on his own in life by the age of seven. Alaska
he had veered to because after a steady growth of
talent from beggary to picking pockets to thievery the
other destination imminently beckoning to him was
fängelse: prison.

So Braaf turned up as another in the 1851 contingent to New Archangel, and at once skinning knives
and snuffboxes and twists of Circassian tobacco and
other unattached items began to vanish from the settlement as if having sprung wings in the night. The Russians vented fury on the harborfront natives for the
outbreak of vanishment, but the coterie of Swedes and
Finns rapidly made a different guess, the new young
Stockholmer among them having set up shop as a kind
of human commissary in the barracks. Because Braaf
stayed reasonable in his prices—interested less in re-

muneration than in chipping the monotony of Alaskan life, which he found to be a rain-walled prison in its own right—and was diplomatic enough not to forage from his own barrackmates, nothing was said against him.

How hard it would have been anyway to lodge a believable case against Braaf. At twenty, he displayed the round ruddy face of a farmboy—an apple of a face—and in talking with you lofted his gaze with innocent interest just above your eyes, as if considerately measuring you for a hat.

The morning after tea was taken outside the stockade of New Archangel by a pair of Swedes, it was taken by a trio.

"Me?" Braaf murmured when Melander loomed alongside him and Karlsson appeared at his opposite shoulder. "No, I was just about to . . . Sorry, I've to . . . Maybe the noon break, I'll . . ."

In his quiet manner Karlsson suggested Braaf had better shove a bung in his spout and hear out Melander's proposition.

"You put it that way," Braaf revised, "and my ears are yours."

On the slope of shore above the canoes, Braaf studied back and forth from Melander's forehead to Karlsson's as Melander once more outlined the plan.

"Austria, I've heard of that. But is it anywhere around here?"

"Astoria," Melander repeated with patience. "It's

the port for a part of this coast the Americans call Oregon."

"Imagine," said Braaf politely through a slurp of tea.

"Braaf, we need your skill of, umm, acquiring. It'll take supplies and supplies for such a journey."

"Why should I?"

"Because you're stuck here like a stump if you don't."

"That's a reason, I suppose. Why won't we drown?"

"God's bones, Braaf, these Kolosh canoes float like waterbugs. You'd need be an oaf to tip one over."

"I've been in company with an oaf or two in my time."

"Braaf, listen," Karlsson broke in. "I go in these canoes all the time, and I am undrowned."

"For all I know you have gills in the cheeks of your ass, too."

"Braaf," Melander resumed as if reciting to a limited child. "You have a choice here which comes rare in life. Join us and leave this Russian shitpile, or stay and be caught one day lifting one snuffbox too many. You've seen what these Russians can do with a knout. That sergeant of the sentries will sign his name up and down your back. Aye?"

"Pretty choice you paint. Rock and stony place."

"What else is the world? Step in with us, Braaf. It'll take your fast fingers to get us from here. But we can get."

"My fingers should ever see the day they're fast as your tongue, Melander."

"Thank you, but we can race another time. With us, are you, or not?"

"You know for heaven-certain that we'll find this American fort at—what's it, Astruria?"

"Astoria. It is there. I have known sailors whose ships have called there. Could be we'll not even need to go that far, maybe meet a merchantman or trading ship or whaler along the way. English, Spanish, Americans, or the devil, won't matter which. So long as they're not Russians. Aye?"

"And the downcoast natives? Koloshes and whatever-the-hell-else they might be?"

"I already said the devil."

Only for an instant now, about the duration of a held breath, did Braaf's eyes come steady with those of Melander and Karlsson. Just before he nodded agreement to join the escape. And that is how they became three.

In the galaxy of frontier enclaves sparked into creation by colonialism, New Archangel was a map dot unlike any other. Simultaneously a far-north backwater port and capital of a territory greater than France and Spain and England and Ireland taken together, the settlement ran on Russian capacities for hard labor and doggedness, and was kept from running any better than it did by Russian penchants for muddle and infighting. New Archangel here fifty years after its founding still stood forth in the image of its progenitor, the stumpy and tenacious Aleksandr Andreevich Baranov.

Of Baranov historians exclaim that, like Napoleon, he was a little great man, for Baranov it was who as first governor of Russian America began in 1791 to stretch Russian strength from the Aleutian chain of isles down the great arc of Alaska's coast, bending or breaking the native cultures along the route one after another: Aleuts chastened into becoming the Russians' seasonal hunters of fur seals and sea otters, people of the Kenai cajoled into allegiance by Baranov's mating with the daughter of a foremost chief, stubbornly combative Tlingits—whom the Russians dubbed Koloshes—at last in 1804 dislodged from Sitka Sound by the cannonades of one of the tsar's gunships.

Baranov had true need of Sitka. Along virtually all of that stupendous southeast Alaskan coast the mountains drop sheer to the Pacific, spruce slopes like green avalanches into the seawater. Except at Sitka, where miles of harbor indent the archipelagic shoreline; an inlet "infinitely sinuous," said an early observer. Sitka, where the deep notch of bay is sided by a handy shelf of shore. Sitka, where in further grudging bequest of topography, at the shelf's southmost hook a knoll of rock some forty feet in elevation and four times as broad pokes up. Amid the coastline of shoulder to shoulder mountains this single odd stone callus was the strategic bayside point: the Koloshes employed the mound as their stronghold and Baranov would lose no time in perching his own thick-logged bastion there. The Russian-American Company's frontier Gibraltar, perhaps say. So turn the issue this way, that, and the other—beyond doubt, Baranov whirled it dizzy—Sitka

Sound represented the maritime ringhold into which Russian influence could be firmly knotted.

In this summer of 1852, the estimable Aleksandr Andreevich three decades dead, a double-storied governor's house still called Baranov's Castle squatted there in the air at the mound end of New Archangel's single street. At the opposite extent rose the onion dome and carrot spire of the comely little Russian Orthodox cathedral. Betwixt and around, the habitations of New Archangel amounted to two hundred or so squared-log buildings, many painted an aspiring yellow as though tint and nearby shore qualified them as seaside cottages. But their rooflines were hipped, the heavy style slanting down in all four directions from the ridgepole; and where gables were fashioned in, they were windowed with small spoked semicircles of glass, like half-suns which never managed either to set or to rise. A burly low-slung squinting town, New Archangel for all its best efforts was, beneath the lording styles of cathedral and Castle.

One aspect further, and this the true civic eccentricity. As large a fleet of ships lay permanently aland in this port of Russian America as was customarily to be found in its harbor. Make-do was the architect here. When they no longer could be safely sailed, hulks were winched out of Sitka Sound onto shore and then improvised upon as needed. ("The tsar's unsinkable squadron" of course is Melander's gibe.) Of the first two, beached into usefulness in Baranov's time, one hulk had been used as a church and the other as a gun battery—a pairing, canon and cannon, which may have caused the Koloshes to ponder a bit about their new landlords. This habit of collecting hull corpses ever since lent New Archangel, as one visitor summed it, "an original, foreign, and fossilized kind of appearance."

The morning after Braaf joined the escape plan, Karlsson emerged from around a corner of the cathedral, on his way from the Scandinavian workmen's barracks a short span to its north, and began to walk the brief dirt street between God's domain and the governor's. So deft with an ax that he often was sent to help with the shaping of a sail timber, Karlsson was delegated to work this day with the shipwrighting crew.

He very nearly could have arrowed to the shipyard with his eyes bound over, merely following the delicious waft of yellow cedar. Yet before reaching the 'wrighting store of timbers the far side of Baranov's Castle, Karlsson veered west toward the stockade gate and the Kolosh village beyond.

Stepped outside and along the wall toward the beach.

Hunkered and began to scour the blade of his ax in the pale sand. Polishing away rust, this conscientious timberwright.

And second work too, for as he squatted, Karlsson from the corner of his eye studied the Kolosh canoes, prows rising in extension like the necks of fantastic horses, in their graceful rank along the beach.

All of New Archangel, stockade and cathedral and Castle and hulks and enterprises and dwellings, sat dwarfed this day by the Alaskan mountains, Verstovia and its throng of minions. Virtually atop the town in the manner that the spire and dome crowned the cathedral, the peaks were those a child would draw. Sharp tall pyramids of forest, occasionally a lesser summit rounded as a cannonball for comparison's sake. Top-knots of snow showed here and there, but the color everywhere else on these stretching peaks was the black-green that only a northern coastal forest enmixes. A kind of colossal constancy breathes at you from form and tone of this sort, the surety that beyond such mountains, wherever you could peer there would stand only more such mountains. Except, of course, west into the ocean, where there was only more ocean.

As Karlsson set at his shipyard hewing, Braaf materialized at the western extent of the settlement, beside the eldermost of two schooner hulks beached there.

When Braaf arrived to New Archangel and it became evident that he was not, as listed on one manifest, a shipwright, nor, as supposed on another item of record, a shoemaker, and Braaf with shy innocence denied knowing how such misunderstandings possibly could have come about, a perplexed Russian-American Company clerk assigned him to the readiest unskilled job, as a cook's helper. Daily Braaf managed to use this livelihood to manufacture free time for himself, much of it spent hiding out somewhere within this maritime carcass. The hulk neighboring it yet was in service as a cannon battery aimed into the Kolosh village, but dry rot had made a casualty of this vessel of Braaf's.

After a moment of endeavor at the doorlock with a small hook of metal, he slipped through the gangway carpentered into the ship's hull when it became a storehouse and crept to the forecastle. Within a particular one of the several stave-sprung barrels there he made a deposit, a walrus ivory snuffbox which hitherto was the possession of a Russian quartermaster.

Then, per Melander's instructions, Braaf began to measure by handwidths the depth and breadth—which is to say, the cache capacity—of other of these abandoned and forgotten receptacles.

Perpetually at combat with the massed mountains around Sitka Sound was the weather, darkening even now, for New Archangel lived two days of three in rain and oftener than that in cloud. "Always autumn," it was said of this diluted climate. One minute, vapor would flow along the bottoms of the mountains to float all the peaks like dark icebergs. The next, the cloud layer would rise and immerse every crag, leaving a broad, broad plateau of forest beneath. Or imprint of stranger sort, clumps of wan light, warmths fallen through chinks in the overcast, now would pinto the forest flanks. Between times a silken rain probably had sifted into the New Archangel air, a dew standing in droplets on clothing before anyone quite became aware of it, and it could be a hundred hours before a man cast his next shadow. Yet the diminutive port within all this swirl was a place of queer clarity as well, its rinsed air somehow holding a tint of blue light which caused everything to stand forth: smallest swags of spruce limbs on mountains a mile off, rock skirts of the timbered islands throughout the harbor, the gold-and-russet trim of seaweed along those stone hems. Voices and the barking of dogs carried extraordinarily.

At midmorning, Braaf reluctantly emerging toward chores for the noon meal, Melander on workbreak presented himself from within the saltery being constructed on the point of shoreline southeast of the cathedral. Sitka Sound shares amply in the wide tides of this region of Alaska, and on the broad exposed tideflat a pig was rooting up clams. His finds, one after another, were snatched from him by crows.

Melander watched for a moment, then laughed.

Other workmen inquired to him over their mugs of tea.

Melander pointed to the raucous gulping birds: "The Castle Russians at one of their banquets."

In complication and unlikelihood, New Archangel's tenantry was fully equal to its architecture and geography and weather. The settlement was ruled by the Russian navy, the governor an officer agreed upon by the Russian-American Company; was administered by a covey of company clerks and other functionaries; seasonally abounded with Aleut fur hunters; relied for most of its muscle work upon creoles—those born of Russian fathers and Kolosh mothers; of New Archangel's sum of about a thousand persons, this added up to far the most sizable group—or upon Russian vagabonds given the push out of Okhotsk; and for its craftwork, such as carpentry and smithing, it imported the seven-year men from Scandinavia. Colony within a colony, the hundred and fifty or so Scandinavians mostly were Finns; one sift more, and the few dozen Swedes such as Melander and Braaf and Karlsson were at last accounted.

Yet not even this social pyramid, sharp-tipped and broad-bottomed as the triangle peaks above the little port, indicated the most numerous populace on Sitka Sound. The Koloshes, the Sitka Tlingits. By their own legend People of the Frog, a restless and vivid clan who had migrated to Sitka Sound with their great-eyed carved emblem in tow behind their canoe fleet. Now their low-roofed longhouses straggled for nearly a mile along the beach west of New Archangel's huddle of buildings; and the stockade wall of defense, strategic batteries of cannon, four blockhouses built of fat logs, and a couple of dozen full-time sentries constantly expressed the colony's wariness of the natives. With cause. This very year of 1852 the Sitka Tlingits had sent word to a Stikine clan that at last a perpetual quarrel might be called quit. When the Stikine peace delegation arrived, thirty-five of them were slain quick as a butchering, the few others managed to beg sanctuary within New Archangel. Long memories on these Sitka Tlingits, then. Of amplitude to recall that when Baranov implanted his first settlement here at their bay, they obliterated it and put the Russian heads up on stakes.

Precisely this prudence toward the Koloshes, the way New Archangel each and every day needed to set its most vigilant face toward those who might scheme to get in, it would take someone of Melander's angle of mind to count on as advantage for getting out.

Steam whiffed around Karlsson as he stepped into the workmen's bathhouse. Every seventh day the vat of water was heated to boil, bucketsful then sluiced onto the hot stones ringing the vat. By this far in the night, man after man of the New Archangel work force having sought to scour weariness from his muscles, the steam densened to one great cube of saturation.

Karlsson stood within the heavy warmth for a moment, slender and very white in his nakedness, before bringing the small woven reed breathing mask to his mouth and holding it there within his cupped right hand.

"At least this cloud is a hot one. We could use a few such outside, aye?"

Melander's voice, deeper for being muffled, resounded from across the room, and in three steps Karlsson could see the hazed man, his body alone in long-boned angles on the bathing bench. Melander's reed respirator mask all but disappeared in the big hand palmed around it, so that he seemed to be covering a perpetual chuckle.

"Are you tasting it yet?" Melander went on. "Our venture, I mean? I find myself thinking of salt air. Ocean air. Better than sniffing fish guts, I can tell you."

"Where's our pickpurse?"

"He will come. The hours of Braaf's day are not like any other man's."

"How far do you trust him?"

"Ordinarily, only a whisker's width." Melander had known Braaf's clan all too well on shipboard, men with the instinct always to vanish just before a topsail needed clewing up. "He'd steal the milk out of your tea, aye? But Braaf wants to shake New Archangel from his boots as badly as we do. He'll do much to manage that. Much that neither of us can do, just as he can't canoe himself down this coast. The three of us are like a shock of rye when your Småland fields are harvested, Karlsson. Together we lean in support of one another. Take any one away and we fall."

"And are trampled by the Russians."

"Aye, well." Melander swabbed sweat from himself with a spruce whisk. "The answer to that is not to fall, nor let each other fall."

"I need to know one matter about you, Melander. Why didn't you stay on with the schooner?"

"Yes, I can see that might be a matter to know. Promise me not to laugh. But I stayed . . . I stayed, I suppose, for a pretty sight. Pretty face, it'd been, you might understand better. But it was this. What took my eyes was the *Nicholas*, these islands and mountains and the Northern ocean. I saw myself on that steam whale, going places of the world here I could never have dreamed of. Up into the high north, there. Ice high as a church eave, they tell of along those shores. And creatures. Carpenter of a brig I shipped on, an old man-of-war's man, had been high north once on a whaler. Said whales stink like Hell's cess, but walruses were worth the trip to see. I've never forgot—'They have noble bones in their teeth,' he said to me. And to sail it all by steam, just this fog around us now. . . . So I looked on the *Nicholas* and saw luck, right enough." Melander's eyes tightened above the reed mask. "What I forgot to look at was the wormy souls of these Russians, aye?"

"And wasn't that a fall, of a sort?"

"A stumble, my friend, a stumble. The strides we'll take together along this coast will make up for it."

"A stumble, that's nothing," said a third voice. "Unless a noose is around your neck just then."

The steam thinned as the opened doorway brought into view Braaf. With his clothes off, he looked more than ever like an outsized boy rather than a man. Both Melander and Karlsson noticed that Braaf did not even pause to accustom himself to the cumulus of heat before crossing the room to them, nor bother to put the steam-sieving mask to his mouth until he was seated, a little way from the other two.

"Our commissary officer. Welcome, Braaf. Let's have no more thoughts than necessary of nooses and the like, though." Now that all three of them were at hand, Melander was, for him, singularly businesslike. "What we need to talk through is our divvy of tasks. Braaf, we're going to want—" and here Melander recited in crisp fashion which would have done honor to a king's remembrancer the list of supplies for the escape. "Any of this you can't put your fingers to?"

Braaf contemplated the steam overhead.

"No. Some harder, some easier. But no."

"Good. Tomorrow, begin your harvest."

"A thing more, Melander." Karlsson, afresh. "How is it we're to get ourselves and all this plunder out of the stockade, when time comes?"

"Oh, aye, did I not tell you? Through the gate."

"Through the . . . ?"

"Well that you asked"—Melander's voice clarifying as he took aside the reed mouth mask to display a growing grin—"for you're the one with the lever to work that gate open for us." Melander instructed Karlsson with monumental joviality now. "It's there between your legs."

In New Archangel's next days, a gleaner drifted about within its walls like a cloudlet of steam freed from the bathhouse. So adept a provisioner did Braaf prove to be that, lest the Russians become suspicious about the fresh blizzard of thievery, Melander had to ration out his stealing assignments.

By the end of July, Braaf's cache for the plotters held a compass, two tins of gunpowder, one of the three-pound boxes of tea the Russians used for trade with the natives, some fishing lines and hooks, a blanket apiece, and a coil of rope.

During August he added a gaff hook, three excellent Kolosh daggers, a number of candles, a couple of hatchets, a fire steel and flint apiece, another blanket each, and a leather map case waterproofed with birch tar.

September's gleanings comprised a second compass —double certain about navigation, Melander wanted to be—a small three-legged iron ketle, a spyglass, another box of tea, and a water cask.

Early in October, New Archangel's month of curtaining rain, the plotters convened about the matter of a canoe.

The Koloshes had them in plenty, the slim vessels lying side by side in front of the longhouses as if drawn up to the starting line of a great regatta, canoes for hunting and canoes to carry trade and canoes for fishing and canoes for families and canoes for war, a navy of all canoes.

Karlsson had eyed out a choice—a twenty-foot shell with a high bold bow, the sheer of its hull rising and sharpening into this cutwater as a scimitar curves in search of its point. High and pointy the stern, too, as though both the ends of this canoe were on sentry against the sea. Gunwales rounded and deftly lipped. Four strong thwarts. And encupping it all, that most beautiful stunt of wood, a great cedar taken down with reverence and wile—*I shall cut you down, tree. You will not twist and warp, tree. You will not have knotholes, tree. Black bear skins have been laid in the place where you will fall, tree. Fall down on them, tree* —and then hollowed and shaped and stretched by heated water into a sleek pouch of vessel, its wooden skin not much more than the thickness of a thumb: exaltation of design and thrift of line, the jugglery of art somehow perfected by this coast's canoewrights. Karlsson's tongue was not the one to say it, but if the standing cedar tree had decided to transform into the swiftest of sea creatures, this craft of alert grace would have been the result.

Too, Karlsson's candidate lay amid the beached squadron of a dozen nearest the stockade gate, convenient enough, and Karlsson attested that he had watched to ensure that its possessor was scrupulous. On New Archangel's rare warm days the native sloshed water over the cedar interior to prevent its drying out and cracking; in normal damp weather, heaped woven mats over the craft for shelter.

A canoe of fit and style and fettle, endorsed Karlsson.

Melander and Braaf took turns at casual glances down the shoreline to Karlsson's nominee.

True, the canoe had so sprightly a look that it seemed only to be awaiting the right word of magic before flying off upward. By any man's standards, a most beckoning tool, keen blade for clearance of a route of water. But Melander believed he too knew something of canoes from having paddled a number of times with Kolosh crews to the herring grounds off the western shorefront of Sitka Sound; indeed, it can be realized now that those journeys were first filaments in the spinning of his decision that seven-yeardom could be fled by water. The fishing canoes were half again the length of this keen-beaked version singled out by Karlsson, and this question of size balked Melander.

Asked his opinion, Braaf mumbled that any canoe was smaller than he desired.

Karlsson maintained that his nominee had all the capacity they needed. What did Melander have in mind, to stuff the craft like a sausage?

Melander could not resist asking Karlsson if he was arguing that his wondrous canoe was bigger on the inside than on the out.

No, goddamn Melander's tongue, Karlsson retorted, it simply was a matter of waterworthiness, this canoe would amply carry their cache of supplies and be livelier to steer than a larger canoe and less weight to propel and . . .

Grinning, Melander was persuaded. Rarely did Karlsson trouble to assert himself about anything, so if he waxed passionate for this particular canoe, that was stout enough testimony.

Braaf requested to know what all the jibber-jabber at the front and back of the canoe was.

Bow and stern, Melander rapidly advised him before Karlsson got touched off again, and the canoe's painted designs, oval outlines with black oval centers to them, like egg-shaped eyes, likely were Kolosh symbols to ward off evil.

Evil whats, demanded Braaf.

Evil minnows that would leap from the sea and piss in Braaf's ear, Melander said in exasperation, how in hell's flaming name was he supposed to know what evil whats the Koloshes were spooked by?

Now: the three of them were of one mind for the canoe, was there any other—

Paddles, Karlsson announced, and insisted they be Haida paddles, a deft leaf-bladed type carved by a tribe somewhere downcoast and occasionally bartered north as far as New Archangel as prized items of trade, and one of them further needed be a long steering paddle of perfect balance.

Hearing this, Braaf frowned.

He had full reason. It took him all of the next week to accumulate a trio of Haida paddles from the natives along the harbor.

"Three?" said Karlsson when they met again. "What if we lose one over the side?"

Braaf cursed in his sweet voice, and went off to start the thief's siege of watching and waiting which would accrue a fourth paddle.

Like the single eye of some great guarding creature, each morning at six the stockade gate near the westmost corner of New Archangel came open, at six each evening it swung resolutely shut.

Only during those hours of day were the Koloshes allowed into the settlement, in scrutinized numbers, and the market area where they were permitted to trade was delineated directly inside the gate, so that they could be rapidly shoved out in event of commotion. Moreover, the first of the four gun-slitted blockhouses buttressing the stockade sat close above the area of market and gate on a shieldlike short slope of rock, miniature of the strong knob uplifting Baranov's Castle. Scan from inside or out, here at New Archangel's portal Russian wariness held its strongest focus.

Except. Except that, bachelor existence on a frontier being what it was, the gate sometimes peeped open in the evenings. Until dusk went into solid night, it was not unknown that a recreative stay might be made among certain bargainable women in the Kolosh village. For those dwelling within New Archangel rather than without, then, the gate's second and unofficial—and by order of the governor, absolute—curfew was full dark.

Karlsson quirked his mouth enough to show skepticism, for him a typhoon of emotion. Melander was one who would have you believe that sideways is always true north. But Karlsson was a vane of stiffer sort. He possessed a close idea of his own capabilities and could gauge himself with some dispassion as to whether he was living up to them. (That he had not much interest in people who lacked either capability or gauge, his stand-off style more than half hinted.) What Melander was proposing in this gate enterprise, Karlsson doubted he could fashion himself to.

"Right fit or not," Melander assured him, "you're the only fit."

And so Karlsson began to increase his frequency of visit to the native village, and by lingering on after the other visitants, to stretch each stay deeper into dusk. Eventually he was nudging regularly against the second curfew, much to the discomfiture of the night watchman at the gate of the stockade, Bilibin.

Bilibin was one of the longest-serving of the Russian indenturees who had been funneled out through the Siberian port of Okhotsk and across the northern seas to New Archangel. Peg him, perhaps, somewhere amid the milder miscreants, without doubt having skinned his nose against one law or another but not the most hellbound soul you can call to mind, either. Simply a burden bearer of the sort life always puts double load onto: in this era when it was said, "Better even to go to the army than to Russian America," Bilibin had ended up at New Archangel and shouldering a musket as well.

For purpose here, however, which is that of Karlsson and Braaf and Melander, Bilibin's significant earmark was his longevity at New Archangel. Like many another, he had stayed on and on in the employ of the Russian-American Company because he was in debt to it deep as his eyeteeth. He also was sufficiently a scapegrace to have exasperated a generation of superiors, so that he now stood the least desirable of shifts, the gravy-eye watch, those heavy hours spanning the middle of the night. Turned about, the matter was that Bilibin's superiors over the years had sufficiently knouted and berated him that he took some care not to rush from under his canopy of dark into their attention.

Thus: the first time Karlsson arrived back to the gate past curfew, Bilibin blustered a threat to march him double-quick to the sergeant in charge of the sentries.

"He'll knout you red, Viking. My scars ache to think of those he'll stripe on you, oh yes . . ."

But did nothing. Rousting out a sergeant because a Swede couldn't finish his rutting on time, well, now . . .

The next time, having conferred beforehand with Melander, Karlsson staggered later than ever from the Kolosh village to Bilibin's gate, singing. Reedily, but singing.

> *The fruit of the heart-tree,*
> *do not eat,*
> *for sorrow grows there,*
> *black as peat.*

Also, he carried a jug of the native liquor called hootchina. Which without undue difficulty he persuaded Bilibin to swig a reviveful mouth's worth from: "Have fifteen drops, Pavel, it drives the snakes from one's boots. . . ."

That his gate performances were credited by Bilibin without more than a first squint of suspicion astounded

Karlsson. Was the world so bait-hungry as this? Was he, Karlsson, so deft of deceit? Well, fair must be fair: the fact here was not hunger but thirst, and the hootch deserved at least equal billing with Karlsson. Under the New Archangel allotment of fifty cups of rum per man per year, Bilibin was a man perpetually parched. "The old sirs up there in the Castle," he groused to Karlsson between swigs, "might's well be spooning out dust to us."

By autumn of 1852, Verstovia now in a yellow-orange bodice of deer cabbage, Karlsson was not departing the stockade until nearly dark.

"Come along and dip your ladle in the kettle," the slim Swede would invite.

"No, no, no," Bilibin would splutter back at him, "I'm limber as a goose's neck, no more women for me, you can have mine as well."

And the gate would wink open.

And wink again, far into the night, when Karlsson returned with a proffer of the hootchina jug.

In early November, Melander announced in his procedural way that the time had arrived for Braaf to acquire the coastal maps by which they would navigate south.

"It'll be the Tebenkov maps we want. One Russian who had something other than cabbage between his ears, Tebenkov was. Made his captains chart all of this coastline when he was governor here, and there's a

set aboard each ship. I had a look at the steamship's
while Rosenberg was bathing his bottom at Ozherskoi.
Those we'll take, they won't be missed until spring or
whenever in hell's time the steamship gets fired up
again. Read Russian, can you, Braaf?"

Braaf shook his head.

"No? Well, less matter, we need the ones from latitude 57° as far south as 45°, and you'll see they're
marked like this."

NW bepera Amepuku, Melander printed carefully.
NW coast of America.

The theft would be tricky, Melander cautioned, because Braaf would need to sort rapidly among all the
maps in the steamship's chart room and—Melander
stopped short as Braaf wagged his head again.

"Aye?" Melander demanded. "What is it?"

"I can't read anything," Braaf said.

The single event certain to irk Melander was the
unforeseen, and this incapacity of Braaf's he had not
calculated on at all. Rarest annoyance crossed that
elevated face. Then Melander swerved to Karlsson
and his disposition righted itself.

"So. It seems to fall to you. This'll at least make a
change from galloping a Kolosh maiden, wouldn't you
say? Now: the maps are kept—"

Karlsson was shaking his head in reprise of Braaf.
"I'm being sent hunting. Perhaps for as long as ten
days."

Now Karlsson looked steadily into Melander's eyes
and for once, so did Braaf.

Under the pressure of these gazes Melander grim-

aced. Scowled. Swore. "Jesu Maria. Need to become a
common sneak thief next, do I? The pair of you . . ."

The pair of them met Melander with the same
square glances two weeks later.

"I've done, I've done," the tall man affirmed edgily.
"But a narrow enough matter it was. Christ on the
cross, Braaf, how you go around like a cat's ghost I'll
never know. I needed to sort and sort, paw through
every bedamned scrap of sheet. Skimpy bastards, these
Russians. Should have figured . . ."

Melander opened his mouth as if to go on, but went
into thought instead. After a moment:

"Aye. Anyway, that's that. Let's get on with our
enterprise. We'll need new sail for the canoe, can't
trust the rotten cheesecloth these Koloshes use. You
are able to recognize sail canvas, Braaf, aren't you?"

It happened minutes after the next morning's work
call. Braaf was making away with the sailcloth, the
folded length cradled snug as Moses beneath an armload of hides he ostensibly was transporting toward
the tannery, when a voice suggested huskily into his
left ear: "Shouldn't't've skinned so deep this time, Braaf.
Let's talk about the bottom of your cargo, there."

Through the cold lightning of fright it did register
on Braaf that the voice at least was Swedish rather
than Russian. Leftward, he inched his head the fraction enough to test the wide sideburn-framed face be-

side him. Recognition unfroze his mind . . . *one of
the blacksmiths . . . vain bastard he is . . . Wenn-
strom, Wennblad:* "Wennberg? Wait, listen now——"

"No, don't stroll off and don't put them down." Not
suggestion now: orders. "We'll have a visit till we see
which happens." Wennberg planted himself in front
of Braaf as companionably as if he had every matter
in the memory of the race to talk over with him.
"Whether you spill that load in front of these Russians, or your long-ass friend Melander lopes himself
over here."

With a lanky swiftness which to any onlooker would
seem as if he had been beckoned over to consult with
the pair, Melander arrived. His dark look met Wennberg's blandness like a cloud against a cliff face, but
he spoke nothing. Nor Wennberg. Braaf was desperate
beyond any saying of it. For a moment, there the three
of them clustered, pegs of quiet centered in the long
rectangle of parade ground between Baranov's Castle
and the stockade gate as if time had snagged to a stop
within their little radius, while around them morning
life eddied, quartermasters and overseers and promy-
shlenniks and shipwrights and caulkers and brasswork-
ers and sailors and Castle officers, New Archangel
humanity in all its start-of-day seeps and spurts of
motion.

"So, Melander," Wennberg snapped their silence.
"Braaf and I're just talking over how much heavier
hides've gotten this year. A man can hardly hold a
pood of them in his arms these days, seems like."

"A man can carry as much as the world puts on

him, it's said," Melander responded crisply, still glowering at Wennberg.

"You're always a deep one, Melander. Isn't he, Braaf?" The blacksmith stepped close and pressed his elbow slowly, powerfully, into Braaf's left upper arm, drawing a strangled gasp from the laden man. "Deep as the devil's pocket, isn't he, hmm?"

"Let's give Braaf a rest, shan't we?" Melander offered rapidly. "Matters of weight can always be talked over."

Wennberg hesitated. Cast a glance into the thinning stream of the workshift. Then as if Melander's words were the first coins down on a debt, nodded.

Braaf lurched his way out of sight in the general direction of the tannery. The other two, Melander more toplofty than ever beside the wide-legged Wennberg, strode toward a building not far inside the stockade gate. The middle of this structure was transected by the smithing shop and within its open arched doorway stood three huge forges, aligned from the outside in like stabled iron creatures. The outermost of these dusky fire bins was Wennberg's.

From where Wennberg stood day-long as he directed the heavy dance of hammer and iron Melander scanned out into the parade ground. All comings and goings there the line of view took in, and most particularly the route into Braaf's storage hulk just across the way.

Rueful, Melander wagged his head in admission. Then proffered: "So?"

"You've plans to crawl out of this Russian bear pit, and I'm coming with you."

"Are you?"

"I am. Else you and Braaf and Karlsson'll be in irons and off to pass your years in Siberia."

"Tsk. Irons, you say. That'd maybe be more burden even than Braaf's armload, just there. More than Swedes ought to have to carry for Russians, aye? What makes you think we're kissing good-bye to New Archangel?"

"Don't come clever with me, Melander. Been watching your trained pack rat Braaf, I have, these weeks."

"Braaf is his own man, like any of us."

"Braaf's operated by your jabber. So's that stiff-cock Karlsson."

"Such powers I seem to have. You'll want to watch out I don't command your sidewhiskers to turn into louse nests."

"You're not the high-and-mighty to command anything just now. You're down the toilet looking up, and don't forget it."

"Come down with this often, do you, Wennberg? Say we wanted to flee, just how would we? New Archangel is the end of the tail of the world, and not much in between it and anything."

"You'd yatter as long as maiden's pee runs downhill, Melander. Time we barter. My silence for your plan."

"Silence I've never much believed in. But school me: why're you interested in notions of fleeing from here?"

"My reasons're yours. Because I'm sick of life under these shit-beetle Russians." Grudgingly: "Because if anyone here is slyboots enough to escape, it's likely you."

"Flattering."

"Which doesn't mean I wouldn't laugh to see you suited up in irons and sent west into snowland, if that's your choice. High-and-mighty can't save you from this, Melander. Decide."

Melander calculated Wennberg. Then the serious smile made its appearance.

"First you preach to poor Braaf of too much weight, now you keep on at me about too much height. Wennberg, I think you maybe underestimate how far a man can stretch himself if he has to. Aye? Can you handle a Haida paddle?"

Melander spent considerable talking that night to convince Braaf and Karlsson that the wisest choice was to shepherd Wennberg into the plan.

Braaf remained indignant about the incident on the parade ground. He volunteered to convert the blacksmith into a dead man, if someone would tell him how it ought to be done.

Melander agreed it to be an understandable ambition, and laudable too, but no. Through and through he had thought the issue, and the death of a valued smith such as Wennberg, especially when the killing would have to be achieved here within the fort, would breed more questions than it was worth. "Besides, he is a hill bull for strength—"

"And stupider than he is strong," Braaf put in.

"—and we can maybe make use of him," continued Melander. "Just maybe we can."

49

Karlsson squinted in reflection, then said shortly that what galled him was to be at Wennberg's mercy in any way. What if Wennberg took it into his narrow bull mind to betray them to the Russians for a reward?

Aye, Melander concurred, that was the very problem to be grappled. "We'll need to set a snare for Mister Blacksmith."

A few nights later, their first time as four.

Karlsson openly appraised Wennberg as if the blacksmith were marrying into the family. Their newcomer was both hefty and wide, like a cut of very broad plank. An unexpectedness atop his girth was the fluffy set of sideburns—light brown, as against the blondness of the other three Swedes—which framed his face all the way down to where his jaw joined his neck. Except for young dandies among the Russian officers no one else of New Archangel sported such feathery sidewhiskers, but then it could be assumed that no one either was going to invoke foppery against this walking slab of brawn. A time or two Wennberg had reedged an ax for Karlsson, but Karlsson knew little more of him than those spaced hammer blows onto red metal. He seemed to find it of interest that the man was amounting to something more than arm.

Wennberg meanwhile tried to reciprocate as much scrutiny as he got, but was at the disadvantage of having to share it around the trio of them: fancy-mouth Melander, this mute fox-nosed one Karlsson, Satan's choirboy Braaf.

"We have a thing to tell you, Wennberg," Melander set in at once. "Since you're new to our midst we can't really know whether your fondest wish is to go with us from here or to sell us to the Russians as runaways. Dance on one foot of that and then the other, a man might. So if you've had wavering, it'll be relief to you to learn we've made up your mind for you. There's no profit whatsoever for you to pigeon off to the Russians."

Challenge of this raw sort was not at all what Wennberg had come shopping for.

"Your goddamned tongue's fatter than your judgment, Melander," the blacksmith flared. "It's not for you to tell me who stands where. You forget. Walk straight out of here, I can, and show the Russians the hidey-hole in that hulk where you've had Braaf stashing, these months."

"But Wennberg, heart's friend," Melander said with such politeness it seemed almost an apology, "there's nothing there."

Wennberg stared at Melander as if the lanky seaman just had changed skin color before his eyes.

"Since you've invited yourself along with us we thought we ought get ourselves a new hidey-hole," Melander went on. "Braaf has the knack of stumbling onto such places, aye? So this new cache now, you can know where it is when we load the canoe, and not an eyeblink before. Trot to the Russians whenever you feel like it, but you'll have nothing in the hulk to show them."

"Except mouse turds." This unexpectedly from

Braaf, whose gaze now floated steadily along three foreheads instead of two. Wennberg shot him a look which all but thundered.

"Yes, except mouse turds." Melander chuckled. "And even the Russians might find it hard to believe that we've been busy storing away treasure of such sort. No, Wennberg, you against the three of us, that's the tilt of it, and we'll see who the Russians choose to believe. Our souls are fresh and there's spring green in our eye, so far as they know. Nor'd you be the first one here to be thought off his head, or a merchant of mischief for some other reason."

Melander paused, then went on in his know-all fashion: "You play a hand of cards now and again, don't you, Wennberg? I suggest you take a second look up the queen's skirt before you wager."

The blacksmith began to retort hotly: "Now listen, you walrus pizzles—" But Melander beat him to speech yet again.

"Careful of your words, Wennberg. If you're coming with us, we have a lot of time ahead together and don't need a sack of bad feelings. If you're going off to the Russians"—an even more eloquent Melander pause—"you don't want your last sentiments to your own dear countrymen weighing wrongly on your soul, do you now?"

Wennberg was boulder-still, in stare at Melander. Fury had him, but evidently something other, too, his mouth now clamped until his lips all but vanished. Words were having their spines snapped there, the other three could see.

Finally Wennberg broke his glower. Swung a heavy look to Braaf. At last, and longest, to the silent one, Karlsson.

"You goddamned set of squareheads may be better at this than I thought," he rumbled. "I'm with you, Christ help me. Now you've to tell me, as if you know down from up. How do we go be pilgrims in the wilderness of water?"

Circle the plan as he would, like a farmer working at a stump, Wennberg found only a few questions to hack at when Melander was finished.

"Why all this fuss with old Bilibin? Whyn't we just cut his stupid throat when we're ready?"

This theorem shifted Karlsson forward in his seat a bit.

"Because if we kill one of his men, Rosenberg will have to have his people chase us," Melander said instructively. "If we leave Bilibin alive, Rosenberg will take it out on him."

"What of rifles? How many can Braaf here lay his fancy fingers on?"

Melander replied that they had the advantage of two ready at hand: Karlsson's long-barreled .69-caliber hunting rifle and the military weapon that would be plucked from Bilibin. Then on the night of the escape, Melander continued, Braaf would gather them a few more. "Six, to be exact."

Braaf blinked rapidly and Karlsson looked mildly surprised, but it was Wennberg who blurted:

"Great good God, Melander, eight guns all together? We're going in a canoe, not a goddamned
man-of-war!"

"Name me a better cargo, can you, Wennberg? Do
you think the ravens are going to feed us on this journey, and the bears will guard us with their kind teeth?
We don't know what in hell-all we'll face, but I want
plenty of ball and powder to face it with. Aye? If you
wish to come along naked, so be it."

Wennberg grumbled, then offered that if Melander
was so fanatic on firearms, he was willing to help out.
A sentry's rifle had been sent into the smith shop for
a new butt plate. He could hold the gun back by saying he hadn't got around to affixing the repair yet.

Gravely Melander congratulated him on entering
the spirit of their enterprise.

"There, Braaf, he's made you amends. You'll need
to pluck only five firepieces when the time is ready."

Braaf said nothing.

Karlsson too stayed unspeaking, but he had begun
to have a feeling about Wennberg. There was something not reckonable, opposite from usual, about this
blacksmith. As when the eyelid of a wood duck watching you closes casually from the bottom up.

Wennberg was not done with the topic of weaponry.

"Just where'll our little storekeeper get these guns,
anyway?"

"You do take three bites at every berry, don't you,
Wennberg? But since you bring the matter up . . ."
Melander turned his long head to Braaf in the manner

5 4

of an indulging uncle. "Braaf, what of it? Where can the guns best be got on our night?"

"The officers' clubhouse," Braaf responded with entire matter-of-factness. "The gun room."

For the single time in all the unfolding of the plan, Melander blanched. Karlsson pulled once at his thin nose. And sardonically, Wennberg: "Next, Braaf, you'll want to parade up to the Castle Russians and ask can we have their underwear for warmth on our little journey."

Braaf shrugged. "Sauerkraut is in the smelliest barrels, guns are in a gun room."

Melander found voice, restrained Wennberg, chided Braaf, and the matter began to be argued out.

It emerged that Braaf likely had it right. That the collection of rifles racked like fat billiard cues within the officers' gun room—on one of his invented errands that wafted him into all crannies of the settlement Braaf had spotted the weapons—and which were used for shooting parties when the governor's retinue went downcoast to Ozherskoi, this small armory was New Archangel's richest trove of firearms unguarded by sentries.

But, as Wennberg demanded, not without suspicion, why unsentried . . . ?

"Because of the padlock on the door and the chain through the trigger guards?" Braaf suggested.

This silenced even Wennberg.

Karlsson at last spoke up.

"There's a second stick to this cross. The officers

and company men coming and going. They flow in
and out of that place day and night."

"I can mark us a safe time," Melander mused. "But
snatching those guns loose . . ."

"Wennberg," murmured Braaf.

"Mister Blacksmith!" Melander proclaimed.

"You squareheaded sons of whores," Wennberg said
unhappily.

The waiting became a kind of ghost attaching itself
within each of their lives, as if a man now cast two
shadows and one somehow fell into his body instead of
away. The outer man had to perform as ever—do his
work, eat, sleep, carry on barracks gabble—while inside, this sudden new shadow-creature, the one in wait,
bided the next six weeks and six days wholly in thought
of the immense voyage ahead.

Melander as he waited studied the Tebenkov maps
ever more firmly into his mind. Before long, their descending coastal chain of islands could have been recited out of him like Old Testament genealogy. New
Archangel's island of Baranof would beget Kuiu Island, Kuiu beget Kosciusko, Kosciusko Heceta, and
Heceta Suemez, south and south and south through
watery geography and explorers' mother tongues until
the eventual rivermouth port called Astoria. Perhaps it
was because Melander had in him the seaman's way of
letting days take care of distance, the necessary nautical faith that there is more time than there is expanse
of the world and so any voyage at last will end, that

these stepping-stone details predominated in his thinking about the escape. Rarely, and then never aloud to
any of the other three, did Melander mull the totality
of the coastal journey ahead. This made a loss to them
all, for Melander alone of the four had traveled greatly
enough on the planet to understand the full scope of
what they would be attempting. To grasp that their
intended ten or twelve hundred miles of canoeing
stretched—wove, rather, through the island-thick wilderness coast—as far as the distance from Stockholm
down all of Europe to the sun coasts of Italy. Each
mile of those hundreds, too, along a cold northern
brink of ocean which in winter is misnamed entirely.
Not pacific at all, but malevolent. And too, each mile
maybe—or maybe not, this was the puzzle of ocean
and oceangoer—each mile maybe working away at this
three-man crew of his, Braaf and Wennberg and
Karlsson. Thief and oaf and clam: or acquisitionist
and draft ox and canoe soldier; whichever each was
now, he perhaps had sea change ahead of him. The
great over-water passage between one life and another.
Melander in his sailoring had been at an edge of the
nineteenth century's immigration tides, the tens of
hundreds of thousands who were the forebears of us,
and so knew how voyage could tower in the mind of a
first-timer. It couldn't not. Treadle of the waves week
on week, the half-coffin berth to try to survive in, re-
liance for that survival on sailors who flew in the mast
trees like clothed monkeys; a compressed existence,
the voyage of a ship, like a battle or a hard illness or a
first failed time in love, lodged in the memory at an

angle not like that of any other set of days. And that
was shipboard; this would be canoe, splinter of a true
vessel. Sea change could come all the more intense. But
then sometimes it never came at all, or again it simply
made a man more of what he was, carved the lines of
him deeper. You never knew. Not even a Melander had
the how of sea change. Yet in this season of wait
Melander might have hinted toward what lay in store
when one went out to live on waves. His knowledge of
water enwrapping the world, the canny force of its
resistance to the intentions of man, he might have used
to put a tempered edge on the escape plan. To have
said, in his silver style of saying, "Hear me on this,
heart's friends. Things beyond all imagining may happen to us down this coast, aye? But we'll have gone free
into our fate. Besides, a man draws nearer to death
wherever he strides. . . ."

But no, and it may be necessity for those who choose
vast risk, even Melander seemed not able to confront
the thought of all the miles at once. Only those from
island to island to island.

In his waiting, Wennberg too spent long spells of
calculation. Turning and turning the question of
whether there could be found a way to betray the
escape.

Certainty did not seem to be anywhere in the proposition. If the Russians could be convinced and then
relied upon to reward him, say grant return to Sweden; but that the Russians would forfeit a blacksmith

so readily did not seem likely, whatever they might promise. If he told of the plan but Melander persuaded the Russians there was nothing to it, Wennberg would never after be safe in New Archangel. Karlsson and perhaps even that stealer of milkteeth Braaf would be steady threat to his life. If he fled with the other three, into freedom—or perhaps into the bottom of that ocean like cats in a sack—

All of it strummed a man's nerves, not to say what fret this place New Archangel played on you anyway. Example, the morning soon after Wennberg added himself into the escape plan. On the way to begin his day of smithing, he'd remembered leaving his new-sewn leather apron back at the barracks and there near Baranov's Castle reversed route to fetch it. Just then gulls on a breeze off Sitka Sound flashed across the breast of Verstovia. White as winter creatures they glided, as if shooed in from the other, snowier crags. Wennberg had cast them a glance—and up there the apparition reared, a Russian cross thrusting out of the dark north slope of Verstovia. A long minute Wennberg stared at this, Calvary arrived to the crest of Alaska, before he picked out that the cross was merely the Russian cathedral's topmost one, that in the morning dark the green-painted spire under it blended invisibly against the forest of Verstovia. As well as anyone, Wennberg knew that if you let yourself dwell on the menace of these mountains you would go around in terror all day every day, like a cowering dog. What jostled his frame of mind, though, was not just the surprise sky-planted cross, but that in his years here he had never noticed this illusion before. Every morning now, despite himself, Wennberg found himself stopping at the spot and casting a look back up there.

And all the rest of the day, if and perhaps. Coax at them how he would, Wennberg could make the pair do no more than somersault into perhaps and if.

This, this damned skitter of a matter—Wennberg did not at all have well-bottom faith in the prospects of Melander's plan. But neither did he see, now, any clear path out of it. What Wennberg imagined was going to be his say over Melander and the other two somehow, by some coil of the escape plan, was turning out to be their say over him.

Since Karlsson went through life anyway in the manner of a man in wait, to him the space of weeks until the escape was simply one more duration, and not so long as most. Time passed, or you put it past. All in all, he showed a good deal less edginess about New Archangel existence than any of the other three. A man built smoke-tight, as Melander had said of him. What then held Karlsson into the pattern of the escape?

Braaf too had wondered.

"Why're you?"

He and Karlsson were dutied, this day, to the warehouse where bundling was done. Beaver pelts had been brought in by the Koloshes. The light task Braaf took, folding each dried hide into a square, fur side in. Karlsson then stacked the bundled pelts into the big screw press, to be squeezed into bales for shipment to China. Quite why it was that Swedes had been brought half around the world to pile together animal skins that would then be cargoed half around the world again to adorn Chinamen, neither Braaf nor Karlsson grasped. But here was the habiliment of several dozen former beavers, and here were they.

"Hmm, Karlsson? Why're you?"

"Same as you, I suppose." Karlsson did not seem much disposed to talk about their leave-taking of New Archangel, which of course focused Braaf onto it all the more.

"So then, why'm I?"

"To kiss good-bye to the Russians, and five more years here."

"Good-bye kisses aren't always happy ones."

"Some truth to that."

"I'll miss the snuffboxes. They hop into a man's hand, here. What of you? What'll you miss?"

Karlsson shrugged.

"What, can't put a name to her?" Braaf queried.

Karlsson gave him a fast look. After a bit, said: "Maybe she has a lot of names."

"All the more to miss."

"Braaf, easy with this. We may be heard."

"Only by heaven. The overseer's gone off to his bottle."

"You'd know."

"That iron puddler, Wennberg. Think he's to be trusted?"

"Do you?"

"I don't trust anyone whose ears are buried in his whiskers."

"Melander has put trust in him."

"Melander isn't you."

Karlsson straightened a bundled pelt into line atop the others in the screw press. "We need trust Melander."

"Not much of a word spender, are you?"

"Not much."

"All right, try this hole: the voyage, can we do it strong as Melander says?"

"Braaf, you've more questions than the king's cat."

"Nothing knocks at the ear if it's never invited in. You still haven't said, you know."

"Said?"

"Why're you coming on the escape?"

Karlsson gave attention to peltry and screw press again. When he turned back, his lean face was as little readable as ever but he peered more interestedly at Braaf. The angle at which the sight of the young thief entered his eyes seemed to have altered. After a bit, Karlsson said:

"Maybe to see how it'll be."

Braaf was not entirely sure whether this constituted answer or not. But he nodded now, as though it did.

The hardest wait among them was Braaf's. Melander forbade him from further stealing until the final flurry of muskets and food on the date of the escape. How, then, to keep his fingers busy?

Melander had a part answer: a hank of hefty rope he passed to Braaf. "Work this in those lily hands of yours, as much as you can every day. Get calluses started, else you'll bleed to death through the palms once we begin paddling."

But a man can't twiddle rope all day, and—

"An Aleut calendar," Melander at last came up with, the fifth or seventh time Braaf asked him if there wasn't just one further item wanted for the cache. "Carve us one, so we can number our time on the way to Astoria, aye?"

Braaf smiled like a boy given a second sugar cake. "I know where there's one, I can get it this after—"

"*No!*" Melander swept a harried glance around, Braaf blinking up at him. "No. Don't steal one. *Carve* one. You may have never noticed, but there is a difference. Keep those damn fingers of yours at home, hear?"

So began Braaf's pastime of carvery, a fine Kolosh slat of red cedar—Melander would not have wanted to ask how it found its way to Braaf—about the size of the lid of a music box and a half-inch thick shaved and shaved by him. Then the twelve rows of peg holes across for the months, and in those rows one hole for every day of month. Braaf next discovered that on the best-wrought of these calendars—Melander had neglected too to forbid borrowing for the sake of a look—the Russians marked for their Aleut converts the frequent religious days, a cross-in-a-circle penciled around four or five of the peg holes each month; the notion being that wherever an Aleut huntsman might roam in his fur harvest for the tsar, he would have along this steadfast guide to orderly obeisance. Lazily crude, though, this penciling seemed to Braaf. He incised his crosses-in-circles. Finally, there was the peg, to keep track of the day of year much as count is recorded on a cribbage board. Braaf made his of walrus-tooth ivory, an elegant knobbed sliver like a tiny belaying pin.

"Aye, well," said Melander when Braaf shyly handed him the polished little board. "May our days be fit for your calendar, Braaf."

"Which is the one, now?" Braaf asked. "When we go?"

Melander plucked out the ivory peg, counted briefly along a row with it, inserted it.

"This one. Just here, Braaf. The day of days."

Night, the seventh of January, 1853. By the Russian calendar, the night after Christmas.

Karlsson staggered from the Kolosh village to the outside of the stockade gate, bounced hard against the wood, propped himself and threw back his head.

" 'Be *GREET*ed joyful *MORN*ing *HOURR*,' " he bawled. " 'A Savior *COMES* with *LOVE*'S sweet *POWERR* . . .' "

"Shush! Christ save us, man, you'll have that sergeant down here," Bilibin called urgently, hustled from the hut sheltering him from the rain, and hurriedly worked the gate. "Quick, in, in . . ."

From the dark beside the blacksmith shop Melander

watched the gate crack open ever so briefly, then close. Two man-shapes bobbed together. Karlsson's slurred mutter and Bilibin's guffaw were heard. Melander swiveled his head toward the end of the smithing shop farthest from the gate and spoke:

"Now."

A piece of the darkness—its name was Braaf—disengaged itself and instantly was vanished around the corner.

Next Melander became motion. Across New Archangel for three hundred yards he hastened, in black reversal of a route he roved one twilit evening a half-year ago. A different being, that Deacon Step-and-a-Half had been, not yet cumbered with a thousand miles of plan.

Outside the Scandinavian workers' barracks Melander halted and drew deep breaths.

For half a minute the rain ticked down on him.

Entering, Melander clattered the barracks door shut behind him, began to shrug out of his rain shirt, mumbled this or that about having forgot his gloves in the toilet, and was vanished out the doorway again.

A person attentively watching this arrival and departure would have had time to blink perhaps three times.

Wennberg had been idly stropping a knife as he spectated the card game being played by three carpenters and a sailmaker. Now he grunted that he too was off to mount the throne of Denmark, if the Russians allowed pants to be dropped on such a festive night, and to the chuckles of the cardplayers pulled on his rain shirt and stepped into the streaming blackness beside Melander.

The pair of them, tree and stump somehow endowed with legs, moved with no word through the night for two minutes, three. Apprehension traveled with them both. Apprehensions rather, for their anxieties were sized as different as the men.

A several hundredth time Melander retold himself the logic by which he had singled this night. On Christmas Eve the Russians had begun, all going around solemn as church mice, crossing themselves until it seemed they'd wear out the air, eating no bite until "the first star of evening." (Which baffled Braaf no little bit: "They wait to see a star over this place, won't they have a hungry winter?") Yesterday, it had been a morning of liturgy murmuring out of the twin-crossed cathedral and then the Russian men paying calls on each other, toasting at every stop until by nightfall the streets were full of crisscrossing bands of them shouting back and forth, "You beat to windward, we'll steer to lee!" Now, the pious and visitational sides of Christmas having been observed, certain as anything this would be their night of celebrating and carousing and dancing their boots off—up there in Baranov's Castle at the governor's ball they'd be, all the officers and any of the company Russians who frequented their clubhouse for card games and tippling and monotony-breaking argument, every breathing one of them. And when the escapees' absence was discovered, what Russian among them was going to be eager to dash from snug activities to chase Swedes through the

6 6

damp black of Alaskan night? And meanwhile the Koloshes would be staying to their longhouses, leaning clear of drunk and boisterous tsarmen. . . . Confusion, alcohol, reluctance, Melander had them all carefully in rank as allies for escape. But late-going Russians yet within the officers' clubhouse . . . racket in the gun room carrying to a sentry at the eastmost blockhouse . . . just here, on such points beyond logic, Melander's months of planning teetered, and the quiver of them touched him through the dark.

Wennberg's perturbance was purely with himself. Until he stood up from beside the cardplayers in the barracks the blacksmith had not been convinced he would go through with the escape. Why risk the tumble, ass-over-earhole, down this bedamned coast? Why trust even a minute to Melander or Karlsson or Braaf, these three orphans of Hell? So how came it that now he was traipsing off with Melander into disaster's black avid mouth?

Abruptly a barrier of building met the two of them.

As Melander and Wennberg hesitated before the officers' clubhouse, a third upright shadow joined them. Into Wennberg's hands it thrust a heavy sharp-pointed pry bar and into Melander's a pair of long-handled smithing snippers, and it muttered: "This way."

In the dark and rain Melander and Wennberg stayed stock-still for a moment, as though the cold feel of metal conferred on them by Braaf had iced them into place.

"Come on, you pair of lumps." Braaf's jab brought them to life, tumbled the big men inside the doorway where he waited. "Stay an arm's length behind me, and try not walk on each other's ankles."

Braaf led Melander and Wennberg through rooms their eyes never really took in, so much focus were the two of them devoting to listening, breathing silently, and creeping.

Which may go to explain how the outer edge of Wennberg's left boot clanked against a hallway spittoon.

Braaf appeared more offended than concerned.

"Plowhorse," came his terse whisper to Wennberg.

The door of the gun room stood like the lid of a colossal strongbox tipped up on end. Heavy hinges, and a corner-to-corner X of strap iron to thwart notions of chopping in, and a powerful hasp, and a padlock the size of a big man's fist.

"Do your digging, blacksmith," Braaf said under his breath. "And pound quiet as you can."

Wennberg pulled from his breeches a mallet and a chisel. He stepped to where the padlock hung heavy in the ring plate of the hasp, put the chisel to the wood of the doorframe a few inches out to the side of the metal, and quickly rapped a groove in behind the ring plate.

"Now the other," Wennberg decreed huskily. "There'll be commotion to this."

"The rain'll drown most of it," answered Braaf. "Don't stand around telling stories, do it."

Wennberg worked the sharp point of the lengthy pry bar into where he had channeled behind the ring plate. Moved his thick hands toward the outer end of

the pry bar for all possible leverage. Was joined by
Melander, grabbing beside him on the bar. And both
strained outward.

The ring plate wrenched loose, its lag screws tearing
wood as they came.

Braaf reached instantly and swung the ring plate
and padlock away from the doorframe they had been
freed from.

"Done, hair and hide," congratulated Melander.
"And we didn't make any more noise than Judgment
Day. Now one job more." The tall leader tugged open
the powerful door.

Somehow rifles racked together multiply their
power, akin to the way that cavalry does by drawing
up abreast. The repeat of pattern, the echoing numer-
ousness it implies, as though this concentrated squad is
just a swatch from bigger trouble—such impress now
met Melander and Braaf and Wennberg, black tubes
of barrel and brass ramrod pipes in legions rising
straight up from the chain that threaded through each
trigger guard. Truth be known, except for an occasional Beaumarchais sportsman's weapon and one
hefty American Hawken with an octagonal barrel, the
guns here were eccentric old Bakers or Brunswicks
bought from Hudson's Bay traders in years past; the
Brunswicks in particular were hard-recoiling, scatter-
barreled specimens given up on by the British army.
None of this could be known to Braaf, Wennberg,
Melander. Blast and thunder were their want, not
ballistic nicety.

In went Wennberg, then Braaf.

Wennberg pushed down lightly, testingly, on the chain imprisoning the rifles and slid his snippers in atop it to the trigger guard of the first gun. An exertion on the long handles of the snippers, and tempered jaws crushed through the softer brass of the trigger guard.

With care, Wennberg now bent the trigger guard out from where he had made his cut, then cleared the chain through the fresh gap in the brass. Braaf plucked the weapon from him and handed it on out to Melander.

Four more rifles the blacksmith clipped and liberated in the same fashion. "Aye," Melander saying softly each time.

Sharing out their new armory, the trio readied themselves. Wennberg shouldered shut the gun room door, pushed the ring plate and padlock back where they had been, tapped them into place in the original screw holes. Any close cast of look would show at once that the lock was awry but a rare Russian it would be who came home tonight with a quick eye.

Braaf moved in front of the other two; advised under his breath to Wennberg, "Try pick up your hooves this time"; and led.

They exited the clubhouse and through the dark set off together, now west across New Archangel toward the stockade gate, Braaf like a bat choosing the most shadowed route.

The noise exploded atop them then.

Palong! Palong!

Braaf was four running strides away from the frozen Melander and Wennberg before he, and they,

realized—*Palong! Palong!*—how cathedral bells resound to those who sneak about the streets at night.

"Your Russian is fond of bells," a visitor who departed New Archangel with ringing ears once noted
down, and the sweet-sad peals from the belfry of the
Russian Orthodox cathedral as the hour was rung followed the tall figure and the shorter two across the
settlement toward the stockade gate.

A few feet from the sentry lean-to the trio halted,
and Melander called in huskily: "Karlsson?"

Out loomed a figure in sentry cap, with a rifle at
port arms.

Wennberg grunted a curse and grabbed for the
knife inside his rain shirt.

In Karlsson's voice the figure mildly chided: "You
don't find Bilibin's cap becoming on me, Wennberg?"

"Speaking of caps," Melander said as if announcing
tea, "the time's come to fling our hat over the nunnery
wall."

Karlsson eased the gate open just enough for them
to slip through with the guns. Minutes stretched, then
the three were back from the canoe and the blackness
of the Kolosh village.

"We're away to the cache," whispered Melander.
"Stand ready with the gate."

Fewer than fifty paces later, Melander and Braaf
halted beside the blacksmith shop.

"What're we doing here?" Wennberg rumbled low
to Melander. "Where's this hidey-hole of Braaf's?"

"Here."

"Here? Here where?"

"In the sill loft. Up over your forge." The sill loft was a narrow platform, like a span of board ceiling, laid across the center of the rafters of the smithing shop. Wood to make windowsills and doorframes was dried there winter-long in the heat rising from the forges, and until the summer building season came, no one paid the loft any mind. Except of course Melander, who observed now: "In Gotland, we say the darkest place is under the candlestick."

"You pissants!" The stun of it set Wennberg back a step, these weeks of the war within himself, escape-or-betray, the lobes of his mind standing and fighting each other like crabs over the question, and all the while—"If the Russians'd looked up there they'd've condemned me!"

"That thought did visit us. But you had luck, the Russians didn't peek. Shinny the ladder, Braaf, and begin handing down to us, aye?"

Six trips it took, Braaf and Wennberg lugging now while Melander stowed and stowed, to convey the trove that Braaf had accumulated like a discriminating pack rat.

Then all at once Melander, alone, was back at the gate.

"We're cargoed," he said to Karlsson. "You'll be our last item, aye?" And was gone.

Karlsson began to wait out a span of becalmed time. The hammer chorale of the bells at last had ceased, and the all-but-silence, just the soft rain sound, was worse. Too, there was an occasional stirring from Bilibin, trussed and gagged and bleary on the floor of the hut behind him. Karlsson decided it was best to keep busy within himself, saying and resaying the word.

There are moments, central moments such as what Karlsson awaits now, which form themselves unlike any that ever have issued in our lives or shall again. Ours might seem a kindlier evolution if what we know as memory had been set in us the other way: if these pith incidents of existence already waited on display there in the mind when you, I, Karlsson come into the world —a glance, and scene *A* ready to happen some certain Thursday; beyond it, *B* in clear view, due on a Wednesday two years and seventeen days off. The snag, of course, is *Z*, the single exactitude we could never bear to know: death's date. In order then that we can stand existence, the apparatus fetches backward for us rather than ahead. Memory instead of foreknowledge. So Karlsson on wait here in the Alaska night is like all of us in life's dark, able to know only that a moment is arriving due and to hope it is not the last of the series.

Then it came, as if in chorus to his silent recitings, the word flying out of the dark, in call down from the blockhouse on the hump of ridge above the stockade gate.

"Slushai!"

One time each hour the word made its relay from sentry post to sentry post. Not much of an utterance, no recital on behalf of tsar or God, perhaps the littlest cog in all the guardful apparatus of the capital of Russian America: simply the traditional reminding call, "Harken!" But try, a time, with throat dry and all of life riding there on your tongue, try then to echo such a word as if born to it. . . .

Having been endlessly rehearsed by Melander, whose Russian was better than his own, Karlsson swallowed. Cupped his hands to his mouth. And as close as he could raise his voice to Bilibin's blurt, cried back the watch call.

Silence from the blockhouse.

Karlsson cracked the gate for himself.

"You're croaking like a raven down there tonight."

Karlsson spun to the resumed voice. Down from the blockhouse, here it blared yet again. "Something got you by the throat?"

Motionless, Karlsson frantically rummaged the times he had shared the hootch jug with Bilibin, tried to draw to mind the old guard's gossipy gab, pluck words out, but what words . . .

Then from beside Karlsson in the blackness, a bray in Russian:

"Nothing fifteen drops won't cure!"

Karlsson's right elbow was being gripped by the largest hand imaginable, which told him what his eyes could not in the dark: Melander.

Fresh silence at the other guard post. Deeper, tauter silence, it seemed to Karlsson, unrelenting as Melander's grip.

At last:

"Swig fifteen more for me and make a start on my woes as well. Christ's season be merry for you, Pavel Ivanovich!"

TWO

A s i f in mock of some dance the Russians just then were gyrating through in the Castle, the Swedes' vast voyage southward started off with an abrupt two-step to the west.

On the first of the Tebenkov maps, Melander had shown Karlsson the pair of south-going channels threaded like careful seams among the islands of Sitka Sound. Karlsson had glanced down and immediately up: "At night? Likely in rain?"

That granite nubbin of opinion pivoted the escapees to the third possible route, veering up the channel from the Kolosh village, around Japonski Island, then outside the shoal of Sound isles. Such a loop was longer than the other channels and unsheltered from the ocean currents, but at least it was not a blindfolded plunge into Sitka's labyrinth.

This was however the inauguration for Braaf and Wennberg into paddling in untame waters, and as promptly as this, it began that these men were brave and afraid and back and forth between the two.

Both Braaf and Wennberg were chocked with anticipation that the canoe was going to buck, slide down nose first, rock to one side and then the other, then start over, on and on in a nautical jig horrifying to join in the wet dark. None such ruckus happened. Ballasted deep by the provisions, the canoe rode steady, almost with nonchalance, in the night water of Sitka. What proved obstreperous instead were the paddles in the hands of Wennberg and Braaf. The pair of novices splashed much, and more than occasionally whunked the canoe side. Then Braaf caught the tip of his paddle amid a stroke, spraying water forward onto Wennberg's back and down his neck.

The blacksmith's devoutly muttered string of curses inspired counsel from Melander. "Steady up, don't beat the damn water to death." But the paddling efforts of the pair in the middle of the canoe still were stabs into the sloshing turmoil until Karlsson directed:

"Spread your hands wide as you can on the paddle and stroke only when I say. Now—now—now—now—now—"

The contrived tick and tock, Karlsson's nows and the breath space between, advanced them through the blackness until Melander spoke from the bow of the canoe.

"Hold up, bring us broadside a moment, Karlsson. We've at least earned a look."

As the canoe swayed around, the other three saw his meaning. Back through one of the channel canyons amid the islands of Sitka Sound, an astonishing wide box of lights sat in the air. Baranov's Castle, every window bright for this night of Christmas merriment, sent outward through the black and the rain their final glittering glimpse of New Archangel.

By and large, a boat ride is a cold ride. From launching the canoe, the men's legs were wet to just above their knees, and it took the first half hour of paddling to warm themselves.

The night was windless, which they needed. The rain was not heavy, and gift above all, it was not snow. A few weeks earlier December's customary snowstorm had arrived, a white time when ice plated the tops of New Archangel's rain barrels and Melander went around looking pinched. But then thaw, and the Sitka air's usual mood of drizzle ever since.

Their course out of the harbor looped the canoe toward the ocean, then swung southeast, to bring the craft along the shore of Baranof. Baranof's coastline the canoemen could estimate by the surf sound, and occasionally by a moving margin of lightness as a wave struck and swashed. Their night vision was decent, accustomed by New Archangel's dim wintertime. But even so, any effort to see to their right, the ocean side, drew only intense black of a sort modern eyes have been weaned from: starless, so much so that it seemed nothing ever had kindled in that cosmic cave, and vast, beyond all reason vast. New Archangel apart, the next lamp in that void flickered thousands of miles across the Pacific, if indeed the residents of Japan lit lamps.

Of all the kinds of toil there are, the ocean demands the most strange. A ship under sail asked constant trussing and retrussing; the hauling about of ropes and sailcloth was like putting up and taking down a huge complicated tent, day and night. Advent of the steamship changed the chore to stuffing a mammoth incessant stove, between apprehensive glances at clockfaces that might but more likely might not indicate whether matters were going to go up in blast. Both of these unlikely sea vocations had drawn sweat from Melander, and now he was back to the ocean's original tool, the paddle. He was finding, with Braaf and Wennberg—Karlsson already had been through the lesson—that the paddler's exertion is like that of pulling yourself hand over hand along an endless rope. The hands, wrists, arms—yes, they tire, stiffen. The legs and knees learn misery, from the position they are forced to keep for so long. But where the paddling effort eats deep is the shoulder blade. First at one, then when the paddle is shifted to the other side of the canoe for relief, the ache moves across to the other: as if all weariness chose to ride the back just there, on those twin bone saddles.

Water rippled lightly at the bow. Against the canoe's cedar length, the steady mild lap of waves. Now and then a Braaf or Wennberg stroke going askew and Haida paddle whacking Tlingit craft.

The four men in the darkness stroked steadily rather than rapidly. Not even Wennberg was impatient about this, for he knew with the others that they needed to pull themselves as far from New Archangel as possible by daybreak, and that meant pace, endurance. The invisible rope of route, more and more a hawser as you worked at it, was nothing to be raced along.

Perhaps fifteen strokes a minute, four men stroking, rest pausing as little they could, seven–eight hours to daybreak: an approximate twenty-five thousand of these exertions and they could seek out a dawn cove for hiding.

Hours and hours later, near-eternities later to Melander and Braaf and Wennberg, darkness thinned toward dawn's gray.

Karlsson, glancing back to judge how far his eyes had accustomed to the coming of day, was the first to see the slim arc of canoe, like a middle distance reflection of their own craft, closing the space of water behind them.

"You long-ass bastard, Melander!" This was Wennberg. " 'The Russians won't follow us,' ay?"

"They haven't," Melander retorted. "Koloshes, those are. We'll see how quick they are to die for the

far white father in St. Petersburg. Braaf, load the rest
of those fancy rifles of yours, then pass Karlsson his
hunting gun."

Carefully the Kolosh chieftain in the chasing canoe
counted as Braaf worked at the loading, and did not
like how the numbers added and added. The half-drunk
Russian officer who had roused the Kolosh crew told
them the escaping men were only three—Braaf at first
had not been missed, his whereabouts as usual the most
obscure matter this side of ghostcraft. But plainly
there were four of the whitehairs, they possessed at
least two firepieces each, and this one doing the loading
was rapid at his task. Against the four and their evident armory the Kolosh chieftain had his six paddlers
and himself, with but three rifles and some spears.

"Fools they are, you'll skewer them like fish in a
barrel," the Russian officer had proclaimed. "If they
haven't drowned themselves first." But fools these men
ahead did not noticeably seem to be. They had paddled far, almost a surprise how far. A canoe chief of
less knowledge than his own would not have reckoned
them yet to this distance. They seemed inclined to
fight, and held that total of rifles in their favor. Tobacco, molasses, even the silver coins had been promised
by the angry tsarman. Those, against the battle these
whitehairs might put up. Once wondering begins there
is no cure, and here was much, firepieces and molasses
and Russians and the nature of promises and tobacco

and coins and four steady-armed whitehairs instead of three exhausted timorous ones, to be wondered about.

While the leader of the Koloshes sought to balance it all in his mind and the exertion of his crew shortened the water between the canoes, the craft in front suddenly began to swing broadside, a bold-necked creature of wood turning as if having decided, at last, to do fight even if the foe was of its own kind.

As the canoe came around, the figure in its stern leveled a long hunting gun.

Startled, the range being greater than they themselves would expend shots across, the Kolosh paddlers ducked and grappled for their own weapons. But the chieftain sat steady and watched. Here was an instant he owed all attention.

The slender whitehair swung his rifle into place, on a line through the air to the Kolosh leader.

The chieftain knew, as only one man of combat can see into the power of another, what Karlsson was doing. The whitehair was touching across distance to the chieftain's life, plucking it up easily as a kitten, either to claim or to let drop back into place.

The other three whitehairs aimed their weapons as well, but not with the slender one's measure.

Rattled by the turnabout of men who were supposed to be desperately fleeing them, the Kolosh crew were trying to yank their rifles into place, the canoe rocking with their confusion.

The chieftain still watched ahead. He knew himself to be twice the watcher here, the one intent on the waiting rifleman across the water and the other in gaze to himself at this unexpected seam between existences. There was this and that to be said for courage and a calm death; life was tasked with a decent departure. But the fact was that here, straddled between the strange tribes of whitehairs and tsarmen, did not seem the ultimate site and audience a canoe warrior of his years had a right to expect.

The decision was out of the chieftain's mouth before his mind knew it had concluded the weighing.

The Kolosh paddlers slid their guns into the bottom of their canoe. Their craft steadied on the water, gentling, a steed of sea cavalry settling into rest.

In the other canoe, the slender man set aside his rifle; as did the big whitehair in the bow. Silently the Koloshes watched as the two of them, strokesmen of power, paddled the canoe away while the other pair maintained rifles.

The Swedes' craft was passing from view around a shorewall of timber when the chieftain said one thing more.

"Let the sea eat them."

Shortly before noon, Naval Captain of Second Rank Nikolai Yakovlevich Rosenberg, governor of Russian America, pinched hard at the bridge of his nose in hope of alleviating the aftereffect of the previous night's festivities, decided that no remedy known to man could staunch such aches as were contending within his forehead, sighed, and instructed his secretary to send in the Lutheran pastor.

The pastor, a Finn from Saarijaarvi who was considered something of a clodhopper not only by the Russian officers but by the Stockholm contingent of Swedes, dolefully had been anticipating his call into the governor's chamber. By breakfast every tongue in New Archangel knew of the escape. The double number of sentries along the stockade catwalk retold the news, and the sidelong glances every Russian was casting at every Swede and Finn this morning bespoke most eloquently of all. The pastor's hesitant entrance into the governor's presence gathered beneath a single ceiling two of the three unhappiest men in New Archangel. The third was named Bilibin.

"Excellency."

"Pastor. As you may have heard, our citizenry is fewer by four this morning."

"I did happen to hear the, ah, rumor."

"Yes. Oblige me, if you will. Were these men parishioners of yours?' Rosenberg intoned through the list of four names his secretary had initiated this blighted day with.

Melander: incredible, that gabby stork of a sailor a plotter.

Karlsson and Wennberg: the governor could put vague faces to them; average slag among the seven-year force.

Braaf: this one he could not recall ever having heard of at all.

The pastor cleared his throat. "Wennberg was. Formerly, I mean to say."

"Formerly? Oblige me further."

The pastor housecleaned in his vocal box some more, then ventured into history. "Wennberg was in the group of artisans who arrived here with Governor Etholen—was it ten, twelve years ago? When I myself arrived to succeed Pastor Cygnaeus, Wennberg was a member of our congregation. He came of a God-fearing family, I believe. But you know how a Swede is, a hard knot even for God."

The pastor paused to sort his words with some care here.

"A turn of mind, you see, happened in him. The devil's mischief, always watching its chance. Sometime not long after my arrival here, it could be seen that Wennberg had slipped from the path of right. When I sought to—to show him the way of return, he cursed me. He also cursed—God. Since then he has fallen, if I may say so, even deeper into harmful ways."

Rosenberg pinched the area between his eyes again. Had Melander's name been able to speak off the list, the governor would have been solemnly assured he had caught the morning-after affliction that they on Gotland called "ont i haret": pain in the hair, aye?

"Drink, do you mean, Pastor?"

"Actually, no. Wennberg, ah, gambled."

At this the governor pursed his lips and looked quizzically at the pastor, who himself was known at the officers' clubhouse as a devout plunger at the card table. The pastor hurried on:

"Wennberg, you see, is—was—long past his seven years of service here, his gambling debts have kept him on. Not the first ever to—overstay. Yes, well, what I mean . . . Wennberg has become, may God grant that he see his erring way, a man destroying himself. Sullen, unpredictable. A loose cannon, I think the naval phrase is? If you would like my opinion, he is capable of destroying others as well."

Rosenberg rose, crossed to a window, leaned his forehead against the glass coolness, and stared out at the clouded coastline south across Sitka Sound. So, now. Send the *Nicholas* to alert Ozherskoi? If the damnable Swedes could paddle at all they likely were beyond the redoubt by now. No, the decision was fatter and homelier than that. Whether to order out the steamship to hunt down a canoe which could hide among the coves and islands of this coast like a mouse in a stable. Or let the bedamned Swedes go, let ocean and winter do the hunting of them. Yet this was no trifle of matter, thank you, the economics in the loss of four indenturees, two dozen or so man-years of service left in them—and the example to the other laborers could be treacherous. One thing certain, steamship or not: can't be remedied but can't be ignored, therefore paper it over. The governor knew the saying that paper is the schoolman's forest, and the governor had been to school. On quite a number of matters been to school, as a further saying had it. Months ago the dispatch had gone off to Russia requesting that he be relieved of his governorship—"ill health . . . family reasons." In truth, a sufficiency of New Archangel and the declining fur trade and the grudgeful Koloshes and the inattention of the tsar's government half the world away. With a resourceful bit of clerkship, this matter of runaway Swedes could slide out of sight into the morass of inkwork his successor would inherit. For his part, Rosenberg would reap one further anecdote with which to regale dinner parties in St. Petersburg.

"Three fools and a lunatic in a Kolosh canoe," he intoned against the windowpane as if practicing.

Then, realizing he had rehearsed aloud, the governor added without turning: "That will be all, Pastor. If you know a prayer for the souls of fools and lunatics, you perhaps might go say it."

"Excellency."

Late that afternoon, securely downcast from New Archangel and some careful miles shy of the Ozherskoi outpost, the four canoeists pulled ashore behind a small headland, in a cove snug as a mountainside tarn.

Weariness burdened every smallest move as they tried to uncramp their legs, shrug the hunch from the top of their backs. Karlsson, evidently going to be methodical until he dropped, at once was unloading the rifles against further risk of accident from one. Wennberg, clumsy from the need of food, lurched to a rock and sat.

Melander, though. Creakily, Melander leaned toward Braaf and whispered.

Braaf nodded and ran a rapid hand into the supplies stowed within the canoe. When his hand came up, it held an elegant dark bottle.

"Karlsson, forgive us that it isn't hootchina. But

champagne from the officers' clubhouse was the best Braaf could manage under the circumstances."

Melander's long face as he spoke was centered with a colossal grin, which now began to repeat itself on Karlsson and even Wennberg.

"We think it may do well enough for a toast to our first day of journey even so," Melander purred on as Braaf worked the cork free. "Braaf, you furnished the ale, would you care to sip first?"

Melander, like the others, expected the young provisioner merely to swig and pass along. Instead Braaf stood looking at the slim bottle in his hands and murmured: "Let me remember a moment. . . . Yes, I know . . ." He lifted his glance to the other three, sent it on above their heads, and recited:

" 'May you live forever and I never die.' "

Then he drank deep.

Permitting the others their champagne sleep, Melander enlists the last of dusk and begins to restow the lesser items in the canoe, taking more care than could be had in the dark and hurry at New Archangel. Fit the spyglass into this cranny, handy to hand. . . . Stowage will be a perpetual chore of these voyage days, all the heavy items such as the water cask and the provisions and the guns unshipped each time the canoe is carried up the shore into shelter for the night, precaution against breaking the thin wooden skin with weight. Pauses now, gives a listen toward the water. Resumes: tucks away a box of tea. . . .

As Melander occupies himself at this, another picture is called for in the mind, large as you can manage to make it. Perhaps larger yet, for this image must be of the northmost arc of the Pacific Ocean: the chill ascendant quarter-moon of that hemisphere of water, from the schooled islands of Japan up to the Siberian coast and across to the Alaskan, then curving south and east along the continental extent of Canada and America.

Vaster stretches can be found on the earth, but not all so many, and none as fiercely changeable. Most of the weathers imaginable are engendered somewhere along the North Pacific's horizon coast, from polar chill to the stun of desert heat. Within this water world the special law of gravity is lateral and violent. Currents of brine and air rule. Most famous and elusive of these is the extreme wind called the williwaw—an ambusher, an abrupt torrent of gust flung seaward from the snow-held Alaskan mountains. But times, too, the North Pacific flings back the wind, gale so steady onto the coast it seems the continent has had to hunch low to keep from swaying.

The North Pacific's most tremendous force, however, is something like a permanent typhoon under the water. Kuroshio, the Japanese Current, which puts easterly push into several thousand miles of ocean. Even here at this farthest littoral, the furrowed southeastern archipelago which on a map dithers at the flank of the main Alaskan peninsula like a puppy shadowing its mother—even here, Melander and Karlsson and Wennberg and Braaf feel Kuroshio's shove against their journey without realizing it. Are touched too by the clemency Kuroshio brings from its origins near the equator, warmth being relayed along this portion of coast by a north-seeking offspring of Kuroshio, the Alaska Current. Snow can find southeastern Alaska and often enough visits it, but more commonly winter is moderated here to rain and fog. Not that these are small elements, tapping and sniffing at man as they do, as if deeply suspicious whether he is substantial. To the worst of Alaska's possible weather, though—true North Pacific storm, storm whirling down out of the Gulf of Alaska where the Alaska Current has collided with chill northern water, storm showing in full the North Pacific's set of strengths— fog and rain can be counted only as lazy cousins.

These four Swedes in a Tlingit canoe are attempting a thousand or twelve hundred miles—something of that range, by Melander's estimate—of this North Pacific world. Not all so much, you may say. A fraction of a shard of an ocean, after all. Ten or a dozen hundred miles: in fifty or sixty sturdy days one might walk such a distance and perhaps yet have a wafer's-worth of leather on one's boot soles. Except that much of this particular distance is exploded into archipelago: island, island, island, island, like a field of flattened asteroids. Except, too, for season being fully against these watergoing men, the weather of winter capable of blustering them to a halt any hour of each day and seldom apt to furnish the favoring downcoast wind needed to employ the canoe's portable mast and square sail. Except, more than that, current too being against them, the flow of the Alaska Current up this coast as they seek to stroke down it. Except, finally, for details of barrier the eye and mind just now are beginning to reach—forbidding bristle of forest on those countless islands, white smash of breakers on rocks hidden amid the moating channels—so greatly more complex is this jagged slope of the North Pacific than the plain arithmetic of its miles.

In this picture, Melander as he raptly stashes his boxes of tea and swags of sailcloth amounts to a worker ant on the rock toe of an Alp.

"Tumble up! Fall onto your feet and suffer morning!"

Melander roused his trio as rapidly as if they constituted the crew of a schooner aiming into storm, and for the ocean-old reason: to steal minutes. Snatch time whenever it was catchable was going to be the policy of his captaincy. Any distance gained here at the front of their voyage served as that much less to be slogged out later, when weariness would be like a weight grown into their bones.

Melander amended their canoe positions from the night before. Karlsson still the stern paddler. But in front of him, Wennberg. In front of Wennberg, Braaf. Melander again in the bow. In such placement Melander of course had reason. Karlsson was the adept canoeman of them, far away the fittest to handle the large steersman's paddle. Wennberg, close by Karlsson's example, would be driven to try to keep pace with him. Braaf, Melander wanted nearest his own scrutiny, to ensure that he shirked no more than could be prevented.

Their early miles went in silence, as if these new canoemen were not sure they could afford effort to talk. And had they been able to bend their vision upward over Baranof's dour foreshore to see what they were traveling on the edge of, their powers of speech might have been appalled out of them for good. A high-standing sea of mountains, white chop of snow and ice and rock, with arms of the Pacific, blue fjords and inlets, thrusting in at whatever chance: Alaska's locked grapple of continent and ocean.

Then—

"Melander, you said these first days we'd only to keep this shore on our left, there's no other land along here. What the hell d'you call that out there?"

Wennberg was pointing southwest, where a dim bulk rose on the horizon.

"You've caught your eye on Cape Flyaway," Melander responded. "Clouds. Sometimes they sit down on the water like brood hens and you'd swear they're land, couldn't be anything but. That Finn skipper spent half of one morning searching our charts for a thunderhead he thought was a piece of Hawaii. We need to take care. This coast would gladly stand us on our ears. Read the map, read the compass, read the landmarks, and not go chasing clouds. That'll fetch us to Astoria. Aye?"

"What'll it be like?" This was Braaf, who took the chance to stop his paddle while asking. "Another wet woodpile like New Archangel?"

"Sailors' buzz I've heard is that it's a proper port but small. Sits on a fat river with Hell's own sandbar at its mouth. The Americans—paddle, Braaf, a scissor of a lad like you is sharp enough to move your mouth and arms at the same time, aye?—the Americans, recent years, have been coming into that country in numbers and they boast Astoria as tomorrow's town of this coast. But all we care is whether ships touch at the place, and touch they do."

Not far into the day, Melander called a pause in the paddling. "Time for a listen," he said.

"A listen—?" Wennberg caught on. "The steamship, you don't think—Melander, damn you seven ways, you said the Russians'd not come chasing after us with it—"

"I still say so. But maybe we'd do well to have a listen now and again, for the practice of it, aye? Close your face, Wennberg."

Melander cocked his long head as if counting the trees of the forested shore. Braaf sat as always but still as a gravestone. Karlsson leaned down toward the water to catch any bounce of sound. Wennberg concentrated so hard his back bowed.

The canoe rolled mildly, moved the heads of the men inches to this side, then same inches to the other, a slow tiny wigwag.

Melander at last turned his gaze, solemn, to Wennberg.

"What—" the blacksmith started, "is there something—Melander, d'you hear—?"

"Aye," intoned Melander. "Clear as anything." The smile came out. "Silence. Which is just what we need to hear, and more of it."

Melander captained them to near North Cape, some thirty water miles downcoast from New Archangel, before stopping. By then Braaf, the least accustomed to exertion, looked particularly done in. But he said nothing, and lent a hand in the unstowing and then in hefting the canoe into shelter among a shore-touching stand of spruce.

Melander stepped over to Braaf. "Let's see."

Braaf held out his hands. "Chafed some just here" —the skin around from the back of each thumb to the forefinger, particular target of sea spray as he'd paddled—"but could be worse."

"So are mine," Melander said. "Three or four days it'll take to toughen the skin there. But then you'll be solid as horn. Braaf, you'll make a deckhand yet."

The sail and mast, fitted onto a pair of long cleft sticks and pegged taut, were put up as tent. Melander had not said so, but he expected shelter was going to be the main service of their sailing equipment.

Wennberg was cajoled into building a fire, Melander apportioned beans and salt beef into a kettle, Karlsson cut spruce boughs to sleep on and spread the sailcloth which would serve as a ground tarp and then their blankets, and dark brought night two of their leaving of New Archangel.

"Cheery as a graveyard, isn't it? The Russians deserve such country."

They were into their third full day of paddling beside the drab-rocked foreshore of Baranof Island, mile of whitish gray following mile of grayish white, and Melander thought it time to brighten the situation.

"Maybe we ought to have pointed north." First words out of Karlsson since breakfast, but at least he was going along with Melander's try. "I've been up the coast a way with the bear milkers and those cliffs are good dark ground."

"You'd see enough gray-gray-gray, white-white-white there too, Karlsson. Go far enough, up past the Aleuts, it's drift ice and glacier, and glacier and drift ice. Cold enough to make the walls creak. No, that's the north slope of Hell up there, the high north. At least credit me with knowing enough to point us the other way. Aye?"

Wennberg jumped for that. "That means you're taking us down Hell's south slope, does it, Melander?"

Melander blew out his breath. "Wennberg, your soul is as dingy as those rocks. Shut your gab and paddle."

Of a sudden, rain swept the coast. Not New Archangel's soft, muslinlike showers, but cold hard rods of wet, drilling down on the men. The downfall stuttered

on their garments—*pit pit pit pit*—like restless fingers
drumming on a knee.

The other three donned well-worn seal-gut rain
shirts, but Braaf sat resplendent in a knee-length
Aleut parka, bright yarn embroidery at the cuffs, a
front ruff of eagle down.

"What're you, on parade?" Wennberg demanded.
"Where'd you come up with that rig?"

Braaf held up a wrist and admired the sewn filigree.
"Round and about, where all good ware comes from,
blacksmith."

"Elegant as new ivory, Braaf," Melander put in
dryly. "If the Koloshes come pestering again, we'll tell
them you're the crown prince, aye? Now paddle."

That day and most of the one after it took them to
reach the southmost tip of Baranof Island, Cape Ommaney.

In that time Braaf and Wennberg and Melander began to realize, though it never would have occurred to
the first two to offer it aloud and even Melander found
the sentiment a bit unwieldy to frame into words, that
in all their seasons at New Archangel they never really
had put eyes on the Alaskan forest. True, timber
hedged the stockade and settlement, furred the isles of
Sitka Sound and the humped backs of mountains
around. But here downcoast, Alaska's forest stretched
like black-green legions of time itself, the horizon to
the left of the canoemen relentlessly jutting with trees
wherever there was firmament for them to fasten them-

selves upright on. Where soil ran out at the shore edge, trees teetered on rock. Fleece-thick as this forest was, it seemed possible that every tree of the coast was in green touch with every other, limb to limb, a continent-long tagline of thicket.

Along this universe of standing wood the Swedes saw not another human—which was what Melander had banked on—nor even sea life to speak of, the Russian-American Company's "marine Cossacks," the Aleuts, long since having harvested these waters bare of otters and seals. What abounded were birds. Lordly ravens, big as midnight cats. Crows, smaller and baleful about it. Sharp-shinned hawks in tree outlooks. Eagles riding the air above the coastal lines of bluff, patrolling in great watchful glides before letting the air spiral them high again. Sea gulls, cormorants, scoters, loons, puffins, kingfishers, ducks of a dozen kinds. At times, every breathing thing of this coastline except the four paddlers seemed to have taken wing.

Cape Ommaney steepened southward into nearly half a mile of summit, evidently detailed to hunch there as the island's last high sentry against the open water all around.

Perhaps the stony bluff put Wennberg in mind of the round-backed mountains near New Archangel, for that evening after supper he nodded out toward the bay between the canoeists' camp and the cape and asked: "What'd you do, Melander, if the *Nicholas* poked around that point just now?"

"After I emptied my britches, do you mean? So then, Wennberg, the *Nicholas* chugs in your dreams tonight, does it? Me, by now I think she's still anchored firm in Sitka Sound and the Russians are in their beds with their thumbs up their butts." The canoe's progress thus far had set Melander up on stilts of humor. "But I've been in error before. Once, anyway—the time I thought I was wrong. What about you other pair, now, what's your guess? Are the Russians panting after us like hounds onto hares as Brother Wennberg thinks? Aye?"

"No," Karlsson offered. "They think we can't survive."

"What the hell makes you think we can?" retorted Wennberg.

"Because we're alive to now, and closer to Astoria each time we move a paddle."

"Your prediction, Braaf?"

"They're not after us. They don't spend thought on us at all by now."

Wennberg snorted. "We dance out of New Archangel practically under their goddamn noses and they don't even think about us? Braaf, your head is mud."

"They need forget us, or we'll mean too much to them. You learn that fast in the streets, blacksmith. The ones who rule never bother their minds with the likes of us. The provisions I took from the Russians, they regret. That they're short of our faces at work call, they regret. Maybe they even regret the Kolosh canoe gone. But us ourselves, we're smoke to them by now."

None of them had ever heard so many sentences one after another out of Braaf and in the silence that followed, it seemed to be taken as truth even by Wennberg that whatever they encountered onward along this coast, and there might be much, the challenge probably now would not be Russian.

They readied in the morning to cross the channel from Cape Ommaney east to Kuiu, the first of the island stairsteps onward from Baranof. On Melander's map Kuiu could have been where palsy seized the mapmaker's hand, a spatter of crooked shores and hedging rocks. Melander said nothing of all this quiver to the other three, simply told them that he judged there'd be stout current up the passage so that they would need to aim mostly south to end up east.

It worked out his way, and by noon the canoe was nearing Kuiu, snow-scarved peaks rising beyond shore. Here, however, the map's muss of dots and squiggles became real, and the coastline stood to them with a rugged headland.

"No hole in the shore, aye?" Surf blasted across rocks not far off the point. "Let's stay away from that horse market," Melander decreed. Avoiding the channel between headland and rocks the canoe stood south again, the paddlers now working directly against the current.

In a few miles a cove revealed itself, but faced open to the weather from the west.

The next break in the shore yawned more exposure yet.

"Damn." Melander's exasperation was outgrowing his epithets. "Is this whole stone of an island unbuttoned like this?"

Two further inhospitable Kuiu coves answered him.

Dusk waited not far by now, and the labor of paddling against the current was sapping the canoemen. From weariness, they nearly blundered into a broad slop of kelp before Karlsson glimpsed it in the gloom.

By now the canoe had reached the southern tip of the island, a rocky point which bade less welcome than any profile yet.

"Bleak as ashes," Melander bestowed on this last of Kuiu. Then reached out the spyglass, to see whether there was any hope out in the channel.

Maybe, he reported. In the water beyond them stood what looked like thin clumps of timber.

Melander lit a pitch splinter in order to peer close at his map. Through the channel hung a thread of line; a ship had navigated here, testimony which was needed now because low rocks and shoals so easily could hide themselves in the gray mingle of water and dusk.

Melander set the craft for the timber clumps. They proved to be small islands, and on one of the narrowest, the kind that sailors said could be put through an hourglass in half a day, the canoeists pulled to shelter just short of full dark.

* * *

That was their first day of stumble, two stair treads of island when but one had been in glimpse. Yet Melander and his three-man navy somehow had alit secure, and after Kuiu the going smoothened.

In the days now, the canoe jinked its way southeast amid constant accessible landfall. The major island called Prince of Wales rests dominantly in this topography like a long platter on a table, smaller isles along its west a strew of lesser plateware of this North Pacific setting. Here the canoeists could cut a course which, while Melander said a snake would break its back trying to follow their wake, kept them mostly shielded from the ocean's tempers of weather. It granted them too a less hectic chance to learn some of the look and behavior of the Northwest coast. How a break in the forest ahead meant not merely gulch or indent of shore, it meant stream and possible campsite. How a bed of kelp could serve as breakwater, smoothen the route between it and shore even when the outer water was fractious. And the vital reading by Melander that alongshore, in a width about that of a broad street, flowed local currents and eddies that sometimes were opposite to a hindering wind or tide. It was not the voyage any of the Swedes had expected, these stints in among the eelgrass and anemones, but they eased the miles.

"New Archangel, there. What d'you suppose they're at, just now?"

"The governor's just done his whole day's labor—taken a sniff of snuff."

"Okhotskans're staring themselves cross-eyed at the bedamned mountains."

"The Finns, they're praying for it to rain ale."

"Trade boots with any of them, would you?"

"No. Not yet."

The spaces between stars are where the work of the universe is done. Forces hang invisibly there, tethering the spheres across the black infinite canyons: an unsee-able cosmic harness which somehow tugs night and sun, ebbtide and flood, season and coming season. So too the distances among men cast in with one another on an ocean must operate. In their days of steady paddling, these four found that they needed to cohere in ways they had never dreamt of at New Archangel. To per-form all within the same close orbit yet not bang against one another.

Meals brought a first quandary. Melander began as cook, but fussed the matter. Perpetually his suppers lagged behind everyone else's hunger. When he could no longer stand Melander's dawdling and poking, Wennberg volunteered himself. That lasted two tries. "You're not smithing axheads here," Braaf murmured as he poked at the char of Wennberg's victuals. Braaf himself, it went without saying, could not be entirely relied upon to prevent food from detouring between his lips instead of arriving at the others' plates. By the sixth day, then, the cooking chore had singled out Karlsson. He was no festal prodigy, but his output at least stilled the nightly grumbling that one might as well go off into the forest and graze.

Wennberg's particular tithe turned out to be his paddling. Not built best for it, much too much ham at his shoulders and upper arms; but Wennberg had the impatience to take on the water like a windmill in a high breeze. Always exerting toward Karlsson's example of deftness, the blacksmith stroked at half again the pace Melander could manage, twice as great as the inconstant Braaf. Day on day the canoe pushed itself through the water primarily on the aft paddles of Karlsson and Wennberg. Melander would have preferred more balance to the propulsion, yet it worked.

To his own surprise as much as anyone's, Braaf proved the best of them at reading the weather. Long before even Melander, the one seasoned sailor among them, Braaf would know a change was coming onto the ocean, as if along with his naive robin face he possessed a bird's hollow bones in which to feel the atmosphere's shift.

And Melander, Melander's personal orbit was detail: Melander navigating, finding fresh water for the cask, fetching firewood, mothering the canoe and its stowage; Melander sew your button for you, treat your blister, sustain you with a midmorning piece of dried salmon, commiserate your ache of knee; the edge strength to hold all into place, Melander provided.

More than this henwork he saw to, though. Subtract parts from this extensive man in their successive value

to the escape, the ultimate item would be his tongue.
For Melander knew what poets and prime ministers
know, that the cave of the mouth is where men's spirits
shelter. His gift of gab stood him well with crews on
all the vessels of his voyaging. Now he worked words
on Wennberg and Braaf and Karlsson like a polish rag
on brass. "Keep your hair on, Wennberg, there'll be
supper quick as quick. . . . Braaf, it would be pretty
to think this canoe will paddle itself, but it won't. Get
the holiday out of your stroking, aye? . . . Karlsson,
that surf looks to me like worse and more of it. Let's
bend our way around, so-fashion. . . ."

Could you, from high, hold to view a certain time of
each evening now—the brink when dark is just over-
coming dusk—you would see a surprising tracery of
bright embers southward from New Archangel: the
fires of each campsite of the canoemen. Only six or
eight, as yet, but trending, definitely trending, draft-
ing fresh pattern along the night coast.

"Too much smoke. We're not signaling Saint Peter
from here." Melander once more. He dropped to his
knees to fan the campfire into purer flame.

"You'd've never lasted over a forge," jeered Wennberg. "A whiff of smoke tans the soul."

Melander calculated. Three camps in a row, this
smoky debate with Wennberg. The tall man made his
decision.

"You need to know a thing, Mister Blacksmith.

Braaf, Karlsson, you also. This I heard from Dob-zhansky, that interpreter who helped me out at first with the Kolosh fishing crews. He came once somewhere into these waters with a trading mission the Russians tried . . ."

The mission had been contrived as retaliation against the Hudson's Bay Company for its practice of slipping firearms to the Sitka Koloshes, so both the Russians and the downcoast natives were in a mood to make as much face as possible. They inaugurated with a night of feast, and Dobzhansky found himself shar-ing a baked salmon and goathorn cups of fermented berry juice with a canoe chieftain. The pair discovered they could converse in the trading tongue of the coast, Chinook jargon. At once the native sought to know of Dobzhansky how many heads the tsar had.

"How many heads? Why, one like you and me."

No, the native made Dobzhansky understand, not how many *heads*. How many *skulls?*

"Skulls? What would the tsar do with skulls?"

Sleep on them, the way Callicum does, the native said, pointing out to Dobzhansky the tribal chief in the middle of the carousal.

"Sleeps on them? Why does he do that?"

For strength, the native answered. Anyone who sleeps on a pile of skulls is a strong man, is he not?

Melander had not intended to tell his crew Dob-zhansky's tale of this coast's people. He was not heaven-certain he should have.

But no more objections were heard about care over campfire smoke.

*   *   *

The water met their daily moods with its own. One morning their channel would drowse, lie heavy, with a molten look like gray bottle glass. Another, it would wake in full fret, white lids of wave opened by wind or current.

The weather could change with knife-edge sharpness. Once they saw to the southeast a pastel fluff of clouds, peach and pale blue, which was directly abutted by an ink cloud of squall: a tender seascape neighboring with tantrum. The join of continent and ocean seemed to excite the weather into such local targeting. Time and time, the canoemen saw a storm swoop onto a single mountain amid many, as if sacking up a hostage as a lesson to all the rest.

Once Braaf pointed out for the others a narrow white sheet of sky, very likely snow, north on the coast behind them. "Stay north and frost the Russians' asses," Melander directed the storm with a push of his hands. It stayed.

A thirty-nosed sea creature poked abruptly from the water, delivered the canoeists a thunderous burp, and sank.

"Sea lions," Karlsson called. When the school surfaced again, each pug-nosed head making steady quick thrusts as if breaking the silver pane of the water, the leathery swimmers held pace for a while alongside the canoe, watching the upright creatures in it.

The past few days Melander had traded about with Karlsson, thinking it well that more than one of them be able to handle the steering paddle at the stern and that these waters were the place to do the learning. Melander once had been told by his Kolosh fishing crew that the practice of some southward natives was to dub the bowman of a canoe "Captain Nose." Accordingly, with Karlsson's move forward Melander bestowed the title on him, and Braaf and Wennberg took the notion up. For the next while, it was all "Captain Nose, Your Honor, what's it to be for supper tonight?" and "May I suggest, Captain Nose, that it's nice to see something ahead besides Melander's back?"

A number of tossful nights passed before any of them could become accustomed to the noise of ocean contending against coast. Surf expelling up the beach and draining back, the increasing crash of tide incoming, the held-breath instants of silence at lowest low tide.

Melander's unease went on longest. An absence of some sort nagged through the dark at him, persistent as the sweet spruce odor of their nightly mattress of boughs. Time and again he would come up in the night, sit a minute in his long angles, propped, and gazing at the blanketed forms on either side of him. Two chosen by him as tools would be pulled from a carpenter's kit, one who had chosen himself. Known casually to one another at New Archangel, but not much more than that. And maybe no more even now, Melander's plan their single creed in common. Behind their foreheads, still strangers to each other. And perhaps would step out at Astoria yet the same. Be it said, among these new watermen waited crosscurrents that, if they were let to flow free, might prove as roily as any of the North Pacific's. Wennberg of course was the oftenest source of tension, for after his manner of wedging himself into the escape none of the others could entirely put trust in him. Then too, as with many strong-tempered men, the anger in Wennberg that could flare pure and fast as pitch fire covered other qualities. A capable enough voyager, able to put up with the discomforts and as steady at the canoe work as could be asked—that was this blacksmith, if some incident did not set him off. But the trigger in Wennberg was always this close to click. As for Melander himself, the problem with so elevated a type is that ordinary men cannot always see eye to eye with him. Difficult to be totally at ease with a man who is thinking so many steps ahead, even though those stairs of thought may be your salvation. Similarly, Karlsson's silent style could be judged a bit too aloof. There seemed to be not much visit in the slender man, and less jokery. "An icicle up his ass," Wennberg was heard to mutter of Karlsson. Braaf? Being around Braaf was like being in the presence of a natural phenomenon, such as St. Elmo's fire or marsh vapors. Braaf simply was there, on his own misty terms, take him for what he was. As if still in echo of their encounter on the parade ground, Braaf and Wennberg it was who were most apt to jangle with each other. Wennberg would suggest that Braaf had about as much weight in the world as the fart of a fly, and Braaf would recommend that Wennberg shove his head up the nearest horse's behind to see whether it held any more exact turds like him. Melander was able to slow their slanging, but never quite to stop it. So it was something to sit up with, the fact of these four separate lives he had gathered under this sailcloth shelter.

At last, amid one of these propped sessions, Melander found the bother to him in the shoresounds of the night. He was listening for the creak of ship timbers, the other part of the choir whenever ocean was heard.

"Sweet porridge with cinnamon," Wennberg burst out one night beside the fire.

The other three broke into laughter.

"Laugh yourselves crooked, you bastards, but you'd give as much for a sweet porridge right now as I would. Trip your own mother to get to it, too, you would."

"Mister Blacksmith is right," Melander admitted with a chuckle. "Though with me it's not sweet porridge, but a feather bed in a sailors' inn I know at Danzig. I could bob in that for a week and never open an eye except to look for more sleep, aye?"

Karlsson nominated next. "A woman I remember in our village in Småland," he said slowly. "Her name was Anna-Karin and her hair was fox red."

Braaf blinked as the other three looked at him, awaiting his choice. "I'll settle just for three paces of headstart on each of you."

To do something about the sameness of their menu Karlsson suggested they try trolling. Out of the canoe, back alongside Melander, was let a line and a hook baited with a sliver of salt beef. On their second day of attempt, Melander yelped when the line whipped taut across his shins. "It's collect the whale or stove the boat," he boomed happily as he hand-over-handed at their catch.

Melander tugged the head of the fish out of the water against the side of the canoe, then halted his grapple. "Mother of Moses," he swore in wonder.

The other three peered over the side at the spiny, reddish mottled lump glaring up at Melander.

"Ugly pig of a thing," observed Wennberg. "What the devil is it?"

"Looks like a toad fathered by a porcupine," muttered Melander. "Could be some kind of cod, my guess. Well, how do you say? Do we try to eat it?"

No one wanted to be the first, repellent as the red snapper looked, to commit one way or the other. Finally Karlsson offered, "I'm the potman, and I'll give a try. But I don't know . . ."

"Hunger is good sauce," Braaf put in dubiously.

"It better be," said Wennberg.

"At least cut off its head first," Braaf prompted.

"Else it looks like it'll be gnawing on us before we can get to it."

"Eat it is," Melander proclaimed. "Somebody reach the gaff and heave the bastard aboard."

"I saw a bear make supper on fish once, near Ozher-skoi." Skinned and baked over coals, the snapper had proved delicious, and Karlsson's relief was such that he was breaking out in words. "He looked big as a bullock. But he swatted salmon out of the water and peeled off just the skin with his claws, skoffed it down dainty as anything."

Melander pretended to ponder. "You'd ought to have invited him for supper tonight. He'd have been welcome to the outside of that sea beast we've just put into ourselves."

A moment of these encamped nights, cherish with Melander the scroll he fetches from its snug place in the canoe.

Hunkered within the firelight as Braaf and Wennberg and Karlsson settle to sleep, he places the waterproof map case beside him. One by one, he polishes four biscuit-sized stones against the leg of his britches. Wipes his fingers down his shirt front. From a pocket digs a stub of pencil. Lays a square of sailcloth the size of a baker's apron, smooths it creaseless. Now extracts the maps and, like a Muslim with a prayer rug, unfurls the roll tenderly onto the cloth and sets a scrubbed stone to weight each corner.

Each time, this unfolding of his set of the Tebenkov maps riffles a profound pleasure through Melander. It is as if an entire tiny commonwealth has sprung to creation just for him. Sprigs small as the point of his pencil denote the great stands of forest. Tideflats are delicately dotted, as if speck-sized clams breathe calmly beneath. Wherever the land soars—and this coastline, recall, abounds in up and down—the rise in elevation is shown as a scalloped plateau. Threaded among the shores and islets go the proven sailing routes, as though an exploring spider has spun his test voyage of each passage. The total of engraver's strokes on each map is astounding, thousands. Melander cannot imagine who among the Russian quill pushers in the Castle possessed the skill and energy for such pin-precise work.

In time since, a poet has offered the thought that it is within civilization's portions of maps now that the injunction ought be inked, *Here be monsters*. Melander's firelit maps represent an instant of balance in humankind's relationship with the North Pacific: after sea serpents were discounted, and before ports and their tentacles of shipping lanes proliferated. To cast a glance onto these superbly functional maps is like seeing suddenly beneath the fog-and-cloud skin of this shore, down to the truth of nature's bone and muscle and ligament. The frame of this shoulder of the Pacific is what Melander avidly needs to know, and the Tebenkov maps peel it into sight for him.

The first map, that of New Archangel and Sitka Sound, Melander particularly gazes at again and again. Detail here comes most phenomenal of all: the exact black speck, slightly longer than wide, which was the Swedes' barracks is shown just above the cross-within-a-cross indicating the Russian cathedral. (That time when Melander unrolled this map to seek Karlsson's opinion about the best route through Sitka's covey of islands, he had been gratified by Karlsson's blink of surprise. "You can see everything but the flea in the governor's ear, aye?") Melander worked much with maps in his sea time, but to be able to trace from the very dwelling where you packed your sea bag, this now is a new thing of the world.

The coastscape at hand just now is not Sitka Sound, however, but the geography enwrapped in the third of Melander's furl of maps. Here these ten or so days south from Sitka the map begins to report a lingual stew, islands left oddly paired—Heceta and Noyes, Baker and Suemez, Dall and San Fernando—from the crisscross of British and Spanish explorations, these names Russified by the New Archangel mapmaker, then notated into Swedish by the pencil of the man above them now: Melander of Gotland gives his centered grin when the full hibble-bibble occurs to him.

Yet seen another way, such a muss of languages is exactly apt, for everything else of this map number three sprawls in pieces as well. Dabs, driblets, peninsulas, spits and spatters, this portion of coastline when rendered into linework looks startlingly like a breathing moil of sea things, jellyfish and oysters and barnacles and limpets and anemones. It takes an effort of will, even for Melander on his knees, to believe they are going to hold motionless, either on the map or in actuality, to permit voyage among them.

The four fresh beards itched. At New Archangel, because the Russians sported beards most of the Finns and Swedes had made it a point to keep clean-shaven. Now Melander's face and Karlsson's were barbed with growth as blond as barley stubble, while Wennberg's ducal whiskers came a surprising rich sorrel shade. Braaf sprouted a thin downy fluff of almost white. "Spread cream on," Wennberg snickered, "and a cat'd lick them off for you."

Melander had started from camp to gather firewood from the drift piles along the top of the tideline when Braaf surprised him by saying, "I'll fetch with you." Braaf volunteering for a chore was an event to put you on your guard considerably, as when a parson might offer to keep you company on your stroll to a brothel.

When they were out of earshot of the others and starting on their armloads, Braaf asked, "Melander, tell me a thing, will you?"

"If I can. What?"

Braaf gave him his upcast look and began. "You were a sailor."

"I was that. Until the Russians set me to putting salt on fishes' tails."

"I had a half-brother. Or at least people said he was,

and we looked alike. He was years older, and a sailor like you. I'd see him on the docks at Stockholm when his ship was in. The *Ambrosius*, a brig, it was. Then I heard the *Ambrosius* had sunk. They said it followed false lights onto the rocks somewhere, England or Spain, one of those places, and every one of its crew was drowned, and then the people there took its cargo from the wreck. Do they do that, Melander? Set false lights so that a ship will come onto the rocks?"

For once Melander's tongue held back. Finally the tall man let his breath out with great slowness and shaped an answer.

"They are called moon-cursers, Braaf. On a black night they hobble a horse and lead him along the shore with a lantern tied to his bridle. The lantern looks like the running light of a ship, and a ship at sea will follow in because it seems a proven course. Follow in to the rocks. Aye, Braaf. They do that."

Braaf nodded above his armload of wood. "I thought they did," he said, and turned back toward camp.

The day Karlsson shot a blacktail deer came none too soon. Melander counted, of course, on appetites being built by the constant paddling. He had apportioned into the provisions the prospect that each man might eat half again as much as usual in a New Archangel day. But they all were devouring more than twice as much, and hungering beyond that; Wennberg in particular was proving to be a human furnace for food. Already the dried salmon they snacked on for energy while paddling was nearly gone, and the potato supply was severely on the wane.

So the venison banquet was glorious, midday on the long slope of beach where the five deer had paused to peer and the biggest of them, a three-point buck, paid to Karlsson for that curiosity.

"Never thought I'd miss all that Russian grease." Fat was a craving of them all. Even as the haunch of the buck was cooking over the fire the Swedes had put their metal cups under to catch the drippings and then spooned them straight down.

"You can fetch us one of these every day, Karlsson, why not."

"You can talk the deer into it, I will."

After the feed Karlsson and Braaf sectioned the rest of the deer meat, Melander and Wennberg then dunking the chunks in boiling sea water to case them against spoilage. "A crime against good meat," as Melander said it, but the other choice was to lose the venison bonanza to the damp weather.

By now, they could notice that daylight, what there was of it, stayed with them a bit longer.

"After Christmas, each day gets a chicken step longer," Melander assured them solemnly.

Even in these sheltered waters the currents sometimes twirled witches' knots in themselves. Once the canoemen watched as such a whirlpool took a drifting tree and spun it like a compass needle in total turn.

* * *

The sky opened entirely one morning, cloudless as if curtains had been taken down.

After days of hovering gray and cloaking rain the sun seemed a new idea in the scheme of things. The fresh breadth of existence was astounding. The nearest mountains stood green as May meadows. The next, loftier group darkened toward black. Then the highest, horizon peaks farthest east and south, were a shadowed blue as though thinning of substance as they extended along the coast.

This fresh light and warmth replenished all four men. "Midsummer Day come early," Melander exulted. "Today we jump over our own heads."

But through the morning the sun hung so low along the southern horizon that the glare made hazard of the water in front of the canoe. An hour or so of the ferocious dazzle left the men air-headed, sozzled with light.

Melander squinted and swore.

"Too much of everything, this bedamned coast has."

By strong afternoon effort when the sun had swung out above the ocean the canoeists managed to make a usual day's mileage.

"Braaf, you piss near me one more time and I'll rub your nose in it like a bitch pup."

Wennberg's warning halted Braaf in mid pull at the front of his thighs. Thoughtfully he arced a look from the item of interest there to the blacksmith seated a few yards away. The look, it could have been, of a marksman calculating windage and declination.

Across the campsite from the pair, ever so slightly Melander shook his head in message: No, Braaf, don't rile the bull.

"I'll wait the day I've enough to drown you," Braaf said offhandedly and eased away into the timber.

A dusk breeze gossiped here and there in the higher-up swags of forest. His wool britches undone, Braaf stood spraddled, any mother's lad with head cocked dreamily to the croon of the great woods.

Abruptly Braaf stopped hearing the wind, all his listening jerked elsewhere. Standing there with his legs wide, Braaf felt the touch of being watched, as when the thief's timbre within him would warn that the instant was wrong for pilferage. But in these woods who—

Braaf spun and met the eyes. Eyes big as his hands, staring at him from either side of an arm-long hooked beak.

In a half moment Braaf recognized that the phantasm was blind, as wood must be: and that up from its carved stare squatted several more stock-still gandering creatures, a ladder of sets of eyes.

Braaf broke to the edge of the trees and urged softly to the other three men, "Come look."

Within and around an opening in the forest they found other acrobat columns of gargoyles, some atilt as if peering more sharply down at the interlopers. Creature upon creature bursting from cedar bole, these carvings annihilated reality, loomed in a middle air of existence as if the knife, adze, whatever edged tool shaved fantasy into form, somehow had flinted life into them as well.

"What's it all?" asked Braaf. "Like those poles the Koloshes stick up, but bigger."

"I'd guess a kind of cathedral," Melander replied.

"Don't give us your hagbag riddles, Melander." Wennberg was reaching a hand up to inspect the joinery of the beak piece onto the column seen first by Braaf. Rather, which first had seen Braaf. In spite of himself the blacksmith was tugged close by the serene craft of these goblin poles. "Next you'll be telling us Braaf is the saint of egg snitchers."

Melander looked steadily at Wennberg. "A kind of cathedral," he repeated. "Whatever it is that these people believe is said in these carvings. Like rune stones, aye?"

Until now, insofar as Melander and company could discern in their clamber down the precipice of coast-line, not another human might ever have existed among these shore islands. Take the matter to truth, though, and their journey more resembled the course a late-of-night stroller might follow through slumbering neighborhoods. In tribal clusters, perhaps as many as sixty thousand residents inhabited this long littoral of what would become British Columbia: Tlingits, Haidas, Tsimshians, Bellabellas, Bella Coolas, Kwakiutls, Noot-kas, peoples often at odds among themselves but who had in common that they put their backs to the rest of the continent and went about matters as if they alone knew the terms of life. For behind the rain curtains of this winter theirs was a Pacific-nurtured existence which asks to be called nothing less than sumptuous. In spawning time the coastal rivers were stippled thick with salmon, veins of protein bulging there in the water to be wrested, fileted, dried for the winter larder. Abovestream the wealth was wood, particularly the cedar whose cunning these people knew how to set free; under their hands it transformed to capacious lodges, canoes the length of a decent trawler, and art, this most startling of art. Tree-sized columns of carvings simply offered the most evident form of how these tribes told stories of the creatures of timber and sea, sang and recited them, danced and acted them behind masks, in chill times wore pelts as if taking the saga animals into themselves.

Out of this vivid swirl wafted, inevitably, the reputation of these coastal people as canoe warriors and slave takers—plus illustrative tales such as that matter of the bed of skulls. These four interloping Swedes knew no specifics of the downcoast tribes, but reason told them this much. If they never dipped paddle into a one of the populated coves where the rain season was being whiled away in performance and potlatch, so much the better luck.

Just now Braaf was the one of them to speak that dialect called if.

"Why's this out here, deserted? If it is."

"Likely they do as the Sitka Koloshes," Melander

guessed. "Hunt from a summer village right around here, in winter pull back to a main village somewhere."

In the dusk, eagle poised eternally atop bear.

Whale stood on end in dive through contorted lesser creatures.

One being, possibly frog the size of calf, pranced merrily upside down.

Every sort of winkless forest changeling, they goggled in unison at the backs of the retreating men.

Later, the others breathing their rhythms of night beside the fire, Melander could not find sleep.

His memory was at a New Archangel market morning, hubbub of Sitka Koloshes and three or four dozen visiting tribesmen from somewhere to the north. Amid the newcomers hawking their wares squatted a seam-faced carver. Word had rippled through the settlement about this man's daggers: blades of power with each hilt carved as the rising neck of some alarming beast. The head topping a hilt neck sometimes was a bear with glinting abalone inlays of eyes and nostrils and teeth, sometimes a long-faced wolf, again a great-toothed beaver; always, angled and fierce and magical as dragons. The interpreter Dobzhansky tried to converse with the northern carver. Dobzhansky's first question received answer, then the native stayed silent. Melander inquired what had been said. Dobzhansky related that he had asked how many years it took to obtain such skill.

"So long as I have lived, so long have I carved," the

daggerman responded. "If the spirit people will let me, I will carve even after I am dead."

Even Melander could not have said why, but that response echoed around in the corners of his mind this night.

Just past daybreak the four men slide the canoe out into surf. Usual bruised-looking sky, tatters of fog in the treetops. This coast's mornings are as if brawl had gone on in the heavens all night.

As ever, trees push down to absolute waterline: boundless green, then immediate blue. You could reach up from swimming and continue your way arm-over-arm through the forest.

This day more, the canoemen pull their way along a lengthy timber-thick island, Dall.

That night: "Sleep deep," Melander advised. "To-morrow we introduce ourselves to Kaigani."

The letters spoke large near the bottom of Melander's third map, and in sober block rather than the finespun script elsewhere on the paper. The space framing them, six widths of Melander's thumb could have spanned. In actuality the plain of water represented there extends twice the distance of the English Channel between Dover and Calais, and no calm white cliffs stand as guides.

Taken all in all, calculated Melander, they compressed into themselves a marathon day of canoe voyage, did those two thickset words: *Proliv Kaigani. Kaigani Strait.*

The water stretched to them out of a horizonless gray, a blob of overcast messily sealing together sea and sky. Melander did not at all like it that no line of land could be seen out there. In the canoemen's island-by-island descent of the coast, Kaigani and the channel which intersected it to the east, Hecate Strait, were the first expanses where the day's shore did not stand steadily in sight. Yet the map vouched to Melander that across in that fume of seawater and cloud the northeast tip of the Queen Charlotte Islands arced toward the canoeists. Hold to a heading of south-southeast and they would aim into its embrace. At least Melander needed to believe that south-southeast could be held to. If not, if current swung them too far eastward, they would be swept from Kaigani directly on into Hecate Strait. One waterstead of distance and risk, Melander reckoned they could manage in the day. Two, he doubted gravely.

From his resumed place at the bow Melander studied back along the canoe at the others. Braaf with his paddle across the gunwales and his fingers restless atop the wood as if absently plucking music. Wennberg eyeing askance at the wide water. Stock-still, Karlsson; the steering paddle needed his skill today.

What was required of Melander now was a division of faith. Certain of himself, confident of what he could

make in his mind, going through life as if he had always a following wind; such had been Melander's history, self-belief. Now he needed to apportion trust into
these other three in the canoe with him, into the coil
of map which promised firm earth out there over the
precipice of water, into the hovering grayness, into the
canoe, paddles, compass. . . .

Melander spat over the side to clear his mouth, not
recognizing the taste of diluted faith but decidedly not
caring much for it. Then he said: "Time for our
stroll."

The powerful rumple of the Pacific made itself felt
to them at once. Swells were spaced wide, perhaps two
lengths of the canoe between crests, but regular as
great slow breathings. Each swell levered up the prow
of the canoe, Melander instantly created even taller, a
foremast of man, then the craft was shrugged downward.

"More beef, Wennberg. Push that paddle deeper,
aye?"

Melander's urging began while the tips of the fir
trees of Dall Island still feathered against the sky behind them. Wennberg he had not expected to be slack
in this situation. Braaf it was who could be anticipated
to scant his labor if high heaven itself depended on it.
But Braaf was thrusting steadily, and onto Melander's
admonition tossed gibe of his own.

"Bashful are you, Wennberg? Reach right down
there and meet the wet, why not. . . ."

Wennberg grumped something unhearable, but his paddling picked up markedly.

What Melander's Russian map here denominated as Kaigani Strait has since become Dixon Entrance, a name engrafted for the English captain who delved the region in the ship *Queen Charlotte*. By whatever christening, the expanse forms one of the largest of dozens of plains of water between the broken lands of the North Pacific coastline. Extensive in its perils as well, this water. "The tidal currents are much confused," navigators are cautioned; in storm the channel can seem to be forty white miles of breakers. All times of year the flood tide east into Hecate Strait can surge as rapid as a man can walk. Small wonder that at the eastern reach of this mariners' thicket, islands are bunched like galleons desperately seeking a lee anchorage.

Not a whit of this was suggested from that calm space between shorelines on Melander's map.

"Got a lump in it today, it has," Melander admitted as a wave shuddered the canoe.

Thirty or forty hillocks of water later, again the heart skip in the rhythm of the boat.

"Wennberg!" Melander's tone crackled now. "You're dabbing at it again."

Wennberg held his paddle just above the lapping waves, as though trying to recall whether water or air was the element in which it operated. His face hung open in surprise. His mouth made motions but no sound. Then with gulped effort: "I'm. Getting. Sick."

"If you don't paddle you'll get dead, and us with

you. Have a puke now and be done with it, Wennberg. We need your arms, aye?"

Wennberg glassily found Melander, seemed to mull the suggestion, then shook his wide head.

"Drag it up," Melander insisted. "You've got to."

Wennberg put his head over the side of the canoe and gaped his mouth as if hoping to inhale better health up from the ocean.

After a minute his gasps managed to be words: "Can't. Too. Sick."

"Wennberg, listen to me, aye? Jab a finger down your gullet, tell yourself you've swallowed baneberries, pretend that Braaf here melted a slug into your tea this morning—do whatever the hell, but heave the sickness out of you now. Do it, Wennberg. Dump your gut."

"Keep on, you'll have me tossing up, too," muttered Braaf.

Just then Melander's prescriptions took their intended effect on Wennberg.

"There now, you're empty and scraped," Melander proclaimed in satisfaction. "You'll be a bull again before you know it. Rest a half moment, we can spare you until you get your breath back."

Wennberg focused woozily toward Melander. "Melander—one time I'll—reach down that—mouth of yours and—" But before long, he retrieved his paddle and, while still not able to stroke in smoothness with the others, was adding push to theirs.

* * *

For a time—say, the first few dozen hundred pad-dlestrokes of this day's journey—a wall of reassurance yet could be seen behind the canoemen, the outline of Dall Island and its greater neighbor, Prince of Wales. Farther though that landline was becoming, the shore of the islands lay as a footing, a ledge to return to.

Then, just after Melander reckoned aloud that they might be a third of the way across, Karlsson glanced back and saw that the landwall was gone. In place of the islands hovered a sheet of storm. Kaigani had en-wrapped the canoe and its men, anywhere about them nothing other than water or cloud or mix of the two.

They had no timepiece, but an onlooker could have clocked Melander's decrees to within two minutes' reg-ularity of one another. Each time he called rest, one man continued to paddle to keep the canoe from back-sliding in the swells. That sentinel then rested briefly while the other three resumed, then plunged to work again. At the next rest, the solitary paddling duty slid to the next man.

Near to what Melander estimated ought to be the midpoint of the channel, waves began to chop more rapidly at the canoe. A fresh sound, a slapping higher against the side of the craft, could be heard, and spray now and again tossed itself over the bow and Melander.

"A fast ship's always wet forward," he called out, the while wondering how much more the water would thicken.

Braaf, though, noticed an absence. The gulls which hung in curiosity beside them in the island waters and the early distance offshore from Dall were vanished. He discovered too that the air felt different, more tooth in it, and that off to the west a particular splotch of weather resembled neither fog nor rain.

Braaf leaned ahead enough to pass the news softly over Melander's shoulder, as it were their secret: "Snow."

"Jesu Maria," Melander said back.

The squall hit them first with wind. Gust tagged closely onto gust, taking the canoe at an angle from the southwest.

Melander watched along the surface of Kaigani intently. *Upon the high seas* is the wrong saying of it, a horizon of ocean all around makes shallow the place of an onlooker, sloshes even a Melander in a basin of the taller water.

Then what Melander dreaded sprung to creation. Wind streaks on the water, long ropy crawlers of white. "Neptune's snakes," Melander knew them as from his shipboard years, and knew too that they are the spawn of a thirty-knot gale.

"Melander!" Karlsson called forward. "We need be steadier with the paddles. That slap the Koloshes do, let's try . . ."

"Be the drum lad," Melander agreed instantly. "Braaf, Wennberg, listen sharp . . ."

127

Karlsson began as the next wave struck the canoe, quivered it. He paddled twice, deep strokes; then rapped his paddle against the side of the canoe, just below the gunwale.

The craft meanwhile mounted the roll of water, another hummock waited to slide under the hull. When it came, again Karlsson's double stroke and rap to signal pause.

The other three took the rhythm and the canoe steadied its pace, two strong climbing strokes up each wave, the tap of waiting, then next wave and same again.

The sky began to fleck, snowflakes like tiny gulls riding down the wind which now strengthened into a constant whirl past the canoemen's ears. Melander looked away from his compass only to monitor the stroking of his crew and to glance at the angle of the swells to the canoe. The compass could not be wrong, daren't be, yet there was constant urge to check it against the evidence of his eyes.

Water was finding its way over the gunwales, lopping in off rollers now mighty enough that when they crested beneath the bow, Melander went so uplifted he had to reach far down to get his paddle to the ocean.

Chop of this sort needed rapid heed. Still struggling against seasickness, Wennberg was erratic at the paddle. But if he lowered his head to bail, he would be sicker yet. So—"Braaf." Water noise made Melander raise his choice to a shout. "*Braaf!* You'll need to shovel water, and quick!"

Three motions fought in the water now: the broad sloshing advance of the waves themselves; the lizardy wrinkle of their texture; and the gale ripple skipping ahead. At odds with all these and with the wind-spun snow as well, the canoe's progress fell to a kind of embarrassed wallow, as when a good steed is forced to slog through mire.

Working the bailer, a cedar scoop which coupled over his hand like a hollowed-out hoof, Braaf pawed seawater from the canoe's bottom.

Karlsson gritted against spray and snow and tried to hold in mind nothing but the pulse of stroke stroke slap, stroke stroke slap. But he somehow did hear the voice of agony in front of him. "Oh God who watches over fools and babes," Wennberg implored. "What am I doing in this pisspot of a canoe?"

Like a prophet promising geysers of honey just there beyond shovel point, Melander preached steadily to his straining crew now. . . . "We're straddling it, Karlsson. No water is wide as forever . . ." Karlsson's face could have been mounted forward as figurehead for the craft, if imagination permits that a Kolosh canoe ever would breast the sea with a Småland parson's profile at its front. Everything, each fiber, of Karlsson was set to the twin grips of his hands on the steering paddle, the portioning-out of effort. If stone profile and mill-work arms could grind a way across Kaigani, Karlsson meant it to be done. . . . Melander: "Dig the paddle, Wennberg. You're strong as wake ale now." (Melander within: May he not go ill on us again, this lumpy water is no place for a cripple in the crew. . . .) But Wennberg yet tussled with a hive of woes. The tipping wave surface was bad enough, and the unending exertion, and the over-the-side-of-the-world absence of land or even horizon. Worst of all, the nausea which hid so sly within him, reambushing whenever he thought the bile might have receded. The blacksmith felt weaker than he could ever remember, listless, yet this uphill labor of paddling demanded and demanded of him. Wennberg too fell into a machined rhythm, jab-pull back-jab, wait, do-it-again, but out of a different drive-wheel than Karlsson's. Overswarmed with doom and unhealth, Wennberg could think of no way to struggle back but to move his arms, which happened to have a flat-faced rod of wood at their end. . . . Melander: "Braaf, can you find in your heart to stroke along with the rest of us?" (Melander within: May the canoe dance as lightly on these waves as it has been. If just they don't rise . . .) Among the larger men Braaf sat small and hunched with caution. He was the one of the four of them most in place in this situation, for at basis, this crossing of Kaigani Strait constituted an act of theft. Of stealing survival from a hazard that held every intention of denying it to you. Afloat you exist in balance between unthinkable distances. Above, the sky

and the down-push of all its vastnesses. Under, the
thickness of ocean with its queer unruly upward law of
gravity, buoyancy. In time the greater deep, that of
sky, must win this pushing contest in which you are the
flake of contention, and you will go down. The game is
to scamper landward before this obliteration can happen. None of this could Braaf have declaimed aloud—
just as there never was a philosopher who could pocket
another man's snuffbox with no itch of conscience—yet
Braaf understood the proposition of Kaigani profoundly: it had to do with dodging life's odds, like all
else. Braaf then did not stroke mechanically in Karlsson's way nor try to fend strenuously as Wennberg did.
Braaf poked his paddle to the water as if using a stick
to discourage a very big dog . . . Melander: "Neck
or nothing, now. Pull . . . pull . . . pull . . ." (Melander within: May this storm hold to the compass
where it is. But oh God if the bastard shifts, shoves us
east into the miles of Hecate . . .) So the matter, like
most of this coast's matters, came down to perseverance.
While Melander urged, Wennberg was grunting dismally and Braaf once in a while shirking, out of sheer
habit when he wasn't reminding himself otherwise, and
at the stern Karlsson staying a human piston: all of
them trying to put from mind the numbing of their
knees and the deepening ache of their arms and shoulders; and across Kaigani Strait the canoe striving
steadily southeast, a dark sharp-snouted creature
stretched low against the gray wavescape, four broad-
hoofed legs striking and striking at the water, running
on the sea.

THREE

MELANDER broke awake on the tamest of terrain.

Anywhere in sight, not a sea cliff nor boulder nor so much as a fist-sized stone.

Beach of sand, all tan satin. Waves did not pound at the tideline, simply teased it, shying tiny clouds of spume along the water edge and then lapping away.

The canoe had taken shore here in the dark, Swedes having prevailed—barely—over storm in the wrestle that went on all day and across dusk and into the first of night. At last dragging their craft onto whatever this place was, the four men groped together the shelter of sailcloth and collapsed to sleep. Now to find, by this morning's evidence, that Kaigani had flung them through the customary coastal geography to an opposite order of matters. Everything flat, discreet, lullful.

No, not everything meek. It registered now on Melander that the treetops spearing up through mist just to the west of him stood twice the height conceivable for trees to stand.

"On the same ocean as last night, are we?" Karlsson was at his elbow.

"Mother's milk this morning, isn't it?" agreed Melander. "Ever see trees to that height, up to the clouds like steeples?"

Karlsson shook his head.

"Nor I. Has to be a rise of land in that fog. We ought have a look there, aye? Wake Braaf enough to tell him, why don't you, so he and Wennberg won't think we've gone yachting off without them."

The tall man and the slim one pushed the canoe into the placid tidewater, turned the prow toward the middle-air mosaic of mist and timber. They found that they were crossing the mouth of a river, a sixty-foot width of black water so dense and slow it seemed more solid than the beach and forest on either side. Lacquered and beautiful, this surprise ebony river, and along its surface small circlets of foam spun like ghostly anemones.

On the river's far side a gray-black rim of rock showed itself over the waterline and just under the bank of mist. Rapidly this dour rim bent outward into a point, of no height to speak of but too sharp-sided to land the canoe.

"On around," Melander decreed, and the pair of canoemen began to skirt the protrusion.

Karlsson glanced inland, drew his paddle into the canoe, and pointed upward.

The fog was lifting from the forest and, abruptly, half a small mountain stepped into view: a startling humped cliff as if one of the cannonball peaks around Sitka had been sawed in half from its summit downward. This very top, start of the astonishing sunder, the pair of men could see only by putting their heads back as far as they could. They might have been peering through the dust of eons rather than the morning's last waft of sea mist. On the sheerness, clumps of long grass somehow had rooted here and there atop basalt columns; together with moss growth, these tufts made the cliff face seem greatly age-spotted, Methuselan.

As the men gaped up, two bald eagles swept soundlessly across the orb of stone.

Around the point Melander and Karlsson pulled the canoe to security and clambered onto the flow of black rock beneath the cliff for a fuller look.

"God's bones, what a place," Melander murmured.

The point had been convulsed into hummocks and parapets, pitted with holes as if having come under siege from small cannon, strewn with a tumble of black boulders the size of oxcarts, and finally riven with tidal troughs.

As Melander and Karlsson stood gawking, surf blasted up from a blowhole behind them. A mocking geyser of white bowed toward them as they whirled to the commotion.

"Aye, well. At least we know what's hung those trees into the middle of the air." Atop the dome of cliff over them, tall evergreens poked forth like feathers in a war bonnet. "Had better find a way up there, I had, and see if I can place us on the map. If any Koloshes show up, trade Wennberg to them for a haunch of beef, aye?"

Melander long-gaited off around the base of the cliff. Staying in range of where they had landed the canoe, Karlsson passed time by exploring into the start of the stand of forest between half-mountain and river. Cedar richly scented the air. To Karlsson, these days of the coast had been a holiday for the nose. No more of the accumulated man-smells of the barracks—damp boots, aged mattresses, tobacco, clothes as winter-stale as the tasks they were worn to . . .

He was beside the bole of a particularly huge cedar when a fat bead of water ticked his right wrist.

In surprise, Karlsson tipped his head until he was peering straight up. He saw another water bead detach from a limb eighty feet above him and drop like a slow tiny jewel, giving him time to step aside before it struck.

Another, another.

Karlsson stepped, stepped again.

Like strange slowed-down rain the droplets descended two, three to the minute. The forest trees had become sharp green clouds, Karlsson upturned to them as a sunflower will seek the sun, the leisured freshet the pulse of attraction between them. Drop and drop and drop Karlsson evaded lithely, stepping back and forth around the girth of the tree, face up like a drunk man at the gate of God. As coal is said to concentrate to diamond, the coastal world of water spun tiny in these falling crystals: flicker of a mountain stream trying to leap from itself, white veils of spray brushing back from the Pacific's wave brows, quick thin lakes strewn by a half-day rain, all here now flying down in sparkle. The moment bathed Karlsson. His mind went free, vaulted the exertions and dangers of the past many days, nothing existed but the beaded dazzles from above and his body, slow-dancing with water . . .

"At least I know who not to stand sentry the next time it rains, aye?"

Karlsson halted in place, looked around at Melander, and was promptly splattered with a dew glob atop his head. The tall man's amusement twitched behind his mouth.

"Moonbeams must have got into me," Karlsson offered, vastly embarrassed.

"I can believe this place sends a man lopsided," said Melander. "Let's get back to the beach before I go chasing raindrops myself."

Melander discovered from the summit that the arc of beach continued some miles northeastward, to Hecate Strait. This intelligence turned into taunt, however, by the time he and Karlsson returned to the campsite. Wind was pushing in off Kaigani. Not wanting a repeat of the crossing they just had endured, the canoemen sat to wait out the bluster.

* * *

And the wind stiffened. By the afternoon, there were roars of air. A sky-filling sound like that of vast flame. The wind itself seemed cross-purposed, now in great speed to one direction and the next moment whooshing back. Kaigani meanwhile turned ice-gray, with slopes and pools of foam everywhere on it.

When firewood was needed the men went out from the shelter in pairs, one to gather, the other to watch against widowmakers flying down out of the shore forest. Often a gust slammed so hard a man had to bend his knees to stay upright.

For three days of this blow they held to the site— gaining no distance, which Melander knew was the same as losing it.

During a lull, Braaf scuffed a boot against something in the sand, close by where the other three sat sheltered. A dead loon, its bill thrust ahead like a bayonet, one checkered wing stiffly cocked a bit as though readying to fly, the rest of the body beneath the beach surface.

"Buried as Bering," said Melander.

"Means what?" queried Braaf.

"It's something the Russian navy men say. Bering was a skipper, an old sir, first one into the islands up where the Aleuts come from. He was sailing in the tsar's hire, a ship called the *Saint Peter*. A true Russian vessel, leaky as a basket. Somewhere up there among the Aleuts they got themselves wintered in. Those islands haven't a whisker of timber, so Bering and his crew dug into sandhills, pulled over sail canvas for roof. Lived in burrows like lemmings, aye? Lived till they died, at least, and then, the Russians tell it, foxes would come into camp and gobble the bodies. Bering himself took frail and they laid him in one of the dugouts. Sand caved down over his feet, but he wouldn't let the crew dig it away. Said it kept him warm. Then sand over his knees. Still wouldn't let them dig. Then up to his waist. Next his belly, just before he died. Very nearly all in his grave before the last breath was out of him. So, buried as Bering, a Russian'll say to feel sorry for himself."

"How about melon-headed as Melander?" Wennberg suggested. "Do the Russians say that one, too?"

Melander cut a quick look at Wennberg. His sarcasm notwithstanding, the broad man did not seem to be in the brownest of his moods.

"Wennberg, Wennberg. Always ready to bone the guff out of me, aye? Tell me a thing, how do we come by this honor of having you in our crew? What sugar was it that kept you on at New Archangel past your years?"

Wennberg studied the tall leader. Then he spat to one side and muttered: "Serving for Rachel."

Melander tugged an ear. "Lend us that again?" Karlsson and Braaf also glanced over at Wennberg.

" 'Laban had two daughters: the name of the elder was Leah, and the name of the younger was Rachel. Leah was tender-eyed, but Rachel was beautiful and well favored. And Jacob loved Rachel, and said, I will serve thee seven years for Rachel.' " Wennberg broke off his recital and spat again.

Melander and Braaf and Karlsson stared at him.

"Never heard Genesis before?" Wennberg resumed. "Doesn't surprise me, you'd all be off diddling squirrels instead of—"

"Wennberg a Bible-spouter!" Braaf looked genuinely shocked.

The blacksmith shifted uneasily. "My family were church-strong. So's I, when I was a young fool."

"This Rachel matter," Melander pursued. "It sounds more like a sweetmeat for Karlsson than for you."

"Judas's single ball, Melander, can't you tell a goddamned saying when it comes out anybody's mouth but your own? Serving for Rachel means—it means being done out of something." Wennberg drew a breath. " 'And Jacob said unto Laban, give me my wife, for my days are fulfilled, that I may go in unto her. . . . And it came to pass, that in the morning, behold, it was Leah; and he said to Laban, What is this thou has done unto me? Did I not serve with thee for Rachel?' " Wennberg glowered across at Melander. "Now d'you savvy it?"

"Aye," said Melander softly. "I just didn't recognize Laban as a Russian name."

"Tell us a thing, Braaf. You've earned with your pockets, as they say. What's the grandest thing you ever stole?"

Braaf blinked in Wennberg's direction. "Your nose, from up your ass where you usually keep it."

"Just trying to be civil, you Stockholm whelp. Some-

thing to pass the time from squatting on this goddamned sand, I thought."

"The pair of you," Melander conciliated. "Don't
make a feather into five hens."

Braaf eyed up into the line of timber, the treetops
nodding this way and that in the wind. "Could tell you,
though, if I wanted. If I was asked right."

The request for etiquette sank through to Wennberg.
"Oh, God's green socks, all right, Braaf, all right.
Would you be so kind as to tell us whatever the hell it is
you have in mind?"

"A time, I was working slow——"

"Working? I thought this is going to be true."

"Near enough the truth for common purposes, as we
say on ship," Melander suggested. "Let Braaf get on
with it, aye?"

"Your little finger's between your legs, Wennberg.
Working slow is a way we go about it in the streets.
Walk as if counting the cobblestones, that's what it
means. Do that, and you see what's around. See who's
forgot a window, or whose purse is sleeping fat in his
coat. So I spied the thimble then. A shopman was sweeping——"

"Thimble? You went round Stockholm stealing thim-
bles? Christ and the devil, Braaf, some tales I've heard
in my time but——"

"The thimble's the chance, ironhead. Means you see
a chance for yourself. Haven't you heard anything in
this world but a hammer?"

Wennberg muttered this or that. Braaf resumed.

"The shopman was sweeping the steps. Had one of

those birch brooms—widow's musket they're called,
isn't that so, Wennberg? So he had his back away from
me, and the door just open, like so. I slipped in, knew
I had to be fast. A shopkeeper likes to be clever. Else
he wouldn't be a shopkeeper. Sometimes he'll stash
money right there, in some crock like any other. Biscuits
here and salt herring there and just maybe riksdaler
somewhere around. This time, there're crocks on parade.
All along there. So I picked one, lifted the lid. And
there they were, riksdaler and more of them. My pockets
had mumps when I went out of the place. I slid behind
the shopman, he's at the other end of the steps by now,
ask him please sir, is the store open? Never to the likes
of me, he says. Runs me off. Tells himself, clever man
like him he'll not let in some street stray."

"The money, Braaf," prompted Wennberg. "What'd
you do with it all?"

Braaf reflected. "It lasted just about as long as it's
taken to tell of it."

Their third morning storm-held on the Kaigani shore,
a gunshot clapped sleep out of the men under the sailcloth shelter. Then another, even as Melander flung up
and out of the tent like an aroused stork and Wennberg
and Braaf were untangling from their blankets.

Melander immediately was back to say that Karlsson
was absent, along with his hunting rifle and Bilibin's
gun. "Bear milking, he must be."

The pairs of shots continued as the three men got
breakfast into themselves. Then after a time of no firing,

Karlsson appeared with a bag of ducks, a dozen or more as he emptied the sack.

"Weathered in, like us," was his report. "There at the river mouth."

"A lazy wind, we call this on Gotland." Now the next morning after the duck plucking. "It goes through you instead of around you."

"Melander, serve you a plate of fly shit and you'd declare it pepper," muttered Wennberg.

"And you'd lend me your soul as salt, aye, Mister Blacksmith? But we have deciding to do. We've been holed here too damned long. The water ahead of us doesn't shrink while we're here. I say we had better chance the next stretch today, wind or no. Karlsson?"

"You're the sailor of us. How much of this wind is between us and the next island?"

"I think six hours' paddling."

"Six hours, we can last. I say chance."

"Braaf?"

The thief glanced out into the white-capped water, then somewhere above Melander's brow. "If you say so, chance."

"Wennberg?"

"The only thing worse than that bedamned water is this bedamned waiting. Chance, Melander. You know so God-all much, teach us how to eat the wind. May it sit better on my stomach than that last ration did."

* * *

For a change, luck puffed on them. Once the paddling men had struggled the canoe around the horn tip of the beach, they came into a wind skewing directly across Hecate Strait. For the first time since their leaving of New Archangel, up went the canoe's small pole of mast and the sailcloth.

"Not much of a suit of sails, more like a kerchief," as Melander said, but the canvas carried them across the strait and once more into a scatter of shoreline islands.

"Even this hardtack isn't as bad as it might be." Melander, musing, their first day of south-paddling after wafting across Hecate Strait. "A time I can tell you on the brig *Odin*, we had to break our biscuits into our coffee and skim away the weevils as they came up. No, not so bad, aye?"

Braaf, at the onset of their second day after: "I know what Valhalla is now. It's where I never again hear Melander say, 'Tumble up.' "

Wennberg, midway of their third day and yet another Melander monologue: "Melander, I wonder you don't swallow your tongue sometime for the savor of it."

* * *

"Good job of work done": Karlsson, startling them all after they hefted ashore into the spruce forest at the close of their fourth straight progressful day.

The river shoved through the land like a glacier of slate. Had the surface been solid as its turbid appearance—one newcoming settler or another inaugurated the jest that in the season of runoff not much more mud content was needed to make the flow pedestriable—a man crossing here from its north shore toward its south would have had to hike steadily for a full hour. That man would have stridden the Columbia, largest river of the Pacific shore of the Americas, and there on the south bank he would have stamped silt from his feet at Astoria.

Another frontier pinspot of great name, Astoria. John Jacob Astor's wealth, not to say intentions for more of it, installed the settlement as a fur depot in 1811. The ensuing four decades had not made it much more of a place: post office, customs house, long T-shaped dock straddling into the tidal flow, cooperage, Methodist church, handful of stores and saloons catering to the settlers sprinkled south and north of the river's mouth, several tall Yankee houses along the foot of a shaggy Columbia headland. A rain-soaked shore-sitting little colony, each low tide showing the shins of the town. Yet also the recognized port of America's Pacific Northwest, tapping the twelve-hundred-mile-long Columbia and its tributaries like a cup hung to gather the sugar of a

giant maple. Month by month a dozen or fifteen vessels
plied here. So yes, if through whatever unlikelihood you
were to find yourself at Astoria, you could handily
enough aim yourself onward into the world.

This night, the four canoe-going Swedes are encamped not quite half the water distance downcoast
from New Archangel to that long T of dock at Astoria.

Trying to yawn the last of sleep from himself, Karlsson eased out through the trees toward the island's
edge. As usual now that the voyaging rhythm had
worked its way into him, he was the first awake and the
earliest to wonder about weather.

This morning he found that the Pacific lay gray with
cold, but no storm sheeted up from its surface. Along
the beach ahead a small surf pushed ashore, idly rinsed
back on itself: low tide. A pair of cormorants amid a
spill of tidal boulders hung their black wings wide. High
up on the beach gravel a hundred or so strides away the
sharp-prowed canoe rested, as if having plowed to a fur-
row end and now waiting to be turned for another day's
tilling.

Between one eyeblink and the next, Karlsson's brain
filled with the jolt of what he was seeing. He and Melander and Wennberg and Braaf had carried their canoe
as ever into the cover of forest for the night: this canoe
sat larger by half: the painted designs entwining the
prow were different, simpler, bolder: and Karlsson by
now was in crouched retreat toward the trees, staring

hard at the wall of forest beyond the canoe for any sign that he had been detected.

Putting his fingers lightly across the tall man's mouth to signal silence, he roused Melander. Melander snapped awake with the quickness learned of arising to some thousands of shipboard watches and crept behind Karlsson away from the camp.

"A big one," Karlsson husked when they had sidled far enough not to be heard. "Eight, ten paddlemen at least."

"Cabbageheads. Why aren't they holed up for the winter like the Sitka Koloshes? What do they think this is, the Midsummer's Day yachting? Aye?"

"We had better hope they're not going to hole up here."

"No, just one canoe, they couldn't be. Seal hunters or a fishing crew or some such, out for a few days. Cabbageheads."

"You already called them that, and they're still here."

"Aye, so. What's your guess, can we get our canoe to the water and slide away without them seeing us?"

"No."

"No. Outwait them without them tumbling onto us?"

"No."

"No." Melander grimaced as if his echo word had hurt his ears, then squinted back toward camp. "You greet Braaf, I'll do Wennberg."

Again fingers of silence awoke lips. Again Karlsson told the situation.

When his words had sunk into Wennberg and Braaf,

Melander sent Braaf, the most accomplished slinker among them, to keep watch on the beach.

Then Melander glanced at Karlsson, and Karlsson, after hesitation, nodded. "Yes, it needs to be him."

The pair of them turned their eyes to Wennberg. Melander asked: "How are you at turning yourself into a sand crab?"

Wennberg's debut into the art of creeping also marked the first occasion in his life that he ever regretted his strength. Regretted, rather, that more of his power wasn't directly beneath his nose, as Melander's was. "This one is your line of country, Wennberg. You need to do it, or those people of that canoe will snore tonight on our skulls." And Karlsson in his rock-faced way agreeing that only Wennberg possessed the muscle for it; Wennberg could not choose between fury at Karlsson for siding with Melander or ire at him for doing it dubiously. Every lens of clarity, Wennberg believed, had slipped from his life when he leagued himself with this muddle of—

A stone nicked Wennberg's right knee and cued his attention back to creeping. Here in the first eighty yards or so he had cover of a sort, a rib of rock and drift logs behind which he managed to scuttle, chest almost down to his knees, without showing himself, much. But next lay a naked distance of thirty yards. An angle across and up the beach, to the unfamiliar canoe.

At the end now of his final driftlog Wennberg squatted dismally, rubbed the stone bruise on his right knee, and glared back toward where he had departed from Melander, Karlsson, and Braaf.

"Puny bastards," he muttered.

From amid the spruce there a hand flashed into sight —Wennberg knew it would be Melander's—and patiently waved him on.

Wennberg braced, unhunched himself, and in a rolling stride ran toward the beached canoe.

He ran with his elbows cocked almost full out and his head sighted low, as if butting his way. Under his boots gravel clattered wildly, avalanche-loud it seemed to him. God's pity, those fish-fuckers in the forest would have to be without ears not to hear this commotion—

Past the stern of the canoe Wennberg plunged, like a ball rolling beyond its target. He hovered an instant, selecting, then stooped to thrust both hands beneath a gray boulder wide as his chest. Gravel roweled the backs of his hands, his wrists, and finally his forearms as Wennberg wrestled the rock. His breath ached in his throat. With a grunt he brought the burden upward. Grappled it into balance on his knees, next across his waist. Now like a washerwoman carrying an overfull tub of water, turned with the boulder toward the canoe.

Five staggering steps to the wooden wall of the craft, Wennberg more certain with each that the gunblast which would close off his life was being cocked behind him.

Above the bow, just there where the interior of the canoe came to sharpness and prow began to rise—just there where Melander had told him to target, Wennberg heaved the boulder within his arms to the height of his neck. Then with one last grunt let it crash onto the cedar craft.

The crunch was not loud, to Wennberg the first luck anywhere in this situation. But the end of the canoe, thin-carved for its sharp slide through water, split open —and back from the rock as well, a fracture wide as the side of a hand sprung toward midship.

Wennberg gave a rapid glance at his sabotage, skirted the stern of the canoe and was running again, a bear in a footrace.

He had just passed the drift log when he heard the shout behind him, and he did not look back.

Ahead of him Melander and Karlsson and Braaf were putting their own canoe into the surf, Melander somehow finding time as well to urge Wennberg to hurry and lend a hand.

They shoved with their paddles just as the first rifle ball tossed up water beside them. Wennberg in puffing agony glanced around to see two natives with rifles raised, others clustered around the bow-broken canoe, more oh God more emerging from the forest.

Karlsson, who had ended up in the bow, turned and hurried a shot at the two riflemen. It missed but caused them to flinch back from the bullet's ricochet among the beach gravel.

"Paddle-JesusJesus-paddle-paddle-paddle!" Melander was instructing. Another bullet's toss of water, this one nearer. The Swedes stroked as if hurling the ocean behind them as a barrier, and the canoe climbed a mild breaker, sped down its seaward side, climbed a stronger wave and downsped again, then slid rapidly southward from the firing figures on the beach.

Out of the fear and excitement of the escape something other began to grope through to Karlsson in the next moments. From his place at its forepart, he sensed a change about the canoe. Its rhythm felt lightened. Not gone erratic as during Wennberg's sickness at Kaigani, but lessened, thinned.

Karlsson turned enough to look straight back.

"Sven?" he called. "*Sven!*"

At the stern of the canoe Melander, almost tidily, lay folded forward, the upper part of his long body across his knees, the back of his head inclined toward the other three canoemen as if to show them where the rifle ball had torn its red hole.

FOUR

Death's credence comes to us in small costs, mounting and mounting.

At first within the canoe, capacity only for the disbelief. Melander gone from life, the long coast snapping down the cleverest of them as an owl would a dormouse.

Like wild new hearts this shock of loss hammered in Braaf and Wennberg and Karlsson, there never could be room for all the resound in their minds, any minds, it thudded around ears and trembled in throats, such concussion of fresh circumstance: Melander's body now a cargo, deadweight, clotting not just the pulse of the canoe but of whatever of existence was left to the other three of them. . . .

After, it could only seem that during this blind thunderous time the canoe sensed out its own course. When the thought at last forced a way to one of them—Karlsson, the displaced steersman in the bow, it happened to be—that to pull numbly on paddles was not enough, that a compass heading and a map reading were necessitated, the needle and the drawn lines revealed the canoe to be where it ought; where Melander would have steered it.

In that catch-of-breath pause, Braaf whitely burrowing the compass and map case from beneath the corpse that was Melander, Wennberg in a sick glaze handing on the instrument and container to Karlsson—in that stay of time, the absence began its measured toll on them.

Melander's sailor-habited scrutiny of the water around, every chance of rock or shoal or tide rip announced.

The reminding word to Braaf when he made his habitual dawdle in shifting his paddle.

Regulation on Wennberg's bluster, which evidently even Wennberg had come to rely on.

The musing parleys with Karlsson, treetop communing with stone.

Day on day and all the waking hours of those days, such losses of Melander would be exacted now, in silences conspicuous where there ought have rung the watchword of that voice—aye?

* * *

Midday, the canoe ashore at the next southward island, Melander's three-man crew yet trying to unbelieve the folded-forward body in the trench of cedar.

Three men, each with new age on him. During the crossing Wennberg had blurted periodic and profound curses, but now said nothing, seemed to be gritting against whatever slunk on its way next. Braaf, too, stood still and wordless as a post. Karlsson it was who stepped first out of the silence.

"We need to bury him."

They managed with Karlsson's ax, the gaff, and the cooking pot to gouge a shallow grave in the forest floor. Then, with struggle, they brought the body from the canoe. Queerly, lifelessness had made Melander greatly heavy to carry, even with Wennberg's strength counted into the task, while at the same time the sense of death somehow seemed to thin the gravity around Braaf and Karlsson and Wennberg. This emotional addle, not a man of them would have known how to utter. But now in each there swirled atop the dread and confusion and gut gall from Melander's killing an almost giddy feel of ascension. Of being up high and more alert than ever before, alert in every hair, aware of all sides of one's self. It lasts not long—likely the human spirit would burn to blue ash in more than moments of such atmosphere—but the sensation expends the wonder that must course through us at such times: *Death singled thee, not me.*

They dared not spare sailcloth for a shroud. Karlsson took up the ax, whacked limbs from nearby spruce. Melander's last rest along this green coast would be under boughs rather than atop them.

Next, dirt was pushed into the grave. When they had done, Karlsson stepped amid the loose soil. Trod down his right heel, his left. Moved sideways, repeated.

Wennberg and Braaf looked loath, but in a minute joined in the tromp.

Firm dirt over Melander, they hefted stones from the beach and piled them onto the gravetop to discourage— more likely, merely delay—animals.

In the unending windstorm of history, how Sven Melander of Gotland and the sea was put to earth could not possibly make a speck's difference. Yet to these three this forest grave seemed to matter all. They had done now what could be thought of, except—

Karlsson and Braaf looked to Wennberg.

The broad man licked his lips as if against a sour taste, and much white was showing at the corners of his eyes.

"No. Goddamn, no. I don't believe in that guff anymore. Particularly after this."

"Just do it for the words," Braaf murmured. "Do the words for Melander."

Wennberg eyed Braaf; Karlsson. Then in a low rapid rumble he delivered the psalm:

" '. . . A thousand years in Thy sight are but as yesterday when it is past, and as a watch in the night. . . . We spend our years as a tale that is told. . . . So teach us to number our days . . .' "

* * *

The next bad time was quick to come.

They needed a meal, and somehow pieced one to-gether. Just after, crossing the campsite on one fetch or another—all the budget of fuss Melander had attended to now needed to be shared out—Wennberg clomped past the sitting Braaf. Stopped, and examined.

"What's here on the back of you, then?" Wennberg demanded.

Braaf glanced dully up toward the blacksmith. Slipping his arms from the Aleut parka, he brought the garment around for a look.

Across the shoulders and the middle of the back showed small dark splats, as if a rusty rain had fallen.

The three men stared at the stains where Melander's blood had showered forward.

At last Wennberg shifted awkwardly. "Maybe it'll wash—"

Twin glistens of tears laned Braaf's round face. "Say anything, either of you," he choked out, "and I'll gut you."

After, Karlsson never was sure what the flag had been between Wennberg and him, how it happened that they faced each other, off along the brink of shore from the weeping Braaf.

Wennberg began fast, as if the words needed to rattle their way out of him. "Karlsson, listen now—we've—

Hell's own dung ditch, we're fallen in now. The lucky one of us may be Melander. So—"

"You didn't trade places with him there at the grave."

"What? No!" Wennberg seemed startled by Karlsson's rejoinder. Then tried to muster: "No, bad choices're getting to be a habit with me. As when I went out that gate with you damned three."

"But out it you are." Karlsson scanned from Wennberg away into the forest, the constant shaggy nap of these islands. Tried to find concentration in the convoking of all the green beings, the way they touched each to each. Karlsson's head swam a bit and ached a lot and he was wearier than all the axwork of his life ever had made him, and here loomed Wennberg to be dealt with, and Melander dead, and . . . "And a far swim to get back in," Karlsson bought a further moment with. God's wounds, think now, how to halter this damned bull of a blacksmith. . . .

"Karlsson, hear me. Just—just hear me, will you? We can't go at each other like cats with tails tied together and slung over a fence. Not now, not after— Someway we've got to make miles along this God-lost coast. So somebody needs to lead. Decide, this way or that, or we'll meet ourselves in a circle in these bedamned islands. Not even Melander's going to make himself heard up through the earth."

Karlsson's weariness abruptly doubled. "So you're lifting yourself to it."

Exasperation flooded Wennberg. "Karlsson, goddamn—you won't see a matter until it lands on your nose and has a shit there, will you?" With effort, Wennberg tried to steady his tone. Karlsson remembered the same ominous tremor through the blacksmith, the earthquake in a man when temper fights with itself, the time Melander informed him the cache had been spirited away. "No, not—not me to lead. You."

As Karlsson tried to lay hold of the seven words he had just heard, Wennberg discharged more.

"It's sense, is all. There're the maps to be savvied and this bedamned canoe to be pointed, and you've done some of so, out with the bear milkers. So it's sense, you in charge of that."

Wennberg scratched his sidewhiskers as he sought how to put his next premise.

"All the other, we'll just—we don't need a sermon at every turn, like Melander gave. Divvy tasks without all that yatter, we can."

Wennberg paused. Something was yet to pry its way. Finally—

"Braaf, there. He'd never take to me as leader. Be happy to see him left here to bunk with Melander, I would, but we need the little bastard."

"And you." Karlsson someway found the mother wit to say this more as statement than question. "You'll take to me."

Another effort moved through Wennberg. He lifted his look from Karlsson, bent a bleak gaze to the ocean. He said: "I need to, don't I?"

Close by that night's firelight, Karlsson in kneel. Untying the flap of the waterproof map pouch.

Bringing out the scroll of maps. Performing the un-
rolling, then the weighting of each corner with an oval
pebble from the beach gravel.

Into view arrived all their declension of the coast, an
amount of trek across white space that surprised Karlsson, as though he were gazing on sudden new line of
tracks across snow.

Only the top map of the lot had Karlsson ever seen,
the one on which Melander's pencil route took its start
at the square house-dots of New Archangel. That once,
Melander had been borrowing opinion, and here was
traced Karlsson's advice, the canoe's side loop around
Japonski Island and then veering down and down, at
last out the bottom of Sitka Sound. The night forest
of a continent ten paces on one side of him and half a
world of night ocean thirty paces on the other, Karlsson
could scarcely credit it—that there had been time when
he, when any of this canoe's adopted men, existed at
that regiment of dots, answered work call, dwelt in
barracks, fought fleas, wintered on salt fish . . . set
honey for a gate guard named Bilibin.

On the next map the penciled line hugged the west
shore of Baranof Island to Cape Ommaney; then, as if
deflected by what waited south, struck east to Kuiu.
Because of Melander's route sketch in the dirt and the
knowledge that their port of destination lay southward
Karlsson had supposed that they were going along the
escape route much like men shinnying down a rope—
maybe a sidle of effort once and again, but the total
plunge into one direction. It was a revolution in his

thinking to see now that all the time they were canoeing south they also were sidestepping east.

More of angling down the North Pacific, map three brought. The Kuiu-Heceta-Noyes-Suemez-Dall skein of islands and the crossing of Kaigani Strait to the horn tip of the Queen Charlottes. Those days of voyage Karlsson tried to sort in his mind. In the waters along Heceta, was it, where they caught the ugly delicious fish? On which island did the carved creatures rear over Braaf? The great trees beside that dome of cliff, the water diamonds dropping in dazzle, had they been—? But the days of this coast blended like its trees, none could be made to stand in memory without the others.

Karlsson unscrolled to the fourth map, the one showing how they crossed Hecate Strait, stairstepped the islands of the past several days, and then, just more than halfway down this chart, at a rough-edged small island with no name written in beside it, Melander's penciling halted. Yes, well . . .

Melander. In every corner of Karlsson's thoughts, Melander. A painful stutter in the mind, him, his death, the cost to it. Melander with that abrupt alert face atop his length, like the glass cabin up a lighthouse; Melander who believed that an ocean can be fended with, ridden by a Kolosh saddle of wood and reined with these Russian maps. But Melander no longer on hand to dispense such faith. Too well, Karlsson understood that he and Braaf and Wennberg, none of them anything of a Melander and as different from each other as hip-high and upstairs and the moon, needed now to find their own resources to endure this sea run.

At least Braaf had wrinkled smooth again. When
Karlsson and Wennberg returned to camp and the who-
ought-lead proposition was put to him, it took the young
thief an instant to realize he was being polled at all.
He blinked then and said as if it were common fact:
"You've to do it, Karlsson. I can't read the maps and
Wennberg couldn't lead his shadow. You've to do it."

And at least there were the maps, these extra eyes
needed to know the intentions of this coast and ocean.
Glancing to the bottom of this fourth map, down from
where Melander's tracery of route left off, Karlsson
saw that the coastline was shown as far as the northmost
tip of Vancouver's Island. *Cape Scott*, Melander had
penciled in beside the ragged thumb of land. Karlsson
recalled Vancouver's Island to be the third of the land-
forms, those wheres of their escape, scratched into the
dirt by Melander the day of last summer. The maps next
would bring Vancouver's shore and then the final southering coastline from the Strait of Fuca to Astoria.

Karlsson slipped his fingers beneath the top and bottom edges to lift away this map to those next ones. And
was fixed to that motion, as if the chill of beach gravel
against his knuckles had conducted petrifaction into
him.

Beneath the fourth map lay nothing but that gravel.

Karlsson drew in a breath which met his heart at the
top of his throat.

Came to his feet, yanked a brand from the fire for
light, and was gone past the sheltered sleeping lengths
of Braaf and Wennberg on his way to the canoe.

There he dug through the entire stowage. Then dug again, and still found only what he dreaded most, confirmation.

There weren't more maps. The fourth map was the last of the scroll.

"Narrow enough matter it was . . . Needed to paw through every bedamned scrap of sheet . . ." Melander's words spun through the months to Karlsson, their shadow of meaning huge behind them now. "Skimpy bastards, these Russians . . . Should have figured . . ." Should have figured—that the pilothouse of the steamship did not hold the further maps; that since the cumbersome *Nicholas* never voyaged far enough south to go beyond these four, the Russians simply didn't provide more. So Melander during his theft himself was robbed; had to glom just these four maps and clamber away from discovery. And then, being Melander, at once fathered a judgment; that when these charts of the tangled top of the coast were expended the rest of the voyage could be borne on by his sailor's sense; that he would bother the heads of the other three escapees with this only at some far-downcoast bend of time, when necessity showed itself. Through and through Melander would have worked it, and when time came would have made the further maps seem as little vital as extra whiskers on a cat.

But Melander was stretched under that heap of stones, and Karlsson it would be to point the prow of the canoe into maplessness.

The sensation going through Karlsson now was of

being emptied, as if his body from the stomach down had vanished, the way the bottom of the fourth map dissolved their route of escape.

This Karlsson now. Circumstance's man.

. . . Do I? Do I say, Braaf, Wennberg, surprise in the pot this morning, we haven't the maps we need? Going to voyage blind soon now, we are. . . .

More than any of the other three runners of the sea, a man too of the countryside of Sweden which had birthed him. Karlsson was of the Swedish dispersion that began with the fifth decade of the nineteenth century, the bitter years of bad weather and worsening harvests. Rye thin and feeble in the fields, cows like walking boneyards for lack of hay, potatoes rotten lumps in the earth—as though the elaborate clock of the seasons was awry, whatever could happen wrong did so sometime in those years, and all too much of it repeatedly. Karlsson's father was confounded by the coil of the times, generations of landholding now crimping to futility before his eyes. But bafflement was no helpful crop either. Like many another, young Karlsson in that harsh time became extra to his home soil of Småland, early was uncoupled, simply cast to drift, from his family's farmstead. The two brothers older than he caught America fever, put themselves into the emigrant stream coursing to the prairies beyond the Great Lakes. At their urging that he come along this brother of theirs shook his head in his parson-serious way and said only: "I am no farm maker."

. . . Melander had reason, whatever to Christ it was, for saying nothing of the maps. Melander had reason for what direction he stirred his tea. So he said nothing. And now I, I'm the Melander of us, is that the matter of it? Or . . .

But just what he was, seemed to take the young Karlsson some finding out. While he turned the question he set to work as a timberman on the largest estate in the parish, and there the forester's first words to him, after a look up and down this silent youngster, were: "Hear what I tell you, lad. I don't boil my cabbage twice." His next: "We do the day here. Up like lamplighters we are, and late as a miser's tithe." Stropped by that forester's relentless tongue—until he encountered Melander, Karlsson thought it the most relentless possible—Karlsson began to come keen, learn all of axwork, of woodcraft, of a pace to life.

. . . First hour on the gallows is the worst, Melander'd have said. We are still three, we're strong enough yet. We've the chance. . . .

The merchant arrived to the estate in the winter of 1849, another crows' winter in that corner of Småland, bleak cold week on bleak cold week, with the announcement that he was looking for supple wood for sled shafts. His true eye, though, was for the grain on men. What he saw in Karlsson suited very well. Karlsson's lovely thrift at work, that knack of finishing an ax stroke and drawing back for the next before it seemed the first could be quite done. The self-sufficiency of him, working his own neighborhood of timber, the forester never needing to hawk over him. Even the still-

water-touches-deep reputation of the lithe young timberman, that parents of blossoming daughters—and
perhaps too husbands of certain ripened wives—would
not weep to see Småland soil go from under Karlsson's
feet; even this augured for the purpose of the merchant.

There was this, too. The merchant was not entirely at
ease about trafficking in men, and Karlsson he could
account as a salving bargain. The Russian-American
Company would gain an excellent workman, a seven-
year man, as consigned; but evidently one with enough
flint in him to maybe strike the Russians a few Swedish
sparks someday, too.

. . . But kill one of us like a rook on a fence, why
Melander? Wennberg there. Bellied into this on his own,
take him. Wennberg broke that Kolosh canoe for us,
maybe earned life with that. Earn life, no, it just happens. Braaf. Never'd have been him, Braaf survives the
way a winter hare knows to hide. Me then. Could easily
been. I was Captain Nose just then instead of steersman
or I'd be under those rocks and Melander'd be here
guzzling this tea. . . .

The recruitment was made and Karlsson rode in the
merchant's sleigh to Stockholm, a place, like heaven,
where he had never been and hadn't much expected to
get to. Then voyage, the passage to the America of the
Russians, if most of a year of patient endurance of tip
and tilt can be called passage. Patience Karlsson possessed in plenty, had it to the middle of his bones; to
the extent where, like any extreme, it ought not entirely
be counted virtue. This forbearance of his kept him in
situations, for instance, when a Wennberg might have

crashed out or a Braaf wriggled out. Indeed, now had done much to deposit him, without overample debate or decision, onto that whittled spot of the frontier shore where the sea months at last ended, New Archangel.

Promptly Karlsson was paired on the timber-felling crew to a stocky Finn as close-tongued as he, the two of them so wordless the other tree cutters dubbed them "the standing stones." The labor was not all that bad—axwork was axwork, Småland or on the roof of the world—although Karlsson had been caused to rethink the task a bit when he overheard Melander state that New Archangel's true enterprise was the making of axes to cut down trees to turn into charcoal which was then used for forge fire to make more axes. Looked at that way, any workman within an enterprise such as the Russian-American Company amounted to something like one slat in a waterwheel. Laboring in a circle, and a damned damp one at that. But the hunting leavened Karlsson's Alaskan life some. And the Kolosh women more so. So Karlsson had been self-surprised by his readiness to hear out Melander's plan of escape. Never would Karlsson have put it as beribboned as this, but what drew him was a new echo of that years-long purl of question. Where ought a man to point himself, how ought he use his ableness? Not the answers Karlsson ever had expected or heard hint of, Melander's: *down one of the wild coasts of the world, to see whether seven-year men could break their way to freedom.* Which maybe was the beckon in them.

. . . Melander. Melander fathered this, and I've to get on with it. So. The maps, do I . . .

Karlsson knew he was not so wide a thinker as Melander. Come all the way to it, he and Braaf and Wennberg together probably were not that spacious. Melander's province of interest was this entire coastline plus whatever joined it over beyond the bend of the planet. "A roomy shore, this, aye? Not like that Russian woodbox, New Archangel. Here's where you needn't open the window to put your coat on." That was all very well, the power in a grandness of view, it sprung the gate of New Archangel and opened the North Pacific to them, skimmed them across Kaigani and through the labyrinth of isles, propelled them these hundreds of water miles. But even grandness has its eventual limits. In Karlsson was the inkling—he had never needed to think it through to the point where it ought be called creed—that realms much tinier than Melander's counted for something, too. The circlet of strength, say, where the palm of a hand went round the handle of an ax. Or the haft of a paddle.

"Tea, you pair," Karlsson called.

As every morning Braaf arrived drowsy, a blinking child somehow high as a man.

Wennberg sat with a grunt, at once fed more wood to the breakfast fire as if stoking a forge for the day.

. . . May as well, get it behind us. . . .

"I'll show you what we face." As the other two slurped the first of their tea, Karlsson opened the map case and pulled out the fourth map.

"We're this place, here"—midway down the map, amid a shattered strew of coast—"and Melander meant to aim us east, over to this channel"—trench of white, inland a way, north-south through the coastal confusion.

"Then we've a sound to cross"—*Milbanke*, read Melander's penciling here—"then more of channel, then another sound"—*Queen Charlotte*, this inscription—"and we're to Vancouver's Island."

Wennberg and Braaf were gazing down at the map with fixation, tea forgotten. The Russians' map, Melander's map, the white-and-ink tapestry of their escape there to see . . . Braaf said softly, "I don't savvy front from back of it, but it's tsar's wealth to us, isn't it?"

Wennberg's eyelines were crinkled in concentration. "Christ sideways on the cross, this's a coast. How we've got this far and only Melander—" That trend of thought treacherous, Wennberg peered to the bottom of the map. "And more of more, ahead of us there yet. The piece here, just a tit of it, this's—what'd you say, Karlsson?"

"Vancouver's Island," said Karlsson, and took a slow drink of tea.

"Only one way to get there," Wennberg rumbled on, "and that's pry ourselves off our asses. Isn't that so, Captain Nose?"

"That's so," agreed Karlsson, and rerolled the fourth map.

As they pushed east, all three men eyed around at the shoreline continually, on watch for another canoeload of Koloshes.

Apprehension wears fast at stamina. Karlsson called an early halt for midday.

He did so again for the night. Melander had been able to stretch men beyond what they thought were their heavenmost limits. Karlsson already was calculating just how much he was going to have to ration his demands on these other two. Both of them were wan by the end of this day, looked hard-used, despite Karlsson's care with pace. But then Karlsson supposed he himself didn't look newly minted.

. . . But there's a day. They're pulling full this way, Wennberg and Braaf, not worrying their hair off about maps we don't have. We've made miles. Melander, old high-head, we're keeping on with it, this voyage of yours. We'll maybe step out at Astoria for you yet. . . .

The next day arrived not yet certain of mood to choose, merely average gray or storm-dark. Behind the campsite the forest walled close as always, and somewhere up in the highest green a limb stammered in the breeze.

Gazing in the direction, Braaf said: "Waste of noise, like a blacksmith."

Wennberg glanced to Braaf, then turned aside and spat.

. . . Melander's line of country, this ocean, not mine. Savvied water, him. To the others of us it's a kind of night. See it but not into it. And try not catch a tumble from it. God's bones, can it be deep under here as Melander said? Some places as far to bottom as these

mountains go high? Take his word for it, thank you.
Sitka Sound a millpond to any of this. If this coast
was other we'd maybe be hiking out. More my journey,
that'd have been. Forest you can thread your way
through, sort for yourself as you go. In Småland lead
me with a mealsack over my head into any wood and
straight out I'd find my way. Toss one foot in front
of another, you know you get somewhere. But water,
can't keep a fix on water. Only keep after it, stroke and
stroke and stroke. Say this paddle work was ax strokes,
how many trees'd been brought down by now? How
many forests, more like. Could've built our own stockade
and town. Called it New Stockholm. No, Melander in
charge, New Gotland it'd be. . . .

Karlsson caught up with his drift of mind. Bothered
that such straying had happened—new wile of ocean,
this—he shook his stare from the backs of Braaf and
Wennberg, purposely scanned the entire length of the
water horizon. Sober anyone, that gray endless seam of
sea and sky.

Wennberg with joy would have been at his forge.
Any forge, anywhere. Glowing charcoal before him,
circle of water ladled around its edge to concentrate the
heat, then hammer courting metal, fire flakes leaping
from the iron as Wennberg imposed shape on it, his arm
decreeing axhead or hinge or bolster plate, now there
was proper work, not shoveling ocean all the bedamned
day. Wennberg went in his mind time and again to that
morning when he strode up behind Braaf in the parade

ground—and each of these remade times, Wennberg deflected determinedly away from the laden thief.

Of course, thinking on it was like trying to undo fire in the forge: raking coals out in hope they would lapse to fresh charcoal once again. Indeed, Wennberg's wishing was of a fervency that amounted to reversing a forge fire all the way back to living tree.

And made, he sermoned himself yet again, as little sense. In this life paths cross paths and there you are, jangled up with a Braaf and a Karlsson. No help for it, who can number the clouds or stay the bottles of heaven?

But oh, Hell take it, if he just hadn't crossed that parade ground—

Braaf, now—Braaf always was a guess. As best could be told, though, Braaf was enduring coastal life something as an ouzel—that chick-sized bird common along the rivers which cut the Northwest shoreline and the streams which vein down from the mountains into those rivers. Slaty in color, peg-tailed, the ouzel at streamside is not much to notice, except as an example of bother; the bird constantly bobs as though wary of some lifelong peril overhead. In actuality the motion must be practice for its livelihood, which is to plunge into the water, immerse, and walk the bottoms of the rivers and streams, picking bits of feed as it goes. A hydraulic adaptee, the ouzel: somehow the bird has learned to use the flow of current to keep itself pinned down into place during this dinner delve beneath the riffles. Much in that way that the ouzel can shop along the cellar of the river, Braaf was held into route, into canoe and camp routine, by the sum of the pressures all around. Weather above, ocean beside, forest solid along the continent edge— each day's life was pressed to him by such powers of the coast, and Braaf had the instinct simply to stay wary while letting the push of it all carry him ahead.

Kelp drifted alongside them in a tangle, a skim of the the Pacific's deep layers of life.

As in the forest when branches become moving wands overhead but the air at ground keeps strangely still, the coastal weather now cruised over the canoemen without quite touching down. Streamers of cloud shot along, would-be storms jostled with pretensions of clearing; the sky all hither and thither in this fashion, Karlsson and Wennberg and Braaf never knew what to expect except that it would be unruly. Putty weather, gray and changeable. True, Sitka with its weather-of-the-minute had accustomed the Swedes to changeableness. But at least at Sitka the concern was not that the next gray onset would cause the ocean to erupt under them.

Crone mountains, these now. Old bleak places gray-scarved above the green shore.

* * *

The weather held stormless, as though curious to watch down at this orphaned crew for a while. At the midday stop, Karlsson's pencil mark on the map moved east. Moved as much again at evening's camp—but south now. They were in the channel.

"Those Koloshes." Wennberg fed a branch to the supper fire. "Those ones that—back at that island, there. What d'you suppose they're in the world for?"

"For?" Karlsson was loading the rifles for the night, standard now since the encounter with the Koloshes at Arisankhana. He stopped to regard the blacksmith. As steadily as he tried to keep a reading of Wennberg, moods kited in and out of the broad man.

"What I mean, how d'they spend their lives?"

"Paddling their arms off," Braaf guessed, "about same as we are?"

"Sit on mine and ride home, Braaf. I mean truth here. This bedamned coast now, like forty kinds of a Finland. What's the use of these fish-fuckers, scatting around here and there? Whyn't it just empty?"

. . . We need to hope it damned well is, here on. . . .

Karlsson aloud: "Maybe people are like crops, come up everywhere."

"Or weeds, if they're Wennbergs," added Braaf.

"Oh, Hell take the both of you. A man tries to figure life and you fart from the front of your faces at him. I'm turning in. A blanket's better company than you pair."

* * *

. . . Still can be as touchy as a poisoned pup, Wennberg can. But at least it's not war. Maybe he's in troth about it, needing me to lead. Or thinking that I'm leading, instead of just tumbling us down this coast . . .

Karlsson came awake just after daylight had begun to hint. Frost on the sailcloth shelter this morning.

By the time Braaf and Wennberg were roused and breakfast was into the three of them, ridgelines and mountains in their cloaks and hoods of dark were arriving to sight all around the channel.

Canoe prow into water, three paddles into the shimmer sent by the craft. The near shore, the western, was coming distinct with trees now. Then within the first few hundred strokes by the canoemen the horizon to the east brightened with low strips of dawn, as though chinking had fallen out between mountains and clouded sky.

The dawn warmed from silver to straw yellow, to peach. Now clouds burnt free by the light began to drift from view over the eastern crags. Karlsson's third day as escapemaster was going to be stormless.

. . . Thank you to this, any day. Sun, easy water. Wine and figs next, aye, Melander? . . .

The paddles dipped, glistened wet on the forward reach of the stroke, dipped again.

Braaf haphazardly hummed. That he seemed to have no acquaintanceship whatsoever with tune mattered none to Braaf. His random buzzes irked Wennberg, sufficiently justifying them.

Wennberg today you would have thought a prisoner on his way to exile. In his armwork showed none of Karlsson's thrift nor Braaf's minimum attention, just the plod of a man wishing he were anywhere else.

Karlsson while he paddled scanned steadily ahead, as though he could pull the horizon of water nearer with his eyes.

The canoe glided higher in the water now, without Melander. Without, too, as much food. Dried peas, beans, tea, corners of biscuit, not much salt horse, less than a quarter of the deer . . . the provisions seemed to dwindle these days as if seeping out the bottom of the boat, and Karlsson spent long thinking how to replenish.

Queer, but with forest stacked high on both sides of them now, the timber put less weight on their day than had the single-sided throng along the ocean. The calm of the channel, stretching lakewide, perhaps made it so. Ocean-neighboring forest never stood quite so quiet as this, there one breeze or another seeking through the upper boughs, birds conversing in the lower limbs, the devil knew what rustling behind the salmonberry and nettle.

Midmorning, the canoemen steered around a flotilla of trees—not drift logs but roots, branches, cones and all—drifting in the channel. Launched by an avalanche, Karlsson guessed.

Clouds stayed few and to the east, no weather galleons from the ocean. Respite of every sort, this channel so far.

At midday Karlsson called a briefer stop than usual. So steadily were they adding mile onto mile that he wanted only scantest interruption.

They landed, stretched, peed, ate salt beef and biscuit, got back in the canoe.

On and on, trough of channel. All of this was less willful country to face into than any of the ocean shoreline. Poised rather than boistering. The forested ridges conforming the channel, and their kin-mountains beyond them, sat as if in arrest; awaiting the next flow of existence maybe, the next pose to assume when the geologic clock chimed again.

Karlsson did not know how it could be, but times like this, concern and fascination now were sharing space in him. The fret of this shore of danger, and yet its allure. Thoughts forking either way, there. The Russians had a flag of this—an eagle, two-headed, peering this side and that. Just so, the lineaments halved inside Karlsson. Terrible, this chasm of coast. And splendid. Monotonous as a limp, this paddling. And clean labor.

Half through the afternoon Braaf asked Karlsson could it be true that the Russians had buried the finger of a saint under the church of theirs at New Archangel?

Wennberg snorted derision.

Karlsson doubted the tale. How would any saintly finger find its way to New Archangel?

Braaf pondered, nodded, hummed.

If anything, green now crowded the waterline beside the canoemen more thickly than ever. When crows and

ravens flew into this timber they disappeared as if
gulped. The repetition of pattern, each green shape
pyring dozens of long branches upward to a thin rod
of top, seemed to have no possible end to it, simply
multiplied ahead to circle the world and join back on
itself here in this mesh beside the canoe. Braaf and
Wennberg long since had ceased seeing individual trees,
only the everlasting shag. Karlsson worked at watching
for changes in this channel forest, but without result yet.

"Don't make a melody of it, Wennberg. Fog's fog,
it'll leave when the ghosts in it want to visit somewhere
else." The sea mist which clung onto the forest and was
delaying launch into the channel this morning had been
the blacksmith's topic of indignation during the past
minutes, Braaf now his moderator.

"You'd know, you've as much fog in that head of
yours as this bedamned coast," Wennberg muttered.

"Drown in your soup," Braaf invited. He glanced
somewhere over the heads of Wennberg and Karlsson.
"Mast paint."

"What?"

"Mast paint, he called it."

Still Wennberg gaped at Braaf.

"Mast paint," Braaf recited one more time. "Melander called pea soup that."

"Melander." Wennberg gave a half-hearted snort.

"At least he was worth grave space, more than can be
said for you."

"You little pile of—"

"The pair of you, douse it," Karlsson inserted quickly.

"My regrets, blacksmith," Braaf offered. "Maybe you're worth grave space after all. But just tell me a thing, you've swallowed gospel in your time. Where is he?"

"Where's—? Braaf, are you moonstruck or what?"

"No, only tell me. Bible-true. Where's Melander just now?"

Wennberg squinted as if Braaf had asked him the exact cubits of the universe. "Melander's buried, you helped tuck him into his grave."

"Not the grave," Braaf proceeded patiently. "After. Away there."

"Oh. You mean, where's he—been fetched to?"

Braaf bobbed yes. Wennberg appeared no more comfortable with this translation than with the original query.

"That's, well, the pastors now, they say it's a matter of how he'd've met judgment, that's all. 'Judge none blessed before his death,' is what they preach."

Braaf blinked and waited.

"Look at it this way," the blacksmith bid anew. "Those balance scales where the Russians weighed out the poods of fur, remember those?"

Braaf nodded.

"Well, then, you know how one too many pelts made the scale go down on that side, or one too few made it go down on the weighted side."

Braaf nodded.

"Well, the pastors say life gets measured out that

way, good deeds and bad, and whichever the judgment scale comes down on, you see, a soul goes either to Heaven or Hell."

Braaf didn't nod.

"You mean its all up to some weighmaster?" asked Braaf with incredulity.

"Well, not, no, not just a weighmaster, so to speak. God does it. The pastors say."

"What if it comes out dead even?"

"Dead—?"

"What if God puts a pood over here, credit to Melander, and another pood over here, his misdeeds your gospel spouters'd call them, and it comes out dead even, balanced?"

Wennberg looked to Karlsson for aid. Karlsson shook his head. "Bible is your rope of knots, Wennberg, not mine."

"I say he'd come out dead even, Melander would," Braaf swept on. "He'd have savvied any scales, known how to wink them into balance."

"So where—" Braafian theology riveted Wennberg. "So where d'you think Melander is, if judgment didn't deliver him either place?"

"Somewhere between," Braaf reasoned. "Up there swimming the air, maybe, inside this fog. If a goose can, Melander could." Braaf turned his glance from the mist to a place just above Karlsson's brow. "Is there more of that mast paint?"

* * *

The morning of what Karlsson calculated to be their final day in this stretch of channel, the highest ridges showed new snow on their timbered tops, like wigs freshly powdered.

. . . Rather have it up there on the roof than down here on us. Hold, weather. We've a job of work this day. . . .

But work different, and pleasanter, than Karlsson had been looking toward. At midmorning he shot another blacktail deer, out of a herd grazing where a stream emptied into the channel.

Karlsson's first shot missed, and the second echoed so long it seemed to be out searching for Koloshes to hear it. Braaf kept watch on the channel as Wennberg helped Karlsson butcher the deer.

"If those cannon shots didn't bring us company, smoke maybe won't either," Karlsson suggested. Braaf and Wennberg scrutinized from the channel water to the fresh meat, to each other.

"I'll have mine with dumplings and ale," Braaf proposed.

"New potatoes and little green onions with mine," voted Wennberg.

The three of them fed on the meat until they wobbled, then took the rest of the day to cut and boil venison chunks for mealtimes ahead.

While yet within what ought to have been sheltered waters, ridge horizon still solid to their west and ahead of them as far as they could peer, the canoemen the next morning began to meet swells. Long swaybacks which trembled the canoe under them with the strong ancient message: the ocean is waiting.

Their afternoon began as if it was of the same wool as the morning. The identical long, even swells which lapped into the channel were ribbed all across Milbanke Sound; a ceaseless rumple moving across the water, the tautness of the ocean skin continually being tested.

These steady dunes of water the canoe met well, rising easily and then dipping, without the staggers and quivers of the Kaigani crossing.

"Ever I get out of this," Wennberg just had said, "the next water I want to see'll fit in a teacup." And Braaf had just advised, "Whistle for it, blacksmith." Karlsson, keeping eye to the southwest where the sound opened to the ocean, saw then the first whitecaps flick among the swells, like snowy dolphins appearing and disappearing.

"Keep steady at it," Karlsson said. "We're half across."

But now each swell wrinkled white as the canoe breasted into it.

Wennberg was sicker, quicker, longer, than he'd been in the crossing of Kaigani.

"Wennberg, your sour guts'll drown us all yet," Braaf began in profound disgust.

"We're not drowned nor going to be," Karlsson told

him. "Paddle, Braaf. We've to do it, until Wennberg gets his belly back."

. . . Sick as a dog on grass, oh God damn, Wennberg, why can't your guts be solid as your head. . . .

And so it became Braaf and Karlsson and their paddles against the second powerful plain of the North Pacific coast; between them in the surging canoe, Wennberg half of himself and struggling to stay even that much; around the three and their slim craft, the hours of strait they had come, the hours yet to cross.

Perhaps bring to thought that trick done with apple and knife—the fruit to be peeled in one stopless cutting, down and down the pare of skin coiling from the blade's glide, the red-white-red-white spiral stair ever more likely to snap away: but yet is it, for each shaving of coil twirls a bond with all the others, the helix holding itself together, spin on spin, by creational grace. Just such an accumulating dangle this Milbanke voyage became. With each effort by Braaf and Karlsson the canoe sliced distance from the North Pacific, making the journey just that much more apt to sunder or just that much more cunningly pliant, persistent—you would not have wagered which.

It was full dark when they tottered onto the shore.

"Tomorrow," came Braaf's voice. "What's the water tomorrow? Not another ocean like that, is it?"

"No," said Karlsson. "Channel again, tomorrow."

. . . and the day after that, and maybe another and another, then it's ocean again, Braaf, bigger yet. . . .

181

And after that, Karlsson knew but did not say either, the expanse beyond the edge of the map.

Days of rain, those four next.

Of channel water like a gray-blue field very gently stirred by wind.

Of clouds lopping the mountains, so that they seemed strange shagged buttes of green.

Of soft rattle of wings as gulls would rise in a hundred from a shore point of gravel.

Of fog walking the top of the forest in morning.

. . . God's bones, look at it tumble. Melander, you'd have had the words for it, you've maybe seen the like, but I . . .

Alongshore to the southeast of the canoemen a fishing fleet stood in long file, sails of many shapes bright against the forest.

As Braaf and Wennberg and Karlsson ogled, the fleet toppled and was folded back into the water for the next stunt of surf.

This time, not ghost boats but round white islets, a pretty archipelago of froth.

Karlsson, Wennberg, Braaf stared on at the vanishment, the magical refashioning—this version, momentary cottages shining with whitewash.

The onlooking three considered that already the voyage had shown them ample surf for their lifetimes. But eruption of this sort was of new order altogether: so

powerful the water in this tidal expanse that it sought
to cavort up into the sky. As shown by the fourth
Tebenkov map this was the part of the coast where the
Pacific abruptly got two harsh pries against the continent, broad rough thrusts of water driven in like
points of a clawbar through the offshore layer of islands.
First of these shore gaps where the Pacific prised had
been Milbanke Sound, the four days before. The second,
and much greater, was here—Queen Charlotte Sound.

"Tomorrow's work, that," pronounced Karlsson, and
nobody arguing this in the least, they made camp.

Usual now, ever since the ordeal of Milbanke, Karlsson waking to the peg of warmth between his groin and
his belly. "Pride of the morning," Melander called such
night-born rearings. "If your britches don't bulge at
dawn it's a scant day ahead, aye?" But from all Karlsson could tell, these particular full-rigged longings
seemed to be put up not by the habited urges of a man's
blood but by his nights of dream. In each dark now
matters chased one another like squirrels, Småland and
New Archangel somehow bordered together, people of
gone years thrust their faces inside his skull. Dream
maybe was a wild sentinel against the clutch of this
coast; perhaps demanded that the night mind of Karlsson hear its howling tales instead of brood on predicament. Whatever, all of it built and built through the
nights into the wanting which he awoke to. Made him
enter each morning in a mood to want any of a variety
of things that were nowhere in the offing—a woman,

time under a roof, fresh clothes, a square meal, existence without Wennberg. Just now, though, the one particular wanting took up all capacity in Karlsson. He wanted not to be captaining this canoe voyage, and more than that, not on this shore brink of Queen Charlotte Sound, and more than that again, not on this day of crossing that Sound.

Karlsson lay on his side, waiting for the longing to unstiffen. Then rose and went into the forest to start the day with a pee.

"We could make a wintering of it."

The words halted Karlsson and Braaf in mid-chew. Carefully they eyed across the fire, as if to be sure some daft stranger had not put on Wennberg's whiskers this morning.

"Keep snug here, we could," the broad man was saying. "You're clever with an ax, Karlsson, whyn't we grapple together a shelter of some sort, wait out this pissy winter?"

Braaf palmed a hand out and up as if to catch rain, gazed questioningly into the air. The sky over the three men was as clear as if scoured to blue base. A moment, it took Wennberg to catch Braaf's mockery.

"Hell swallow you, Braaf. So it's not pissing down rain just now. That only means it will tomorrow and the forty days after." Wennberg broke off, evidently finding his way back to his original sally. "Why not a wintering? Wait till better season, not fight this god-damn ocean at its worst—"

Rapidly as he could Karlsson was fitting angles to a reply. But meantime Braaf chimed, as if to the air:

"Wait till better season the way the Koloshes are, d'you mean, ironhead? Last time you were in the company of a few of them you ran your legs to stubs. What if spring brings canoe and canoe of them?"

Wennberg cut a glare to Braaf, but the look he fastened again to Karlsson still came earnest, and more. Karlsson realized he was being met by something he had not thought to be Wennberg. A plea.

"—could get by on ducks and deer," Wennberg was proposing.

"—maybe get us a milk cow and a few chickens, too?" Braaf was amending sweetly.

The realization drove sharper into Karlsson. These plains of water, the sounds bare to the ocean, Wennberg was not merely leery of. He held a horror of them. Of their wide swells. Of the teetering gait of the canoe atop them. Of the nausea they pumped into him. Kaigani had invoked the distress in Wennberg, hour on plunging hour of it, and Milbanke Sound a few days ago must have revived it. These past days of sheltered channel Wennberg's new reticence had been taken by Karlsson as amen to the miles they were achieving. Instead it must have been a time of dread building silently toward panic. . . .

. . . Ready to lick dust, the bastard . . .

"—want to roost, whyn't you stay to New Archangel?" Braaf was goading. "—just till better season, that's not goddamn eternity," Wennberg was arguing back.

"Wennberg, hear us," Karlsson set out slowly. "Say the prettiest of this voyage, and it's still going to be grindwork. But it has a bottom end somewhere, like all else." He watched Wennberg's eyes. The plea yet hazed them, still needed the cold airing. "A wintering could be a wait on death, Wennberg. Braaf says truth. With spring the Koloshes will swim solid along here. And the first canoe of them will be apt to have us with Melander."

"But—" Wennberg pulled a face, as if he already could smell the gall being brewed for him by Queen Charlotte Sound. "This weather, all the bedamned miles —if we'd just wait—"

"The miles'd still be there," Braaf murmured.

Karlsson dug for more voice.

"Waiting we've already tasted," he said with decision. "We spat it out at New Archangel."

Braaf turned to speculate just above Karlsson's brow. Wennberg cocked a look as if a matter was dawning to him. Somewhat near as much as the other two, Karlsson had surprised himself.

What he just had come out with was not far off the sort of thing Melander might have delivered, aye?

The least necessary instruction of his young captaincy was issued now by Karlsson—the need to veer well clear of that tideline turmoil—and they set forth onto Queen Charlotte Sound.

This day, sun was staying with them. Wisps of cloud hung above the shore, and a few thin streamers out over the ocean, westward and north. But the Sound itself was burned pure in the light; water blue-black, an elegant ink in which every swirl showed perfectly.

Along here mountains did not thrust so mightily, except some far on the eastern horizon. A lower, more rumpled shore, this, than the canoeists yet had seen, and the effect was to magnify the Sound—its dark sumptuous water and wild bright edge of surf, and then the blue dike, low and distant there, that was Vancouver Island.

Straightway Karlsson and Wennberg and Braaf discovered that between them and Vancouver lay some uncountable total of instances of monotony. Wave upon wave, the canoe was met, lofted at the bow, then let slump, in a half-fall rightward, into the water's trough. A new law of seagoing this seemed to be, stagger-and-dive.

Karlsson questioned to Wennberg.

Wennberg half-turned. He was grim but functioning.

Braaf, though, announced into the crystal air: "Might as well bail up your breakfast now as later, iron puddler."

"You crow-mouthed bastard," Wennberg husked.

Minutes later, he clutched the side of the canoe, leaned over, retched. Then grasped his paddle again, cast a glare around at Braaf, and plowed water in rhythm, more or less, with the other two.

Their crossing was seven hours of stupefying slosh, under the most winsome weather of the entire journey.

* * *

"Cape Scott, off there," Karlsson called as they were approaching the south margin of the Sound.

Across Karlsson's lap lay the fourth Tebenkov map, with etchwork that presented him an identifying silhouette of the cape ahead. Several inches of crinkled rock inked in series there, dragon's grin it might have been, precise miniature profile of the westward jut of shore now showing its outline in front of the canoe, and the broken rampart of sea rock that thrust beyond the cape.

"Cape Snot, may's well be," Wennberg retorted thickly. "That map quits off, you showed us. So where d'we bear from here?"

A forcible part of Karlsson wanted to shout out and have done with it: . . . Wennberg, where from here isn't anything I can know, we've run dry not just of this map but all maps, put your finger to any direction and you'll choose as clever as I can. . . .

The rest of Karlsson struggled and said: "Tell you when I've pulled the next map, it'll take a bit."

Karlsson did up the fourth map. Reached the map case to himself and put the roll of paper in. Braaf and Wennberg were paddling steadily, studying ahead to Vancouver Island. As though plucking a new broadsheet from the scroll in the map case, Karlsson unrolled the fourth map once more.

Same as a minute ago, the silhouette artistry still there like a farewell flourish, across at the lower right the last of the mapped coastline itself, that ragged thumb of land beside which Melander had penciled in "Cape Scott"; and then white margin.

. . . So now I go blind and say that I see. Braaf, Wennberg, forgive this, but we need for me to aim us as if I know the shot. . . .

Braaf put a glance over his shoulder to Karlsson, attracted by his stillness.

A wave worried the canoe and Braaf went back to his fending manner of paddling.

One more time Karlsson looked up from the map to the cape ahead, checked again his memory of Melander's sketched geography in the New Archangel dirt. Then said, offhanded as he could manage: "To the right, there. West."

Tʜᴀᴛ bump of land at the bottom of Karlsson's final map nudged not only the water of Queen Charlotte Sound. Cape Scott was dividing, once and all, Karlsson-as-escapemaster from Melander-as-escapemaster.

For there on the next of the coastal maps—had Karlsson possessed that cartographic treasure—Vancouver Island lies angled across most of the sheet like a plump oyster shell, blunt at each end and nicked rough all along its west with inlets and sounds and bays. An expansive and stubborn mound of shore, fashioned right for its role: largest island of the western coast of North America, dominant rampart of its end of what then was christened New Caledonia and now is the British Columbia shoreline. Nearly three hundred miles in its northwest-southeast length and generally fifty or more miles wide, this ocean-blockading island; and there along its uppermost, the vicinity of Cape Scott, Tebenkov's mapmaker has continued that thread of route followed by Melander in most of the journey of descent from New Archangel, and down out of Queen Charlotte Sound that threadline of navigation weaves, past the prow of Vancouver Island. But past it east, not west.

Melander's penciling has shown Karlsson that he amended from the mapped line of navigation whenever he thought needed. To leap Kaigani. Again to shear across Hecate Strait. And Melander's last amendment ever, to jink among the islands that included Arisankhana. But now, here at the northern pivot of Vancouver, say you are Melander, a bullet once whiffed nearer your ear than sailor's luck ought to permit but your concern just now is a judgment you parented in the pilothouse of the *Nicholas*—the judgment to sell risk then and buy it back later. Later is here, and it has spent your four maps, and Cape Scott looms. The formline of this vast coast you know traces off to the west; the outshore of Vancouver Island, then the Strait of Fuca, and next, last, the American shore down to the Columbia River and Astoria.

But—"We're all of us weary. As down as gravediggers, even Karlsson and Wennberg."

And—"Wennberg there. Any tiddle of ocean has him tossing up, costs us hard in paddling."

So—"We've maybe had enough of ocean. Go the lee of this place, we could, aye? That navigation line has to touch to somewhere. . . ."

An eastward tilt in such musings as these, do you feel?

And so you/Melander in perhaps three days, not more than four, bring your canoe and crew to the stretch of Queen Charlotte Strait where the Hudson's Bay Company in the past few years has installed a trade post called Fort Rupert. Chance is strong against it, but perhaps Fort Rupert eludes you, dozes in fog or storm as you pass. In another dozen days along this inner shore you are rounding the southeastern tip of Vancouver Island and there poises the British New Archangel, the Hudson's Bay command port called Fort Victoria. Say, somehow, you do not happen onto even this haven. From here amid the Strait of Juan de Fuca where you now are paddling, chimney smoke might be seen there over the southern shore, or the canvas of a lumber vessel standing forth against the dark coast—either smudge marking the site of the fledgling American settlement at the mouth of Puget Sound, Port Townsend.

All this, then, is the sort of eventuating interrupted by that chance bullet at Arisankhana. Karlsson, with his nod west, has leaned into his own eventuating.

At length . . . we again saw land. Our latitude was now 49° 29′ north. The appearance of the country differed much from that of the parts which we had seen before, being full of high mountains whose summits were covered with snow. The ground was covered with high, straight trees that formed a beautiful prospect of one vast forest. The southeast extreme of land was called Point Breakers, the other extreme I named Woody Point. Between these two points the shore forms a large bay, which I called Hope Bay, hoping to find in it a good harbor and a comfortable station to supply all our wants, and to make us forget the hardships and delays experienced during a constant succession of adverse winds and boisterous weather ever since our arrival upon the coast of America.

The line of route of Braaf and Wennberg and Karlsson now was also one of the Pacific's meridians of history. In 1778 Cook, the great English captain, explored north through these waters, journaled this outshore of Vancouver Island, put names on the land as points and inlets won his fancy. Cook's expedition, and forays by the Spanish, and the roving Yankee captains who rapidly appeared, they arrived as an empyrean newness to this coast. Indelible people, these European and American explorers and traders proved to be, the broader wakes of their sailing ships never fading from the traditional waters of the canoe tribes.

Like men following a canyon unknown to them, then, Karlsson and Wennberg and Braaf began their descent of this Vancouver shore where past and future had seamed.

. . . It is like trying to bend rock. We pull at these paddles until we ache and always there's more ocean. We do make miles, Melander. Wennberg complains like a creaky gate and Braaf slacks, but we earn distance, more than I'd thought the three of us could. More than possible and less than enough, you'd have said. . . .

One thing only about this Vancouver coast was Karlsson certain on. But like the sum of what the hedgehog knew, it was one big thing. Karlsson savvied that they must not blunder into a downcoast Sitka, come nosing one evening into some fat sheltered sound where a blinking look would show the shore to be a sand street, and longhouses backing it, and Koloshes standing there just in wait for Swedes. None of such as that, thank you. The outmost crannies of this island Karlsson would rein the canoe to.

—And so looped them past Quatsino Sound, and around Cape Cook of the Brooks Peninsula.

Nights now, the trio of canoemen camped at places that might have been the forgotten upper crags of Hell. Ledges of shore just wide enough to grapple the canoe onto and wedge a spot to sleep. Grudging beaches, sometimes a gruel of gravel and surf, sometimes stone for stone's sake.

The while, salt rings from sweat crusting in a three-quarter ring where the men's arms met their shoulders. Their clothing terrible, they knew, and their smell undoubtedly worse.

—And ran them wide of Kyuquot Sound, and of Esperanza Inlet where Cook left that wistful christening, a bay named for hope.

Days, there was the ocean, perpetual paintpot of gray. And broken shore. Now and then a dun cliff, green gently moving atop it as the forest stirred in the ocean's updraft. Of course, rain, and with it, murk. No sunrise, nor sunset, only grayings lighter or darker. Not even mountains relieved the eye, for clouds broke off the peaks and weighted the horizon up there to flatness, a wall along all that side of the world.

Three times it snowed, swarm of white from out of the gray.

The while, their appetites growing and their bellies shrinking. The pinched shore and the snow days and the drizzle kept Karlsson from hunting, and fishing too came scant, a half-dozen smallish bass and two more red snappers the total catch of this Vancouver voyage.

—And past Nootka Sound, named too by Cook; Nootka, where another colossal Englishman, Meares, in 1789 brought Chinese crews to build fur-trading schooners; Nootka, where in the 1790s the British and Spanish empiremakers entangled like mountaineering parties clambering in from both sides of the same precipice, and nearly came to war; Nootka, home harbor of a vibrant canoe people who just now were passing the winter in their style of frequent feast and potlatch, a seasonal rain-trance of song and drama and dance.

The constant push of the North Pacific was wearing deep into the three canoemen, up their wrists and arms, across their effort-bent shoulders. True, once in a while the wind granted them a few hours' use of the sail, and they had the greater luck that their creature of sea run, the dark canoe, was one of the most fluent craft for its task. But the task along Vancouver was no less remitting for such facts. This was slog, nothing but.

The while, Karlsson showing answer to the single doubt Melander had held of him: whether he had lasting edge. The biting surface to put against life, to strop and set to whatever dangerous angles were necessary. The Karlsson of New Archangel could be seen as cause to wonder a bit about that, and depend on it, Melander missed no bit of wondering. All very well it was to go about life as unobtrusively as the quiet Smålander axman—some of that could be recommended to most of humankind—but what of when life began to go about him? Then would be the test of edge: whether the man bent or broke; or worked his salients back at life, made a thrust where he could, a nick as possible. Karlsson was not heaven-made for all that he needed do along Vancouver; spoke as little as Melander had much, at time when Braaf and Wennberg could have heard regular encouragement; let the deceit about the maps take up too much of the inside of his head. But life is mostly freehand, and this Karlsson of the outmost Vancouver shore was verifying Melander's guess of him that under the silence lay some unused edge.

—And past Sydney Inlet, and Clayoquot Sound.

"Karlsson, aren't we about done with this fucking island? The damned place's longer than perdition."

"About, Wennberg. About."

. . . One way or other, about done, yes. . .

—And looped them at last past Barkley Sound, where yet another canoeing people read weather from the behavior of frogs and mice and had concluded this to be a wet, gusty moon of winter, a time to sit snug in longhouses yet a while.

Since Cape Scott, the peg of Braaf's calendar had advanced half a month.

Before the canoemen a channel several miles wide angled, and across its breadth another rumpled coastline, more of the dark world-long pelt of forest.

. . . Must be. Can't be any other. Can it? . . .

Karlsson raised his contemplation from the compass to the water. "Fuca's Strait, this must be."

"Must be?" Wennberg eyed him. "Must be is fool's prayer. What's the map say?"

"Fuca's Strait. I was skeining wool."

"Have a care you don't skein yourself a shroud, and ours with it." Wennberg waited—a count all the way to four could have been done—then demanded: "So, Captain Nose? Where're you aiming us next? There's coast all over the kingdom here."

. . . That much I know, thank you all the way to Hell, ironhead. It's all else I don't. . . .

"We cross right over. For that corner of shore." Karlsson pointed to a long reach of bluff which came down from the higher coast to shear into the ocean, a sort of bowsprit of land. "But we need go past it a way before we put in. It's places like that the Koloshes maybe roost."

"Noah's two asses! Is there no end to the damned Koloshes? I thought Rosenberg had too many of them there at the back porch of the stockade, keeping them like hounds on scraps. But he hasn't made a start on the bastards."

"Figure what the Koloshes'd say if they come onto us, blacksmith," Braaf put in. " 'Noah's two asses! More tsarmen yet, and smelling like a heifer's fart as well!' "

"Braaf, shove your head—"

"The both of you, put your breath to paddling. Or do we squat out here until Koloshes happen along and prove Braaf right?"

They made a scampering afternoon of it. The strait lay as a smaller, dozing version of Kaigani, and the canoe stole mile after mile without the gray water arousing. It even happened that Wennberg managed to stay unsick.

Across, a high sharp cape with waves boiling white at its base took over the continental horizon.

"What's that called, there?" Wennberg asked.

"Cape . . . Etholen." Duping Bilibin those nights at the gate had been short work to this endless piece of performance as mapmaster. "One of the old sirs, wasn't he? Governor when you were a young blood at New Archangel?"

"The one. Cold as a raven, but a fair man. None like him, since."

Off the point of the big timbered cape stood a sheer-cliffed island, as flat on top as if sawn. The passage between continent's wall and the island's lay broad as several fields, but Karlsson, trying to think Melander way, decided to be leery of any currents hiding in there. Around the seaward side of the isle and its guardian reefs he steered the canoe.

Abruptly now Karlsson, Braaf, Wennberg could see ahead to the coast which was to lead them south, the last footing of their climb down from Russian America.

Forest, as ever, but neighbored with rock. Talons of cape rock, haired on top with timber, clutched down into the bright surf. Everywhere offshore were strewn darker blades and knobs of rock. Stones of the sea standing in pillars, in triangles, in shapes there were no names for.

No one said anything. They paddled on.

Melander dabs that bit of stick to the New Archangel earth. Baranof Island he draws, and the Queen Charlotte group, and Vancouver Island, and fourth, last, this coastline between the Strait of Juan de Fuca and the mouth of the Columbia River. One hundred fifty miles lie between strait and river, although Melander did not possess that sum when he drew, nor does Karlsson have so much as a cross-eyed guess of it as he arrives here to the top of this final coast.

Even had either of these unfledged canoe captains known the total, the miles of this shore do not so much resemble those of the Alaska–British Columbia coast to the north, that crammed seaboard of waterside mountains and proliferated islands. In certain profiles, in the ancient pewtered light of continent and ocean alloying, this cousin coast does stand handsome; but strong in detail rather than soaring gesture. Tide pools, arches of rock, the tidemark creeping higher on its beaches with each surge of surf—ditties of coastscape, not arias, here touch the mind. Almost, it seems the usual mainstays of coastline were forgotten. This shore's upper two-thirds lacks not only fetching harbors but honest anchorages of any sort; is in fact a rock-dotted complication of foreshore which sailors kept their distance from, unless they were the adept local Indians or blindly venturesome European explorers. Even such beaches as exist on the section the Swedes are reaching now come as quick crescents between headlands—bites that the ocean has eaten of the continental crust.

In political terms too a coastline of erasures, contentions. Late in the eighteenth century the Spanish arrived to christen melodious names onto geography the local Indians long since assumed they had adequately denominated; next, the British editing severely over the Spanish. Some honest drama was gained in that last transaction. Destruction Island for Isla Dolores. Cape Flattery—just now momentarily rebaptized yet again by Karlsson as Cape Etholen—for Punta de Martinez. But some poetry lost, too: Point Grenville for Punta de los Martires. And even as Karlsson and Braaf and Wennberg have arrived to it, one more incongruity, American now, is being affixed over all. This upper-outside corner of the United States is about to be dubbed Washington Territory, making this ancient sea margin the Washington shore.

Nomenclature and latitude and logic say in chorus, then, that here south of the Strait of Juan de Fuca the canoemen at last have trekked down from the crags of the North Pacific's coast to its lowlands. Yet there was that first view of disordered coast ahead, as if lower shore was not necessarily less troubled shore.

At dusk's start, the paddling men were just to the north of a procession of close-set seastacks out into the ocean, like a caravan of cliffs and crags crossing the canoe's route. Older than old, as though preserved by the Pacific brine ever since creation's boil, these pyramids and arches of rock appeared.

Day-worn as the canoemen were, Karlsson did not want to risk rounding this coastal salient into whatever its far side might hold.

"Shore," he called to Braaf and Wennberg above the surf noise. "We've done the day."

. . . Moon. First in—God's bones, how long? Since New Archangel, and an age before that. "Stone on the stomach of heaven'll make the weather mend." That we could use. In plenty. Mend all night every night, I wouldn't mind, moon. . . .

Sometime in these days the canoe had slid them out of winter into not-winter.

No calendar can quite catch the time, and the cluster

of moments themselves is as little possible to single out as
the family of atoms of air that pushes against the next
and has begun a breeze. Yet the happening is unmiss-
able. Out of their winter rust, ferns unroll green. Up
from the low dampnesses of the forest the blooms of
skunk cabbage lick, a butter-gold flame and scent like
burnt sugar. The weather calms, sometimes as much as
a week of laze and non-storm. Seals bob forth in the
offshore swells. Salmon far out in the Pacific reverse
compass, start their instinctual trace back from under-
ocean pastures toward the rivers where they were
spawned and must now seed spawn in turn. Baja Cali-
fornia has been departed by gray whales, the Bering
Sea is to know them next. Geese and ducks and whis-
tling swans write first strokes of their calligraphy of
flight northward. To the north too, glaciers creak with
the earliest of the strains which at last will calve icebergs into the azure bays. Within the white rivers,
Yukon and Stikine and Susitna and Alsek, Kuskokwim
and Kvichak and Nushagak, currents begin to pry at
their winter roofs of ice.

In stirrings tiny and mighty, the restive great coast
was engendering spring.

. . . One meal of deer left. Then beans. Two, three
skoffs of those. And biscuit corners, maybe a meal's
worth. Already Wennberg is saying his guts think his
throat's been cut. An idea there, Braaf tells him, how'd
he like help? The two of us to hold Wennberg into
bridle, it takes. . . .

The moon reminded Karlsson of an egg, and his stomach regretted that he had looked up. But the shine on the waves compelled it, a soft dazzle that began to be gone even as it showed itself; an eye could not help to wonder where that flitting sheen had been borne from.

Just from the chance at last to do so, stroll a spacious beach in moonlight, Karlsson had wandered south along the silverline of tide to where the file of seastacks anchored into the continent. Out into the water in front of him now the great loaves of stone loomed in succession, until at their outermost a last small whetted formation, like a sentry's spearpoint, struggled with the ocean, defiantly tearing waves to whiteness. Some mad try here at walling the Pacific, all this looked, the line of rock having been fought by the waves, overrun by them, left in gaps, shards, tumbled shapes, but the attempt of the rocks enduring.

. . . Need a hunt again. Anything, deer, goat. Beaver, God's bones, we could learn to think beaver was a manor lord's feast. Costs time and time to hunt, though. And risk to a gunshot, Christ knows whether there're Koloshes along here. But so's there risk to starving ourselves down. Pull to shore early tomorrow, try a bear milking. . . .

Back north along the shore Karlsson could see the campfire, even could discern the arc of the canoe, the bumps of form that were Wennberg and Braaf. At first, when the canoe nosed in here for the night, Karlsson could not make himself feel easy about this fresh manner of coast. Three leisured windrows of surf and

the beach wide, gentle, full-sanded; a carpet of ease
after the stone shores of the past weeks, it ought to
have seemed. Yet through dusk and supper a constric-
tion somehow clung to this mild site, an unexpected
sense of squeeze which kept with Karlsson even when
he strode the length of beach to the seastacks. Maybe
it was the surround of land here, after their Vancouver
nights of precarious perch. The battled wall of searock
reared as barrier at this end and the cape the canoemen had rounded wide of after crossing the Strait of
Fuca extended considerably into the ocean at that
other. Inland the forest stood high—Karlsson had
studied and studied that venue for sign of animals; in
the weave of evergreen and brush, nothing moved—
and behind the north end of the beach the terrain
sharpened into a long clay cliff. For all the broad in-
vitation of its sand this particular beach made a kind
of sack mouth of the coast, the sort of place where you
more-than-half-expected something unpleasant to be
scooped ashore at any time.

. . . A man can worry himself ancient. Step them
off, the days, that's what we need do. Keep on keeping
on, Melander'd say. Earn our way to Astoria yet, we
just may. . . .

The ocean was bringing a constant rumble and
within that a hiss, the odd cold sizzle as the tide edge
melts into the sand. Left in the air was a smell of
emphatic freshness—a tang beyond mint or myrtle,
more a sensation than anything the nose could find
recipe of. And over and through it all, the surf sound,
here so solid it seemed to have corners: the unremitting

boom on the seastacks, a constant crashing noise
against the shore northward. The surf. No other energy on the planet approaches it. On any planet? The
remorseless hurl of it, impending, collapsing, upbuild-
ing, and its extent even beyond that of thunder, that
grave enwrapping beat upon all shores of all continents
at once: how is there any foothold left for us? Braaf's
wonderment, he recently had confided to Karlsson, was
that the power of the ocean didn't rip big chunks from
the land all day long. Braaf figured probably in great
storms it did just that, which must have been how the
islands of their route from New Archangel had been
chewed into creation.

. . . A far place now, New Archangel. Far as that
moon, it seems. How long's it been? Braaf's calendar
will tell. But we're where we are. Last coast, this. . . .

Near the campfire Wennberg and Braaf were sitting
at angle from each other, as if they had a treaty
against face-to-face to be honored.

At Karlsson's approach Wennberg threw on a
branch from the firewood pile beside him, sparks rock-
eting upward. In the heightened light Wennberg
looked somehow more thunderous, and Braaf's eyes
were higher out into the night than ever, seemed to be
appraising the moon.

. . . They've been gnawing back and forth again,
what now. . . . "A silver night," Karlsson offered.
"First in a while. Maybe it'll bring sun on us tomorrow."

Wennberg stared at Karlsson. Then he brought up from behind the firewood the map case, open.

"Tomorrow, yes, that's what's to be studied on here. Braaf and I want to know of tomorrow. Where the goddamned map of it is, say. Yes, whyn't we start with knowing that."

. . . So it's come. . . .

Karlsson drew breath, heard the surf contend against the wall of seastacks. Heard his own silence.

Wennberg's glare to him was joined by a gaze from Braaf. "Karlsson," Braaf said distantly. "Where is it?"

More silence, silence so strong in Karlsson it covered the surf's crash, lifted him inside his ears back to where he stood numbed by the sentry's query into the New Archangel night . . .

"You both know the where of it." His own voice; make it work, silence was testimony for Wennberg. "Back somewhere in New Archangel, where Melander judged it could stay."

Wennberg stood, faster than such heft should have been able. "Then you don't know fuck-all about where we are! You're running us blind down this coast!"

"I know Astoria is ahead. That's enough."

"Hell take you, it's enough! You think you're too goddamn keen to be among us, Karlsson. You've had that about you since we touched away from that Russian dungpile. Afraid maybe I'll smudge off on you, or long-fingers Braaf here'll pick your pocket, you act like. But play us the fool like this—we're hopeless as

Methusaleh's cock, without maps to go by! This coast'll—"

"Wennberg, I can't have maps when there aren't maps. Melander reckoned we could make our way after the steamship's maps gave out and that's what we're doing."

"Whyn't you tell us?" Braaf, the question soft. "Melander would've."

"Because I'm not twin to him, Braaf. Can't be. And what was the gain in telling? To have Wennberg here every hour declaring us dead, might as well have climbed in the grave with Melander? To have you give up, too, maybe? Take a sharp look at telling. Melander held off from telling, when he couldn't lay hand to all the maps."

"Melander, double-damn Melander!" Wennberg had sidestepped, was clear of the fire now instead of across it from Karlsson. "Melander was so fucking clever he jigged his way in front of a bullet. And you're the whelp of him—I'll finish you, you fucking fox of a Smålander—"

Wennberg rushed.

Karlsson had an instant to fling up a forearm against the blacksmith's throat, then they were locked. Wennberg's arms around Karlsson, seeking to crush: Karlsson's forearm in pry against the front of Wennberg's neck. The both, grunting: staggering: Karlsson bending like a sapling to stay upright, Wennberg tipping him, tipping him: desperately a Karlsson hand exerted to a Wennberg ear, maybe twist will slow. . . .

At its target, the hand came against . . . metal? rod, some sort? How could . . .

The grip lifted from Karlsson's ribs now, he and Wennberg stock-still, face to face. But not eye to eye: Wennberg was trying to see around the side of his own head, not to Karlsson's hand which yet was beside his ear as if ready to stroke there, but to Braaf and the rifle.

The mouth of the rifle barrel stayed firm against Wennberg's ear as Braaf spoke.

"Not the first one to jig in front of a bullet, Melander wasn't. Or last, maybe."

"Braaf, wait now." Wennberg labored to suck in breath and spill out words at the same time. "It's Karlsson, played us fools—running us blind down this hell-coast—"

" 'Right fit or not, he's our only fit.' Melander said that once about you, didn't he, Karlsson?"

Karlsson nodded, tried to think through the ache of his ribs, work out what he ought to be saying. But Braaf was doing saying of his own:

"Let's think on that, Wennberg. Melander maybe had truth there."

"Braaf, the bastard's been diddling us along—pretending he knows what the fuck he's doing—"

"So far, he has," murmured Braaf. "Blacksmith, you only ever had a thimbleful of sense and now you've sneezed into it. Back there, after—Melander. You said it needed be Karlsson to find the way for us. He's done it. How, I don't savvy. I'm not sure he does. But we need let him keep on at it. Else we're dead meat."

Braaf peered with interest at the side of Wennberg's head, as if concerned that the gun barrel rested comfortably there. "So, blacksmith? Back at New Archangel, you wanted a sleigh ride down this coast. Ready to join us again?"

"Braaf, I . . . you . . . yes, put the damned gun off, I—I'll let the bastard be."

Braaf stepped back carefully, the rifle yet in Wennberg's direction.

. . . Saved my skin, Braaf. But there'll be Wennberg at me again, first chance, unless . . .

"Wennberg. Hear me out." Karlsson made himself stride to within a step of the burly man, with effort stood steady there. "This is our last job of coast, all the others up there north behind us. We've been making the miles without maps. We can make as many more as we need."

. . . Careful with this now, make it warn but not taunt. . . .

"Wennberg, maybe I chose wrong, not telling about the maps. Maybe so, maybe not. But turn it either way, I've got us this far, all the corners still on us. They say it takes God and his brother to kill a Smålander. So far I haven't met up with either on this coast."

Wennberg rubbed his ear, spoke nothing. Somehow, a very loud nothing. Then scowled from Karlsson to Braaf, and back again. His eyes seemed empty of fury now but neither man could tell just what else dwelt in them, acceptance or biding. In the fireshine Wennberg looked more than ever like a bear with a beard, and who can read the thoughts of a bear?

Wennberg shook his head one time. Again, biding or acceptance, it could have been either or neither. Then turned and aimed himself off down the beach toward the seastacks. The other two watched his bulky outline shamble away in the moonlight.

"There goes a fool of a man," Braaf said.

"Before we've done," said Karlsson, "we may be wishing Mister Blacksmith is nothing worse than fool."

He picked up the map case, out of habit tied it snug, tossed it into the canoe. "We won't load the rifles tonight. And unload that one."

Braaf once more was a spectator of the moon. "It's not loaded. There wasn't time."

Karlsson woke to rain sound. Except for the triple windrows of surf the day's colors were all grays, sea and sky nearly the same, rocks and forest darker. The tint in it all was fog. The big cape to the north was obscured.

Wennberg this morning looked as if he was trying to pick the bones out of everything said by Karlsson or Braaf. He offered no words of his own, however, until past breakfast, and then turned loudly weather-angry. "Pissing down rain again!"

Braaf slurped tea, gazed to the grayness. "Could be worse, blacksmith."

"Worse? How's that, worse?"

"Could be raining down piss."

* * *

Again now, that wait to see when the fickle weather would lift itself from them.

After a few hours of Wennberg squinting resentfully into it and Braaf putting wandering glances up at it and Karlsson calculating whether the gray of it was as gray as an instant before, the murk was agreed to be thinning a bit.

They pushed off from the beach sand, paddled carefully out around the end of the seastack wall, and had a moment when they could see more seastacks along the coast ahead. Then the rain took the shoreline from them.

"This's like having our heads in a bucket," Wennberg complained nervously.

"The high rocks will steer us," Karlsson said with more calm than he felt. "They're near shore all along here. Pass just outside them and we're keeping to the coast."

There was no midday stop. No visible ledge of shore on which to make one. Karlsson divvied the last of the dried meat and they took turns to eat, one man doing so while the other two kept paddling.

Sometime in the afternoon—the hours of this day, gray strung on gray, were impossible to separate—a timbered island some hundreds of yards long loomed out on their left.

Karlsson steered along its outer edge, with intention to turn to shore beyond the island. But then at its end, through the rain haze rocks bulking in the water between island and coast could be made out, stone knuckles everywhere.

"The island," Karlsson chose, and gratefully they aimed to shore on its inland side.

After the sopping day, a sopping camp.

The canoemen had come in near the south reach of the island, where several high humps of boulder weighted the shore. Into this rough outwall of rocks they lodged an end of the mast shelter and so kept that corner of the weather out. But others got in, this rain evidently willing to probe toward humankind for however long it took to find some. The Swedes managed to coax a choking fire long enough to heat beans and tea, then gave up on the evening.

Surprise it was, then, when Karlsson woke sometime later and saw that the sky now held stars.

. . . One gain, Wennberg's a mute these mornings. No knowing what's prowling in his head, but at least it's not jumping out his mouth. . . .

Wennberg was fussing the breakfast fire to life. The weather seemed to have cleansed itself the day before, was bright as a widow's new window today. Karlsson wanted the canoe to be on the water by now but for once he had overslept, Wennberg's fire was proving a damp and balky proposition, Braaf had drifted off north saying he would check the ocean horizon for lurking storm—dawdle eats hours and Karlsson decided all three of them were feeding it more than enough this morning.

"You've about found fire"—an oblique urging sometimes would lodge in Wennberg—"so I'd better fetch
Braaf." Karlsson started away toward the north end of
the island.

"If I'd arms for three paddles y'could leave the
little bastard there and yourself with him."

. . . Coming awake, is he? Count on Wennberg,
hammer for a tongue and the world his anvil. . . .

Just then Braaf arrived to sight. Running, bent low.

Past Karlsson he raced, toward the squatting Wennberg. The careful stack of sticks Wennberg just had
managed to puff into blaze, Braaf kicked to flinders.

Wennberg gaped, sputtered. "Braaf, I'll braid your
guts—"

"Koloshes," panted Braaf. "Whole village. Across
there."

Karlsson grabbed the spyglass out of the canoe and
followed Braaf back around the beach rocks.

A high round little island, like a kettle turned
down, sat upcoast perhaps a half a mile from where
Karlsson and Braaf and Wennberg crouched now behind a boulder on their own island, and just inshore
from the kettle island, gray and low under the coastal
ridge of forest the longhouses were ranked.

Karlsson flung a look along their own beach to be
certain sure: the canoe and camp were from sight behind the tumble of rock. Then with the glass Karlsson
counted. Fifteen of the almost flat-roofed structures.
If these Koloshes lived as many to a longhouse as the
Sitkans, families all the way out to Adam . . .

"People on those roofs," Karlsson reported in puzzlement. "Children, looks like."

"Upside down bastards anyway, these goddamn Koloshes," Wennberg stated. "What're they squatting up there for?"

Karlsson studied further. "Watching the sea, seem to be. They—"

Just then commotion erupted atop the roofs. Its reason already was found by Braaf, pointing into the stretch of ocean they'd paddled through in yesterday's cloud.

Craft were coming in there, a line of them. Blade forms on the water. But all aimed the same, one after another, straight as straight, toward the kettle island.

The glass ratified what was in the minds of the three Swedes. "Canoes," Karlsson reported. Braaf and Wennberg were tranced beside him, watching the flotilla. "Several paddlers each."

The way the canoes stayed a steady space from each other . . . Karlsson puzzled at the pattern. As if they were strung into place. Or harnessed—

"Something in tow, there."

The tiny tunnel of sight brought it then to Karlsson.

. . . Melander, Melander, this you ought've seen. Fishers of monsters . . .

"Whale."

The news did not register on Braaf and Wennberg. Karlsson repeated.

"They're towing a whale."

"Whale? Whale, my ass." Any manner of doubt not known to Wennberg had not been invented yet. "Where'd they get a whale? You've come down with the vapors, Karlsson, hand me that glass—"

Wennberg focused in turn and the same marvel traveled the tube of the glass to him. The canoe fleet was bringing behind it a glistening length, buoyed with floats that looked like puffed-up seals.

"Working like Finns at it," observed Braaf. "Digging paddles that deep, you'd think their arms'd pull off."

Wennberg, still not wanting to accept: "But how in Judas—?"

Karlsson had plucked the glass back from him and was studying again. "Laying up over the prows there. Harpoons. They paddle out and kill whales."

. . . And small fish we'd be for them. Holy Ghost and any of the others, what'll we . . .

Karlsson felt a dry clot form hard at the top of his throat as he watched the long canoes—five, six, seven all together. Six paddlers at work in each and two further men, a steersman aft and likely the harpooner forward, to scan the ocean like fish hawks.

Rare for him, Braaf was openly perturbed; his right leg jigged lightly in place, as if testing for run. Wennberg sought to look stolid, but Karlsson noticed him swallow at his own throat-pebble of fear.

In the next hour or so the canoe procession angled between the three watchers and the kettle island, closing slowly on the beach in front of the village. A strenuous chant—"bastards sound like hell let loose," Wennberg appraised—could be heard now from the whalemen. Braaf was first to see what was intended: they would employ high tide to beach their sea creature.

The towline soon was taken from the lead canoe by quick hands ashore and the villagers leaned back in pull as the canoe crew carried their craft high onto the beach. The harpooner, a man larger than the others, was followed to the surf's edge by a swirling attendance of women and children. Canoe followed canoe now in swift unharnessing, the hawser at last only between the whale carcass and the people of the shore, tug-of-war between nature's most vast creature and its most pursuitful.

Slowly the gray form, a reef of flesh, crept toward tide line.

Just short, the tugging ceased. The children of the village ran to the towline and took places, small beads among larger. Then as it is said, a long pull—a strong pull—and a pull all together—the generations of the village drew the whale the last yards up onto their beach.

"So?" This was put by Braaf, in confoundment.

"Yes, so." If this portion of coast was populated with such sea hunters, the problem was beyond any ready words. Karlsson was casting for anything more to say when Wennberg blurted:

"This is a how-d'ye-do we don't need! You bastard,

Karlsson, you touched us in at this island, is there nothing you can't make goose shit of?"

"Rather be ashore there to welcome those Koloshes, would you?" That held Wennberg for an instant, and Karlsson used it to go on: "One thing we can do. Need do. Travel from here by night."

This notion set Braaf to chewing at the corner of his mouth. Wennberg meanwhile tried to lurch the argument sideways.

"But these whale chasers—whyn't they be like other Koloshes, lay up now and celebrate themselves silly? Eat and drink and tumble one another in the bushes and the like, won't they now? Reason it, Karlsson. What if we paddle wide of them here, right now, out from this island and swing to shore downcoast?"

. . . A notion, there. Get away maybe while they're prancing around that whale. But . . .

"This lot may cut capers for a while," Karlsson allowed, "but what if there're more crews, still out there running down whales? Which risk would you rather, dark or meeting a pack of those canoes?"

"Dark," voted Braaf rapidly. "And blacker, better."

Wennberg stared morosely toward shore, where the whale had been lashed into place and the village people seemed to be standing back and admiring.

"Oh, Judas's ball," he at last gritted out. "Dark, dark, dark. These fish-fuckers down this coast, whyn't they just squat on their asses and look wise all the while like the Sitka Koloshes?"

* * *

A watching day, they would need to make it.

Wennberg claimed the top of the island where the seaward side could be scanned for further canoes. "Spares me some hours with you pair," he rapped out, and went.

Karlsson and Braaf stayed to where they could see across to the village. One Kolosh—Karlsson thought he might be the big harpooner from the lead canoe—had sliced a saddle of flesh from the whale's back and with his train of admirers disappeared into a longhouse with it. Otherwise, though, all the come-and-go of the village still was around the long blunt-nosed carcass.

Sentried for the day this way, life maybe depending on what he and Braaf could bring into their eyes and calculate from it, Karlsson felt the dividing come to him again. The kettle island, green flow of the shore horizon, the water span around, the might of the whale, the speckle of white barnacle scars along its vast skin, the festival the Koloshes were going through, all this pageantry of what the world could be held a side of his mind even as he sorted at predicament.

"Sweden." Evidently Braaf's mind was in two, as well. "Tell me truth, Karlsson. Think we'll see it again?"

Karlsson studied the kettle island as if it were Braaf's question. Then answered:

"I won't."

Braaf turned to him in quick regard. "What, you think we can't keep in life? Those Koloshes across there—?"

"No. Not that. I'm not going back."

"But then, why're you—the place Astoria, what about—?"

"Astoria, we all need find. And will. It's the foothold of this part of the world. Only one, so far as we know. Or Melander knew. But once there I'll stay to America."

"And do what?"

"New land, here. Christ knows, we've seen skeins of it along this coast. Melander said the Americans are taking this shore. Reason for Astoria, must be. New land is land to clear. A timberman can find a place in that."

On the foreshore the Koloshes were gathered close around the whale. They seemed to be listening raptly to one of their number, the big harpooner again. Among the New Archangel whites it was lore that no Kolosh could so much as glance up at the weather without feeling the need for a speech.

"What d'you suppose he's preaching, Parson Kolosh there?"

"I don't have any glint of it. Maybe saying what it's like to hunt a mountain of creature like that."

Another whaleman seemed to be marking off the carcass into portions. Six or eight old men, still as cormorants, stood watching him.

"Are they brave, Karlsson? To chase whales? Or just fools?"

"Might be more than one yes to that."

The oration at last concluded, the villagers circled the whale and began to cut at the great form.

"Butchering it, looks like they are! Not going to *eat* that thing, can they be?"

"This is all Dutch to me. Just count it luck that they're busy over there, whatever the Christ it is they're doing."

Blocks of blubber began to be stripped from the carcass. The whale was open now like a hillside being mined; a few of the women disappeared entirely inside the carcass.

"Must have stomachs like leather," Braaf marveled. "I'm hungry as a hawk, but walking around in that thing and then eating it—"

Braaf was quiet awhile. Then confirmed: "So you'll stay to this coast?"

"This end of America, anyway. Across the world from Småland and out from under the Russians."

"Along here with these Kolosh whale hounds?"

"They can't be everywhere of this coast. It just seems so, today."

Braaf shook his head slowly. "Stockholm for me. These years away, they'll have forgot me, the shopkeepers and the high ones. There'll be my new land, their shops and purses."

The two men turned squarely to each other a moment, as if a good-bye was about to be offered. Instead, Karlsson gave Braaf the quick serious smile and said: "Life's harvest to us both, Braaf."

Meeting the ocean swell at the mouth of the Strait of Juan de Fuca, the brig rocked and dipped as though in introduction. A bob and curtsy, it may have been, for the vessel was christened the *Jane*.

A quick ship, the *Jane*, as a Cape May brig will be; but also being of Yankee registry, a working and earning one too. Within its hold lay eleven thousand feet of recent forest, freshly taken aboard at one of the sawmill settlements that were popping into existence along Puget Sound the past year or so. Piling stock constituted this particular cargo, plump round Douglas fir to underpin the docks of one of America's new ports of the Pacific.

Now, outbound, the *Jane* rode clear of Cape Flattery, let out full sails on both its masts, then bore away in the direction of the most robust of those ports —San Francisco–ward, south.

Three hours from then, off the top of the island Wennberg came tumbling.

"Karlsson! Braaf! Christ-of-mercy, out there—!"

Respectful of the turbulent coast, the *Jane* was ranging two miles or more out from shore, and by the time Karlsson and Wennberg and Braaf clambered up to Wennberg's sighting point the ship already was drawing even with the island.

In Karlsson's mind the choices ran: Canoe . . . no, full sails bent that way, the ship couldn't be caught or even gained on. Even could the Swedes paddle into view of the vessel, logic would account them Koloshes from this village, all the better to be left back there sniffing wake. . . . Signal fire . . . same. Even build one instantly, what sane captain would heave in along this howling canyon of a coast? But the whale people, they were more than guaranteed to be attracted across by any such smoke. . . . Gunshots . . . same again, only quicker doom. . . .

Evidently at different pace and route the same sorting had been racing in Braaf and Wennberg. Wennberg was yet squinting dismally toward the ship when Braaf swung to Karlsson.

"Sailcloth," agreed Karlsson, and Braaf was gone for it.

Careful to be always below the seaward brow of the island, walled from any Kolosh glance from the mainland, they flapped sailcloth. Flapped it as if trying to conjure flight, a man at each end of the length of fabric, third man jumping in whenever a pair of arms gave out, the fabric bucking as if in anguish to join that clan of sheets kiting atop the *Jane.*

Whichever of the three was not pummeling the air performed the steady yearning toward the *Jane* with the spyglass, rifle of vision aimed in search of a lens ogling back. But found nothing but portrait of a ship on the wing. Wennberg's wishful curses ran steady as incantation, ought in themselves have wrought some drastic change in the brig's glide. Caused the mainmast to split and crash over. Tumbled the cabin lad overboard. Invoked Neptune to rise and shoo the ship back north. Tugged loose the sails and tangled them so thoroughly the captain would trice her right around. Any miracle, whatever style, would do.

Those sails continued to waft serenely southward.

Leaving Wennberg and Braaf and Karlsson to stand and watch the distancing ship like men yearning to dive to a cloud.

The day at last declining toward dusk, Karlsson took the glass and eased to the downcoast end of the island to study the shoreline ahead. Wennberg was staying atop the island to brood, Braaf was back at watching the Koloshes demolish the whale. Since the passing of the ship, both wore a look as though they had just been promised pestilence.

. . . Danced right by us. Damn. All the days since New Archangel, and a ship chooses this goddamned one. Damn, damn. Hadn't been for the Koloshes we'd right now be . . .

With the glass Karlsson checked back on the villagers and their whale festival. Wood was being piled up the beach from the carcass. Evidently the celebration was going to rollick on into night.

Something flitted, was down among the shore rocks before Karlsson could distinguish it. Birds of this shoreline evidently had caught motion from the surf. Sanderlings, oystercatchers, turnstones, dowitchers, snipe, along here always some or other of them bobbing, skittering, dashing off; the proud-striding measured ravens of New Archangel were nowhere in it with these darters. Contrary another way, too, this southering coast was beginning to show itself. Its clouds were not the ebb and flow skidding about above Sitka Sound, but fat islands that impended on the horizon half a day at a time. Here it seemed, then, that you could navigate according to the clouds' positions, and that the routes of birds had nothing to teach but life's confusion—which it would be like both weather and wingdom to deceive you into.

Karlsson one more time put his attention south.

The withdrawing tide was lifting more and more spines of reef to view. But no beach was coming evident, just a broad tidal tract of roundish rocks, as if the farm fields of all the world had been emptied of stone here. Or, cannonball-like as these rocks looked to be, it might be said battlefields.

Beyond the stone clutter no islands stood to sight, only the bladed outlines of seastacks. Many of them. All in all, Karlsson saw, this appeared the rockiest reach of coast yet, and it needed be paddled past by night and a landing made on it somewhere in earliest dawn.

. . . Day this has been, even that can't be much damn worse. . . .

"Burning the goddamn world over there. What in the name of hell d'you suppose they're up to?"

The villagers' beach fire just had flared high, a puff of sun against the dark, from a bowl of whale oil flung onto it.

"Whether they mean to or not, they're making us a beacon to steer from awhile," Karlsson answered Wennberg. The three canoemen hefted, and the canoe left land, caught the water's pulse.

Not since taking their quit of New Archangel had they paddled at night, and the memory of that stint did not go far to reassure anybody.

Ordinarily dark was Braaf's time, the thief's workplace. But here in the canoe with blackness around, Karlsson could sense Braaf's distrust of the situation, feel how his paddling grew more tentative, grudging, than ever.

Wennberg at the bow meantime seemed in every hurry to yank them through the night single-handed; *his* paddling was near flail.

Karlsson drew breath deep, exhaled exasperation oh so carefully, and decreed:

"Hold up, the both of you. We need to flap our wings together. At my word, do your stroke. Now . . . now . . . now . . ."

The night Pacific is little at all like the day's. With the demarking line of horizon unseeable the ocean draws up dimension from its deeps, sends it spreading, distending, perhaps away into some blend with the sky itself. If stars ever kindle out there amid the wavetops we need not be much surprised. And all the while every hazard, rock, shoal, reef, shelf, snag, is being whetted against the solid dark.

In their watch for collision Wennberg and Braaf and Karlsson stared tunnels into the black. From Wennberg's harsh breathing and undervoice curses, every instant that catastrophe did not occur only convinced him that it was overdue.

"How far are we going in this?" Braaf this was, his

tone suggesting that he for one had gone a plentiful
distance.

"Far enough past those whale stabbers. Unless you
want to sail in on them and ask breakfast. Put your
breath to work. Now . . . now . . . now . . ."

. . . There's a night I don't need to live again. But
now there'll be tonight. That ought do it, put us past
the country of those whalemen at least. Then we can go
by day, like men with eyes. . . .

As if it was nothing to yacht along this coast, gulls
were drifting up a current over a headland to the
south. Karlsson was studying the rock-cornered shore
beneath the gulls, a half mile or so from this crescent
of beach where the canoe had put in at dawn. The
credit of the night was that the canoe and its men
survived it, not met with stone in the dark. Its debit
had been the interminable wait offshore for daybreak,
the canoe tied to a patch of bull kelp, Karlsson keeping
a watch while Braaf and Wennberg tried to doze, before the coast could be studied for a landing site and
any sign of Koloshes. Now it must have been noon or
past, all of them having slept deep as soon as the canoe
was lodged from sight behind shore rocks. Afternoon
would have to be waited through, until the launch into
dark again. Meanwhile this thrust of shore to their
south . . .

. . . Might be. Just might by Christ be. Chance to
go shake the bush and find out, anyway. . . .

"We've maybe been looking the wrong direction for game," Karlsson mused aloud. "Forest instead of ocean."

"What, then"—Wennberg—"go shooting at fish, are you? About like you, that'd be." By now even the blacksmith had thinned drastically, his blockiness planed away to width. Their last few meals had been beans and mussels and clams, the shellfish a slow pantry to find and gather. Without fresh meat all three canoemen soon would be husks of themselves.

"Fish, no. But a hair seal, maybe. If they've followed season to these waters . . . that point across there, it's the sort they lie around on."

"Gunshot, though?" This doubt from Braaf.

"A lot of noise from surf there, all that rock. And we can gander around the headland for Koloshes before getting onto the point."

Wennberg hitched his trousers, maybe calculating all the new room in them. "I could eat a skunk from the ass forward. If you think you remember which end of the goddamn gun to point, Smålander, I'm for it."

Karlsson checked Braaf, received a slow nod. And made it decision: "Let's go find supper."

Plump jetsam on the outmost of shore, the seals were there.

So was a new style of coast to any the Swedes had seen yet. Having clambered downbeach to the point, the three found themselves at the inshore edge of a rock shelf high and flat as a quay—although no one but nature could employ a quay some two hundred paces wide and that much again in length. Odd in this, too: in the blue and brown afternoon, the Pacific tossing bright around the somber rock face of the coast, this huge queer natural wharf lay thinly sheeted with wet, like puddles after rain.

By now Braaf had tides in his bones alongside the weather. "The high drowns all this, then," he stated, nodding the attention of Karlsson and Wennberg to the remnant pools. "We'll need be quick." Even as Braaf said so, earliest waves of the incoming tide tried to leg themselves up over the seaward edge of the rock quay.

"Quick we'll be," Karlsson responded and was in motion while the words still touched the air. "Over here, that horn of rock."

Onto the tidal plateau he led the other two, to where a formation the height and outline of a sloop sail bladed up. Beside this prong, from view of the seal herd, Karlsson studied out ambush.

Leftward, the rock shelf lay open and bare. Any least twitch of invasion there would be instantly seen by the seals.

To the right, close by Karlsson and Wennberg and Braaf, the ocean with undreamable patience had forced a tidal trough—a lengthy crevasse bent at the middle, like an arm brought up to ward off a blow. Every insurge of surf slopped a harsh compressed tide through this shore crack, a hurl of water as if flung from a giant pan, and the crevasse gaped wider than a man would want to try to jump. No surprise to the seals from this foaming quarter either, then.

The sea end of this trough, though. There a fist of boulder met the ocean, and just inland toward the men bulged a low knurl of rock off that formation. A wen on the back of the tide-rock wrist, you might think of it.

. . . Little help but some help. I'll need make it be enough, won't I. . . .

"I'll shoot from there," Karlsson indicated the wen site ahead to Wennberg and Braaf. He made the short crawl to the hump, Wennberg scrabbling behind on the left and Braaf vastly more agile to the right. They hunched either side of Karlsson, Wennberg breathing heavy, Braaf soundless, as the slender hunter peered to the seals.

"What do they taste like?" Braaf wondered in a whisper.

Karlsson's shake of head confessed lack of acquaintance.

"Pork," reported Wennberg. "The liver's just like a hog's."

The other two looked at him. "Spend the years I did at New Archangel," Wennberg said, "a little of goddamned everything crosses your plate."

The seals lay idle as anvils. Some had been lazing in the sun long enough that their fur had dried pale, others yet were damp and nearly as dark as their rock promenade. All of them were toward a hundred paces from where Karlsson lay sighting. He disliked the dis-

tance for the shot, but decided to amend what he could
of it by singling out a seal that lay a bit inshore from
the others. A young bachelor, bullied into solitude by
the older harem-masters of the herd.

"Tickle luck's chin," Braaf said softly as Karlsson
aimed.

"Or it's smoke soup tonight," Wennberg muttered.

Karlsson's shot struck the seal in the neck, not far
beneath the base of its head.

A lurch by the animal. Its foreflippers and tail
flapped briefly. Then the head lowered as if into doze.

. . . Fetched him! Shot-and-pot, we'll surprise our
bellies yet. . . .

Meantime, the other seals writhed rapidly toward
the rock edge, were gone.

"Square eye, Karlsson!" Braaf congratulated. He
was first onto his feet, stepping to the right of the
bump of rock Karlsson had shot from, Wennberg and
Karlsson up now too, the three of them setting off in
hurry toward the seal, the tide in mind.

Of what happened next, only this much is sure. That
amid a climbing stride by Braaf as he began to cross
the wrist of rock, surf burst its power in front of him.
That a startling white weight of water leapt, seemed to
stand in the air. That it then fell onto Braaf.

Comical, this ought to have been. A drenching, an
ass-over-earhole tumble as Wennberg might have said,
and there the sum of it, Braaf bouncing up now with a
grin of rue. But the topple of water slung Braaf backward more than that and the hand he put down to halt
himself met the wet slickness of brown rockweed.

Braaf slid on into the tidal trough.

Above, Karlsson and Wennberg, half-turned in stare to the crevasse water, were twins of disbelief.

Braaf was vanished.

Then, and a long then it began to seem, up through foam bobbled Braaf's head. For a breath space, his eyes held the affronted look they'd had when Wennberg's boot clattered the spittoon in the officers' clubhouse.

Next the insurging tide shot him from view of Karlsson and Wennberg around the bend of the trough.

. . . Rifle, reach the rifle to him, only chance . . .

Down toward the trough Karlsson clambered, Wennberg heavily at his heels and cursing blue. The footing along the top of the trough was treachery itself. Karlsson and Wennberg skidded like men on soapstone as they tried to approach the edge.

The out-slosh of the tide brought Braaf whirling back below them, grabbing with both hands at the walls of the trough, barnacles and mussels denying him grip and costing him skin. This time it was around the trough's seaward bend that the riptide tossed him from sight.

"Hold me," Karlsson directed Wennberg.

The burly man clamped his arms around Karlsson's knees as Karlsson stretched himself flat, down toward the spilling water. Like a man peering down a well, Karlsson now. With both hands he held the rifle at its barrel end, thrust the stock into the channel as Braaf popped to sight once more.

"Braaf! Grab! We'll pull. . . !"

A wrath of water—it bulged a full three feet over all other froth in the channel, as if some great-headed creature was seeking surface—careened in. Surf spewed over Karlsson and Wennberg, both of them clenching eyes tight against the salt sting.

When they could peer again, Braaf bobbed yards past them on the landward side, his boy's face in a grimace. He seemed to shake his head at them. Then the tide abruptly sucked back toward the ocean and Braaf was spinning toward his rescuers once more, his arms supplicating in search of the gunstock.

But short, a hand's length short . . .

. . . God's bones, it never behaves the same twice. Need be quicker, make ready . . .

"This time, Wennberg! Lower me more, there, now'll reach . . ."

The pair of them stared expectation toward the seaward corner of the trough, bracing themselves for the riptide's return and the hurl of spray over them once more.

It arrived, crashing high along the trough walls, hard spatter, runnels down faces, now eyes could open again . . .

This time the tide had not brought Braaf back with it.

"Braaf!" demanded Wennberg. "Braaf, where the hell—?"

Karlsson scrambled wildly for the ocean edge, banging knees and hands on rough rock, Wennberg lurching after him.

The coastal afternoon's same royal colors of blue and brown were all about the two men, the horizon brow of the planet untroubled out there in front of them, the Pacific's flume of surf flowing as ever to their left and right; the single absence was Braaf.

In the surf's froth, very white beside the rock shelf, Karlsson and Wennberg scanned frantically for other color. Occasionally they glimpsed it, as you might see a bright-headed dancer a quick moment across a crowded room. The straw yellow of Braaf's hair, all but concealed in the tumult of the water and being banged north along the jagged rock shore.

SIX

Two now. But why that. God's bones, why, *why?*
Why one slip and Braaf's gone from life? That how
it'll happen, each by each of us? This coast snare us
each like that? But Braaf. Braaf, oh Christ, Braaf. I'd
give half my life to have it not happen, what did. Gone,
though. Taken water for a wife, the schoonermen say
of it. Why. And pair of us now, we're not much better
off than him. You were the tip weight of us, Braaf, kept
us level. Turn on me, Wennberg had you to worry about.
Go for you, there'd be me sharp on him. But now . . .
Wennberg'll be trouble's trumpet now. Can hear him
over there, what must be whispering in that head of

his. "Oh Christ—the doom on us—the fish-fuckers shot Melander, Braaf tumbles in a millrace—now just the pair of us and I can't trust this Smålander any farther than I can fart—not after the maps—not after this—" Need to tamp him. Someway. Else we're dead men too, waiting to fall. Not the way of it, this shouldn't be. We've done the work of the world, since New Archangel. Done Melander's plan this far, every hair of it. Ought be enough. But always more. Wennberg, he's the first work now. Working slow. Braaf told of that. Braaf, Braaf. Swimming the air with Melander, I hope to Christ you are. And now I go over to that bull and work slow. . . .

"I should've. Oh, I should've done you the other night. Slit you loose from life. Braaf and I'd kept on somehow, we'd've managed. But you, you're black luck if there ever was. The maps, and then those Kolosh whale hounds, now this—"

"You do me, Wennberg, and you've done yourself. Fed yourself to ocean or Koloshes, choose your devil."

They were either side of the canoe, the afternoon graying away, the coast gone somber. Tide was still high, covering the point where Braaf had been lost—and the seal as well, slosh up to the knees of Wennberg and Karlsson when they struggled toward the animal, before they saw a retreating wave swash the gray form back into the ocean. Then the wrangle, on and on—"fucking squaw rider you, if you'd had the maps none of this"—"maps are wish, Wennberg, miles are what we need, so just"—until every word seemed to be out of the both of them. They were weary, groggy, lame in the head. Being deprived of Melander had been like the stiffening of an arm or leg, they somehow learned to function in spite of it, gimped their way onward as they had to. This loss of Braaf was more a warp of the balance within the ear. Nothing stood quite where it had before. And when the lurch of argument and temblors of predicament at last shook the two men silent, Karlsson knew he needed to begin his true labor. And so did.

"Can't paddle in daylight, you say yesterday," Wennberg had responded somewhere between bafflement and fury. *Beware the goat from the front, the horse from the rear, and man from all sides*, ran a saying of the New Archangel Russians. Everything of Wennberg recited this caution into Karlsson now. Yet Wennberg had to be worked back to the journey, into the canoe, brought around from Braaf's . . . "Now it's can't paddle at night. Tell me this one thing, Karlsson. This one goddamned sideways thing. Where're you going to find us hours that aren't one or other, day or night? Whistle up your ass for them, are you?"

"Dusk." Karlsson had repeated it carefully. "Dusk, Wennberg. We need make a short run of it, until we figure we're clear of any Koloshes along here. Just the two of us paddling now, we've got to learn about that, too. So we need do it. Steal enough twilight to paddle an hour, maybe two, we can. Whatever we make is gain toward Astoria."

Now, the day stepping down toward dark, Wennberg sighed dismally, squinted to the ocean, gray and steadily grayer, as though it were dishwater and he were being asked to drink it at a swallow.

"Wennberg, we need do it."

As the two canoemen paddled they could make out that timber still spilled like a dark endless waterfall over the rim of the continent, but all else here looked more and more like old outlying ruins of the vigorous mountain coast behind them to the north.

The growl of the surf was constant on their left. Ahead, a high-sided squarish island, like a fort just offshore, stood in black outline. Two big sharkfin seastacks guarded its oceanward side.

"Country you wouldn't give the devil," Karlsson heard Wennberg say.

Through the near dark they achieved a half-handful of miles, put behind them the fortlike isle, before Karlsson, hoping he was reading this scalloped shore aright, pointed the canoe in between two headlands.

He strained now to pick shapes in the water before them, felt Wennberg ahead doing the same, heard him mutter.

Three, four, half a dozen rocks humped to view in an area the size of a commons field—and none more.

The route clear, the canoe drove in to one more haven of shore.

The camp this night, without Braaf, was like a remembered room with one wall knocked out.

Almost nothing was said during eating, and less after. Karlsson watched Wennberg occasionally shake his head and tug at his whiskers, as if in wonder at where he found himself now. But none of his usual almanac of complaints, nor any newly-thought-up blaze to hurl at Karlsson. Just those grim wags of head.

Trying to hear into that silence, Karlsson knew, was going to be a long piece of work.

The morning showed the two that they were on a beach as fine as velvet, gray-tan and nearly a mile long. At either end of the sand arc rough cliffs rose and pushed a thick green forest up into the sky.

On the cliff rim directly over Wennberg and Karlsson one small tree stood alone in crooked dance, as though sent out by the others to dare the precipice.

Here the surf was the mildest they had seen, only a single wave at a time furrowing in from the ocean. Yet the crash of the water came large, entirely outsize. And out on the horizon the Pacific was playing with its power in another way as well. There white walls periodically would fling up and at once disintegrate in spray—waves hitting on reefs. Unnerving, these surprise explosions as if the edge of the world were flying apart.

This landing spot presented them what Karlsson had hoped profoundly for, a deep view of the coast ahead. What the two of them saw was a shattered line of headlands, shadowed by seastacks in shapes of great gray shipsails and dark tunnel mouths; sea rock various and jagged as a field of icebergs.

"Not that jungle, Karlsson." Wennberg licked his lips, wiped a hand across. "Not in goddamn night nor even dusk, we can't."

A pair of kingfishers chided past, sent a jump through both men with their raucous rattle.

Karlsson returned his look to the tusked coast ahead.

. . . "Chose wrong," Melander told the bastard a time. "Brought you instead of your forge and anvil, they'd been easier to drag along this coast than you." Still, Wennberg's right. Two of us can't handle the canoe well enough. And if there's luck at all in life we ought be down far enough from those whale chasers. . . .

The two were keeping obvious distance between one another this morning. And the dagger was a new feel along Karlsson's left side, inside his rain shirt where he had slipped it the night before; where he would be carrying it from now on. He figured Wennberg was doing the same.

"Then the other time is now," Karlsson answered the blacksmith.

That day and all the next Karlsson and Wennberg pulled past shattered coast, watching into the seastack colonies and the warps of shore for Koloshes as boys would peer through a forest for sight of one another.

. . . Like trying to see through a millstone, this line of coast. There's this, the Koloshes don't seem to fancy the place either. Maybe better tomorrow. It's all dragging work, though. Here on, just the two of us to paddle, that's what it'll need be. All dragging work . . .

And each dusk, came ashore like old women stiff in the knees. Wennberg encouraged a fire while Karlsson gathered mussels or clams, whatever could pass as a meal. Only after they had food in them were they able to face the chores of night, finding water, wood supply, putting up the sailcloth shelter, laying groundcloth and blankets, covering the canoe against possibility of storm finding their night's cove. And after those, face the loneliness which occupied where Braaf ought to have been.

. . . It needs to be the pair of us against this coast now, blacksmith. Ironhead. Just that, no other load on our backs. You're five kinds of an ox but that much you can see, when your temper isn't in the way. If just Braaf . . . "If" is fairy gold. Make it past, what happened. Ahead, we need to point. Wennberg, though: can I keep you damped down. . . .

And again in the morning, nerved themselves and pushed the dark canoe into the surf of the North Pacific.

"Beach!" Wennberg was pointing. "Beach like heaven's own!"

"What was that?" Night down over them now on this sand shore, Karlsson was at the fire boiling clams for supper when Wennberg came and tossed something into the flames.

"That Aleut calendar of Braaf's, found it in the bottom of the canoe." Wennberg picked up a drift branch to add to the fire. "Won't be needing it in eternity, him."

Karlsson reached, plucked the branch from Wennberg, with it flipped the little rectangle from the fire. Its edges were charred and the day-peg browned, but the wood was whole.

"What's that for, then?" demanded Wennberg. "Every damned day along here is every other damned day. It helps nothing to keep adding them up. Why count misery?"

"Maybe not. But this ought be kept." Karlsson set to shaving the char off the calendar with his dagger, then moved the peg the three days since Braaf had gone into the tide trough. A cross-within-a-circle. Russian holy day, Pure Monday or St. Someone's birthday or who knew what . . . Karlsson realized Wennberg still was staring at him. "It's all we have of Braaf."

"All we—? Of *Braaf?* That hive of fingers—?"

Karlsson stopped work on the char but held to the dagger. He took long inventory of Wennberg. Finally, as if not at all keen on the result:

"Braaf happened to be a thief, and he happened to be as high a man as any. I know there's little space in there for it, but try to get both those into mind."

"Karlsson, I'll never savvy you—" Wennberg's eyes slid from their lock with Karlsson's. The dagger had come up off the charred wood.

It paused. Then the blade thrust under the bail of the kettle.

The slender man hoisted the mealware from the coals and set it to the ground.

"Food," said Karlsson.

The coast uncluttered itself for them for the next three days. The beaches stayed steadily sand, and ample, while the ocean and continent margined straighter here, as if this might be a careful boundary of truce. Waves arrived cream-colored, then thinned to milk as they spilled far up the barely tilted shore. Once in a while rocks ganged themselves along tide line, but nothing of the dour constant throngs of the days just past. The dolloped stone islands quit off too, except the one early on Karlsson and Wennberg's second morning of this new coastscape, a long stark bench out a few miles in the ocean.

One last new reach of coast, then, and its visible population only these two kinned against their will, the one family of the kind in all creation, slim Swede and broad Swede arked in a Tlingit canoe.

The beach at the end of the third of these days was widest yet. Wide as kingdom after the ledgelike wecks to the north, somehow a visit of desert here between timbered continent and cold ocean. Five stints of pushing, each a contest against an ever more reluctant sledge, it took the pair of men to skid the canoe in beyond the last mark of the tide.

Scoured shore, too. Between surf and high tide line

nothing but a speckle of broken clam and sand dollar shells, suggesting that only sea gulls prospered here.

Inland, the sand began to rumple. Over the line of dunes, like the spiking on a manor wall the top of forest showed.

"I ought go have a look," Karlsson offered.

"Look your eyes out, for what I care."

The dune grass poked nose-high to Karlsson and he climbed the crest of a sand wave for better view. Before him now, swale of more sand, a couple of hundred strides across. Then a second rumple of slope, scrub evergreens spotting this one. Tight beyond that, forest thick as bear hair.

Southeast, though; southeast, the magnetic direction of this voyage: southeast the spikeline of timber barbed higher. Two plateaus of forest spread into the horizon.

Karlsson hadn't the palest inkling of what would mark the river Columbia, whether some manner of Gibraltar attended it—from what Melander had told of the river's mightiness and to go by this coast's penchant for drama of rock, that seemed fitting—or whether sharp lower cliff, as at the Strait of Fuca, simply would skirt away and reveal Astoria. A considerable opening in the coast earlier this afternoon had shown the Swedes disappointment. Only bay or sound, not vast river mouth. Wennberg still was in a grump from it.

And here, put as wishful an eye to this set of bluffs as he could, Karlsson could not believe them into likelihood as river guardians. They rose inland from the shore a half mile or so, and did not shear away as if a river was working at them. Greater chance that they were just two more of all such continental ribs he and Wennberg already had peered at on this coast.

. . . Not there then, where to hell is it? God's bones, how much farther? . . .

Eyeing around, Karlsson found himself unexpectedly longing for the narrow northern beaches, the wild scatter of seastacks, the tucked coves where they had made grateful camp. Even the clatter of gravel being shoved by the surf, he missed here. These milder beaches promised ease but nicked their prices out of a man. Mussels had vanished with the shore rocks, so desperation's larder here was clams, dug laboriously with Karlsson's ax. Pawing like twin badgers down into the tide line holes, Karlsson and Wennberg were all agreement on one thing, a desire for a spade. No, two things: the other, that boiled horse clams were furnishing survival but they were tough dismal fare after a day of paddling.

. . . Maybe tomorrow. Day of Astoria, maybe it'll be. Some day or other will be. . . .

Karlsson faced back toward the Pacific. There was this, too, in his lack of preference for this new run of coast. On the sand expanse where the canoe stretched at rest and Wennberg was propping the sailcloth shelter, there was nothing whatsoever they could do to put themselves from sight. This beach held the canoe and its two men prominently as three sprats on a platter.

The rough tongue of the wind started on their shelter early in the night.

Noise of the sailcloth bucking woke Wennberg a minute after Karlsson.

"Blowing solid, sounds like," the blacksmith imparted. And the next minute, was slumbering again.

Karlsson, though, still lay awake when rain began to edge into the wind sound.

By morning, the storm was major. The tide was up so alarmingly that Karlsson at once went and drove a stake of driftwood into the sand with the flat of his ax, as a mark to watch the inflow against. Sails of spray flew in off the wave crests, and the wind struck so strong now that even its noise seemed to push into Wennberg and Karlsson. And all that day as the two hunched under the shelter when they weren't having to foray out for firewood or to try to dig clams; all that day, downpour. At New Archangel they had known every manner of rain, but none of it anything to this. This was as if the sky was trying to step on them.

The Indian arrived at the Astoria customs house with an item and a tale. South from the village his people called Hosett he had gone to hunt seals but soon sighted instead a great tangle of kelp brought inshore by the tide, and the kelp had seined in with it the body of a white person. Now he had adventured downcoast aboard a lumber ship to report of this find. "Tole," the native said, the coastal jargon word for "boy." Not until he pantomimed and pidgined the description of a downy fluff of beard did the customs collector grasp that a grown man was being depicted.

With thought of the days of sloshing canoe travel it would take to reach the coastal spot and return, the customs collector prodded hopefully: And . . . ?

And the Indian had done the disposition, rapidly buried the corpse in hope that the spirit had not yet got out of it. But had thought first to clip proof for his report. He handed the customs collector a forelock of straw-colored hair.

That the weather since Christmas had been violent against vessels trying to cross the bar into the Columbia River was all too well known to the customs collector. *Merrithew, Mindoro, Vandalia, Bordeaux*—two barks and two brigs, they all had gone to grief along this rageful coast in these weeks.

Taking up his pen, the collector wrote the native his paper of reward: *The bearer of this, Wha-laltl Asabuy, has assisted the duties of the Astoria District of Customs Collection by his report of* . . .

He then turned to his daybook and began the official epitaph of Braaf: *A body, supposed from one or another of the vessels wrecked north of Cape Disappointment during this fearful winter, has come ashore near the Makah village of Hosett.—It is that of an unknown young seaman, light hair, round-faced* . . .

By the end of the day, rain still blinded the coast.

Karlsson took out the Aleut calendar from the map case where he was keeping it now. Moved the peg rightward one hole. A moment, contemplated the little board.

. . . Might as well know as not. Pass time by counting time, that's one way. . . .

It came out a few weeks worse even than Karlsson had thought. Since they had left New Archangel, sixty-four days.

Russian Christmas more than two months into the past. In the woods edging Sitka Sound, now buds of blueberry would be beginning to swell.

Karlsson looked across to Wennberg; decided the arithmetic of their situation would not be welcome news in that quarter; and put the calendar back into the map case.

"Småland," said Wennberg, startling him.

Karlsson waited to see what venture this was.

"Småland. What sort of place's that? What I mean, what'd you do there?"

Karlsson eyed the burly man. There had been a palisade of silence between them, the only loopholes Wennberg's curses against the weather and Karlsson's setting of chores. All other conversation the storm's— low grumble of surf, whickers of wind, drone of rain on the shelter cloth. Into the night now, Wennberg evidently was at desperation's edge for something other to hear than weather.

. . . Come off your tall horse, have you? . . .

"Farmed. My family did." Melander's description of farming arrived to mind. "Tickled rocks with a plow, more like."

" 'If stone were hardbread Sweden'd be heaven's bakery,' " Wennberg quoted.

247

"Yes. And the family of us, living at each other's elbows. Left the farmstead when I was thirteen, me."

Karlsson reached a stick, tidied coals in from the edge of the fire. These days and weeks of his mind always leaning ahead, aimed where the canoe was aimed, it had been a time since he thought back. But memory, always there in its bone house. What can it be for, remembering? To keep us from falling into the same ditch every day, certainly. But more, too. Memory we hold up and gaze into as proof of ourselves. Like thumbprint on a window, remembering is mindprint: *this I made, no one else has quite the pattern, whorl here and sliver of scar there, they are me*. Karlsson was in Småland now, hills of pine forest, cottages roofed with sod and bark—and yes, stone in the fields and rye short as your ankles and a Karlsson tipped from the land to find what livelihood he could. . . .

"On a forge by thirteen, I was," Wennberg was saying. "Apprenticed, so I had to hammer out plowshares. Thought my arms'd break off. Bad as this bedamned paddling."

Wennberg when young—he was the fifth son, the last and stubborn and brawlsome and least schoolable one, of an inspector of mines in the Nordmark iron district —Wennberg when young already was a figure that might have been knocked together in one of the red-glowing forges of Värmland. Who can say how it is in such instances, whether the person simply has chanced into the body that best fits him or whether the body has grasped command of that mind: but Wennberg as boy looked just what he was, a blacksmith waiting to happen. A beam for shoulders, arms plump with strength. A neck wide as his head. Very nearly as thick, too, in all senses.

"At least there's an end to this paddling."

"Maybe. Could be wrong kind, though. Melander's had his end, and Braaf his."

"And chewing over their deaths doesn't undo them. Wennberg, each day we pull ourselves nearer to Astoria."

"Or to drowning or to Koloshes or to Christ knows just whatever. I ought've taken my death and been done with it, the day somebody spoke 'Merica to me."

Of that continent which had begun to pull Swedes as the moon draws the tides, the young blacksmith knew only the glittering pun its word made against the Swedish tongue. America, 'Merica: *mer rika, more rich.* That there somehow was a Russian 'Merica besides the one that the Swedish farm families were flocking to mystified Wennberg only briefly. He imagined the 'Mericas must be side by side there the other end of the ocean, that the ship made a turn like going down one road fork instead of the other. Then word arrived to the Nordmark region, in the person of a merchant over from Karlstad, that the Russians were recruiting blacksmiths to work iron in their America. Wennberg's father, heartily weary of a son with temper enough in him to burn down Hell, managed to see to it that Wennberg was one of the three smiths chosen, and that Wennberg went off south across the Gulf of Bothnia with the others to meet the Russian ship at Sveaborg. They were joining the voyage of Arvid Adolf Etholen, a naval man of

Finnish-Swedish lineage serving as an officer of the tsar and now to become the new governor of Russian America. Wennberg never worked clear how it was that Etholen could be simultaneously Swede and Russian and captain and governor, but then Wennberg had ahead of him years of finding out that double-daddle of such sort was not rare where the Russians were concerned. A Russian system, at least as he found it practiced in Alaska, did not need make any too much sense, it simply needed be followed relentlessly and the effort pounded into it would eventually force result of some sort out the far end.

"You can't close your ears always," Karlsson said.

"Maybe not," concurred Wennberg. "The trouble is to know when the devil's doing the talking."

Finns predominated in the number that voyaged for Russian America during the term of Etholen; weavers, masons, tanners and tailors, sailmakers, carpenters. But for ironwork a Wennberg was wanted. The forge must have been the cradle of these Värmland Swedes. So Wennberg was shipboard with new governor Etholen's entourage those nine months from the Baltic to New Archangel in 1839–40. Etholen with his prim little divided mustache and those hooded eyes which seemed to see all over the ship at once; he was said to know more of Alaska than any of the tsar's men since Baranov. And Etholen's big-nosed young wife, pious as Deuteronomy recited backwards; and Pastor Cygnaeus, and the governor's servants, and the naval officers; oh, it was high carriage and red wheels too, for a blacksmith to be journeying in company with such as these.

"Tell me truth, Karlsson," Wennberg blurted now. "How many more days d'you think it can be? To Astoria?"

Karlsson, carefully: "There's no count to what you can't see, Wennberg. I'd give much to put a finger a place on Braaf's counting board and say, 'Here. Astoria day, this one.' But we can't know that. We can just know tomorrow will carry us closer to it."

Wennberg shook his head. "I've played cards against men like you, Karlsson. They count too much on the next flip from the deck."

"While your style won you the world?"

Wennberg's embarkation to Russian America carried him to a fresh corner of the planet, a familiar livelihood and religion, and a doom. At first, curiosity was all there was to it, a way to ease hours—watching the card-players. Then he edged into the gaming, merely an evening now and again, which in a feet-first fellow such as Wennberg truly shows how guardful he was being. Some money vanished from him in the first years but not all so much, no amount to keep a man awake nights. Besides, Pastor Cygnaeus was one to inveigh against waywardness, the devil's trinity of drink and cards and the flesh; and as it is with those who have some of the bully in them, Wennberg by close-herding could be bullied in the general direction of moderation. But came the spring of 1845, Pastor Cygnaeus departed New Archangel, sailed back for Europe with Etholen at his end of term as governor. Wennberg yet had two years of indenture and during them his gaming, and all else, changed.

"Back there at the tide trough."

Karlsson waited, impassive.

"If I'd been to the right of you and Braaf to the left, I'd've gone into that millrace instead of him."

. . . If that'd been, my ears would get rest this night. . . . Aloud: "If the moon were window we could see up angels' nighties, too. Lay it away, Wennberg." Less than anything did Karlsson want to discuss the perishing of Braaf. "Tomorrow paddles will still fit our hands, and the canoe will still fit into the ocean. Live by that."

Wennberg moved his head from side to side. "You can wash your mind of such matters, Karlsson. I can't. Death this side of me and then that, I need think on it. See through to why I was let live."

"Maybe God's aim is bad."

"No, got to be more to it than that." Wennberg would not be swerved. "Maybe like sheep and goats. 'And He shall set the sheep on his right hand, but the goats on the left—' No, Braaf was to the right—"

"Wennberg. Stow that."

Wennberg peered earnestly through the firelight to Karlsson. "You know what the pastors'd say, about all this."

. . . No, and I damn well don't give a . . .

"They'd say I'm being put to test. All this, bedamned coast, you other three, Koloshes—" Just now a thought could be seen to surprise Wennberg: "Maybe even you, too, Karlsson! Being put to test!"

Proclamation of his eligibility did not noticeably allure Karlsson. "Wennberg, I know at least this. We're not playing whist with God along this coast. Either we paddle to the place Astoria or die in the try. One or other. Just that."

Wennberg shook his head. Not, as it turned out, against Karlsson; the pastors. "But they don't know a thumb's worth about it either. Found that out, I did, when it happened with—with her."

Karlsson looked the question to Wennberg.

"Katya," the blacksmith said.

"Katya?" Karlsson echoed.

"My wife." Wennberg wiped the back of his hand across his mouth, as if clearing away for the next words. "Think you're the only one ever looked at a woman, do you? You've fiddled your time, north there. You know what the creole women can be, the young ones. Black diamonds, the Russians call them. Katya was one, right enough— But why'd she die?" Wennberg's look was beseeching, as if Karlsson might be withholding the answer. "If she hadn't, I'd not be in all this. God's will, the pastor said. God's swill, right enough, I told him back. What kind of thing is that to do, kill a man's wife with whooping cough? Didn't even seem ill at first, Katya. Just a cough. And then—'O satisfy us early with Thy mercy,' that clodhopper of a Finn preaching when we buried her on the hill. Mercy? Late for mercy on Katya. And me. How's I to go through life with her grave up there on the hill from me all the while? If I could've bought my way out of that Russian shitpile, back to Sweden. If the gambling'd worked—"

Evenings, that summer of 1845, a particular plump Russian clerk sat into the barracks card games. Three times out of five now, when this clerk departed the table he took with him just a bit more of Wennberg's money than Wennberg ought to have let himself lose. Nor was Pastor Cygnaeus' successor any help as a vigilant; he too suffered from that same soul sweat, New Archangel ague, the fever of cards at night and clammy remorse by day. Before Wennberg quite knew any of it, then, the fetters of debt to the company and of more years in Russian 'Merica were on him, and Wennberg had turned with fury against a God who let such chaining happen and a God's man who stood by mumbling while it did. Against, it might be said, life.

"—but no, oh no, and God's little Finnlander telling me, 'Steady yourself, Wennberg, keep from the cards,' and himself squatting at the table with the Russians half the night. Man of God. God doesn't have men, he has demons of some kind to strangle women with the whooping cough and blast the back of the head off Melander and drown Braaf like a blind pup—"

Wind flapped the shelter cloth behind Karlsson's head, rain still was pelting. He and Wennberg in shared life those hundreds of days at New Archangel, now these dozens in the narrow canoe and beside the campfires, they had wrangled and come to blows, might yet come to worse, how was it you could be wearily familiar with every inch of a man and know not much of him at all? Unexpected as winter thunder, something like this, and as hard to answer.

"Wennberg, I—"

"What you said, just then." Wennberg was looking harshly across at Karlsson. "That about the cards. More than style is in it. Luck. Luck I haven't had since Värm-

land, except the goddamn black sort that ended me up
with you."

It had quickened past them, the moment. They were
plowshare and rock again. Karlsson heard himself saying as stone will answer iron—

". . . you've had some in plenty, recent days."

"What, dragging along this boil-and-goiter coast?
You call that luck?"

"The two of us who are dead, neither of them is you.
There's your luck, Wennberg. Now shut your gab and
get some sleep."

At morning, sky and shore showed hard use by the
storm. Both were smudged, vague. The rain had dwindled and the wind ceased, but less than a quarter mile
in each direction from Wennberg and Karlsson and the
canoe, fog grayed out the beach.

. . . Fog ought mean the wind is gone, we won't
swamp. But this cloud on our necks we won't see along
the coast, either. Stays sand beach, that won't matter.
Rocks though. Rocks'd matter. Can't mend it before it
happens. Rocks we'll face when they face us. . . .

"Whyn't we go it afoot, here on?"

Say for Wennberg that in his tumbril way, he had
come this far past Braaf's death, past the rock-spiked
coast, past the end of regular food, before balking. Not
that Karlsson could see any of the credit of that, just
now. What he turned to face was an unsailorly weary
man who did not want to set forth in a canoe into fog.

This new corner of reluctance on Wennberg took all

of the early morning to be worked off. Karlsson's constant answer was question back: what when they hiked themselves to a river, or another sound, or headland cliff? Swim, Wennberg? Take a running jump at it? Fly?

"But goddamn, out into that cloud—beach here like a street, maybe there won't be water in the way—"

"Wennberg. Ever since New Archangel, there has been. Wish won't change that. There'll be water."

When at last the jitter wore out of Wennberg, he looked spent. So much so that Karlsson came wary that the man's next notion would be not to move at all. As wan as a man of his bulk could be, Wennberg this day. Plainly, the clam ration and the dreariness of hunkering in from the storm had exacted much from him.

Wennberg cast Karlsson up a look, though, and fanned enough exasperation in himself to blurt:

"Karlsson, one more time I hear 'need to' out of you and—"

"You'll be that much closer to the place Astoria each time you hear it. Off your bottom now. This's as close a tide as we'll likely get."

By the time they pushed the canoe the distance across the sand to the tide line, both were panting and stumbling. Wennberg hesitated, looked back at the beach. Then surf surged in, swirled up his shins. Wennberg shoved the canoe ahead, half-clambered half-fell into the bow.

The most wobbly launch of the entire journey, this one, the canoe nearly broaching into a wave before Karlsson managed to steer it steady.

Straight out to ocean they paddled, until Wennberg stopped stroking and turned to demand: "Where to hell're you taking us? Shore's almost out of sight."

"We need to stay out from those surf waves or your belly will be visiting your mouth again. I'll head us by compass the way the coast has been pointing."

Wennberg could be seen to be choosing. Seasickness, or swallow Karlsson's notion of voyaging all-but-blind.

He said something Karlsson couldn't catch. And dipped his paddle.

Fog, gray dew on the air. During a rest pause Karlsson touched a hand to his face and found that his beard was wet as if washed.

Fog, the breath of—what, ocean, sky, the forest? Or some mingling of all as when breath smoked out of everyone at New Archangel the morning after the December snow?

Fog, and more of it as the canoemen labored southeast. Through this damp sea-smoke the shore was a dimmest margin of forest, now glimpsed, now gone.

This day, different eyes had been set in the heads of Karlsson and Wennberg. Nothing they saw except the beak of the canoe had sharpness, definite edge to it. This must have been what it would be like to drift across the sky amid mare's tail clouds.

. . . Got to be near, Astoria. All the miles we've come. Can't have gone past. River mouth would tell us,

Melander said it's a river of the world, big as Sitka Sound. Can't have missed that. . . .

In the slim space of the canoe the two of them now were the pared outlines of their New Archangel selves. The canoe, though, seemed to have grown; looked lengthened, disburdened, with a pair of men astride it rather than four.

As best they could, Karlsson and Wennberg settled to terms with the shadowless, unedged day. Their paddling was slow, with frequent need to rest. In what might have been the vicinity of noon they ate cold clams from the potful Karlsson had cooked the night before. Two-thirds of the total vanished into them, and each man could have immediately begun the meal over. But Wennberg said nothing to Karlsson's policy that they needed to save the remainder for midafternoon.

The close fog. Somewhere in it over there, the sand haunch of coast they were trying to trace along.

Paddle swash and silence, silence and paddle swash. Untended, a mind let them take it over. Karlsson shook his head sharply.

* * *

Cold clams again, sips of water. Then two pairs of callused hands, resuming paddles.

End and beginning, land and water, endurance and task; the Pacific's fusions seemed to distill up endlessly, persist into the mind as if the fog was the elixir of all such matters. Into a belowstairs corner of this ocean— the year, 1770—another of Cook's vessels nosed. An inlet was about to be dubbed Botany Bay and the moment was history-turning, arrival of white exploration to an unknown coast of Australia. A hundred five feet long and thunderheads of canvas over her, Cook's *Endeavour* swept in from the sea, while the black people on the shore and in the bay registered—nothing. Past fishermen in dugout canoes the great ship hovered, and the fishermen did not even toss a second glance. A woman ashore looked to the *Endeavour*, "expressed neither surprise nor concern," and squatted to light her meal fire. Too strange for comprehension, Cook's spectral ship to the aborigines; *in the dreaming*, they accepted it to be. An apparition, a waft of the mind. Just so, here on their own gable end of the Pacific, was the fog taking Karlsson and Wennberg into a dreaming of their own. Through the hours it shifted, and diluted, then came potent again: the vast hover of coastline north behind them, Alaska to Kaigani to Vancouver to wherever this was, the join of timber to ocean, islands beneath peaks, tsarmen beside seven-year men, Koloshes beside whales; it curled and sought, then to now: Melander's vision of how they would run on the sea, and Braaf's single stride wrong on this inexorable shore, and Karlsson day by day finding dimension he never knew of, and Wennberg in over his head as he always would be in life; it gathered, touched its way here in the mind of one paddling man and there in the mind of the other: all a dreaming, and not.

Somehow the two canoemen stretched what was left of their strength, did not give way until the day at last did. Dusk and fog together now, shore as well as canoe clasped into their cloud.

Watching how sluggish Wennberg had become, Karlsson was not certain he was any better himself. Thirty more, he vaguely heard himself decide. Aloud, to Wennberg? He wasn't sure.

Those thirty strokes numbly done, Karlsson turned the craft toward where the compass said shore ought to be.

"How to hell far out'd you take us?"

"Ought be almost in now."

"Where's shore, then?"

"Just ahead."

"Maybe that compass's gone wrong, maybe you've steered us to sea—"

"We're with the tide, Wennberg. Can't be taking us anywhere but in."

"This goddamn fog."

"Wennberg, listen."

"So? You think you can say anything that'll bring shore, fetch it out—"

"Not to me, goddamn it. Listen for rocks."

"Rocks? What, you—?"

Karlsson and Wennberg both had stopped paddling, the canoe being carried by the tide, the slosh of surf now near in the fog. Both listening, listening until it seemed each ear must narrow as a squinting eye would.

But the slosh around them stayed steady, no under-drum of tidal rock anywhere behind it, and the canoe continued to be carried in.

The sightlessness seemed to extend time, the ride through slosh went on and on. Still no beach, no dark bank of forest.

They were onto shore before they ever saw it. The canoe simply stopped, as if reined up short.

Karlsson and Wennberg lurched out of the canoe and sank ankle deep into tideflat. "Muck," said Wennberg as if it was exactly what he had expected. And then they pushed, the canoe asking shove and shove.

Amid one, Wennberg slipped. He fell from view, splatted somewhere below the wooden wall of the canoe.

Karlsson labored around the craft.

Wennberg was elbowing himself from the mire, like a person trying to rise out of a deep soft bed. Karlsson got him up. Mud coated Wennberg's legs and his left side to the shoulder.

They went back to shoving. Finally the canoe was beyond water and mud. Only then could the leaden men beside it see the forest, a tangle at the edge of the fog and near dark.

Something of the landfall nudged at Karlsson. But couldn't surface through his weariness. It was as much as he could manage to grasp that the fog had not fed Wennberg and him to the coast's rocks, that they had fumbled the sailcloth and blankets out, that Wennberg already had sagged off under them, that he too now was being let to sink from the day.

It shot clear to Karlsson as he woke in the morning. . . . Wrong side. Sweet sweat of Christ, water's to the wrong side of us, how . . .

Water east rather than water west, and water that was not ocean but a broadsheet of bay, miles of it.

Through the hills across the bay a silvery haze hung, but Karlsson could make out that those hills and the shore forest all around were like the Alaska coastline pressed down and spread: rumpled and green but low.

Karlsson clambered across the beach toward the tree-line for higher view, turned, scanned fervently. Beyond the canoe, across the broad brown tideflat, into all the blue of water, his search: and nowhere in it, any steady move of current which would mark a great river flowing out.

. . . Drifted us in, blind as kittens. But in to where? . . .

Its scatter of water across greatly more geography than it had depth for gave name to the bay: Shoalwater. A startling washout in the southern Washington coast,

Shoalwater Bay pooled across nearly ten miles at its widest and managed to stretch itself southward another twenty-five. A kind of evergreen fen country, Shoal-water, taking some eons to decide whether to remain tideflat and marsh or to danken into forested swamp. Tide, current, channel, seep, all were steadily at work on the decision, sometimes almost within splash of each other. Shoalwater's modest rivers, though, along the eastern bayside, seemed ambivalent. During the sleep of Karlsson and Wennberg those streams had been flowing into themselves, turned backwards by the Pacific-sent tide advancing between their banks; for some hundreds of yards at each mouth, the Willapa, the Querquelin, the Palux, the Naselle were slowly creeping back toward their origins, like bolts of drab cloth surreptitiously trying to roll themselves up.

Karlsson's eyes were correct. Shoalwater Bay was not the mouth of the great river of the west of America, Astoria's river. No, it still was beyond the southern squishy extent of Shoalwater that the Columbia shoved forth into the Pacific. Four miles beyond.

Something in Wennberg had gone slack. Karlsson's rouse of him took minutes and when at last he was upright, he looked pale and bleary. Caked mud from last night's tumble covered his britches like scales.

Wennberg shivered and sat with slow heaviness onto the gunwale of the canoe. "Caught a chill, must've."

"Here." Karlsson teetered a bit himself as he shawled a blanket over the blacksmith's shoulders. He noticed there even was a clot of mud in the man's sidewhiskers. "Wennberg, get awake. We need to make a fire and try this tideflat for clams."

Wennberg sat staring along the rippled mud and tidewater. "Where to hell are we?"

"In a bay, looks like."

Wennberg hugged the blanket more snug around him. "Are we there?"

"In a bay, yes. Get up now, we'll fetch firewood."

"Astoria. Are we at Astoria?"

"Not yet. Get up."

Wennberg still was staring out along the tide line. "Karlsson," he intoned. "Karlsson, what're those?"

Karlsson turned for a look.

"Is it? Got to be—" Wennberg was haggard, hung between hope and alarm. "Karlsson, is it?"

Karlsson still studied into the bay. He and Wennberg had slogged a few hundred yards north for a closer gaze. "I—don't think so."

"Got to be! What the hell are those, if there aren't whites here to put them up? Karlsson, this's got to be the Columbia mouth, people here—"

Karlsson tried to make his mind work past Wennberg's insistences, figure what the thin shapes rising from the water could signify. Four wands of them, like long, peeled willows implanted out in the tidewater, their small bare branches forking to the sky. Standing like four corners of a plot of —water? Tidal muck? Wenn-

berg had the point that they'd never seen anything of
the sort done by Koloshes. But if whites had markered
here, why? And where was sign of anyone, except these
skinny corner posts of nothing?

. . . Still no river current. Can't be the Columbia,
this. We need go on. But why four sticks, middle of
nowhere . . .

All the desperation in Wennberg seemed to be coming out at once. He swayed around wildly scanning the
bay. "Whites've got to've done those. Marking off some
goddamn thing or other. Around here somewhere—"

. . . Wennberg, easy with this. There's no . . .
Karlsson realized he was not saying aloud, began to:
"Wennberg . . ."

"Karlsson! Give a look!"

. . . Oh Christ, he's moonstruck about this, how'll
I . . .

"No, there!" Wennberg was pointing farther north
along the low shore. "There, there!"

The cabin sat in the mid-distance, on the far side of
where the tideflat made a thrust into the beach.

Not since New Archangel had they set eye on such a
dwelling, a spell of houselessness which asked some moments of blink to cure itself, to allow in the news of
peaked green roof, weathered gray walls, hearth,
warmth—

"Those markers out there!" Wennberg, all over himself with excitement. "Told you there had to be whites
here! Fishermen of some sort, must be, planted those
sticks! Christ-of-mercy, let's get ourselves across there!"

Into the muck the pair of men plunged.

Impetus of all the voyage moved their legs now. The distance down the precipice of coast since New Archangel, the pieces of ocean like an endless series of waterfalls, the cold burn of North Pacific wind and current, all now pushed these two grimy men like pebbles in a torrent.

Whenever he had breath Wennberg hallooed, his calls hoarse and lonely in the stillness.

The prospect ahead lensed everything around Karlsson. The cabin yet held back within the dim tones of mud flat and sea grass around it, but spatters of muck flying up from his boots, the motions of his own arms and hands as he lunged forward and forward, the mud man who was Wennberg beside him; Karlsson was aware of the crystal memory of each as they arrived into him.

Twice more Wennberg hallooed. "Got to be someone about, got to," he insisted.

They labored two-thirds of the distance to the cabin before Karlsson could make himself bring out what was wisping in his mind.

"Doesn't look right."

"We don't give a fly's shit how it looks," Wennberg panted. "Just so it's roof and walls."

"Wennberg. Wennberg, it's not."

"Not? Skin your goddamn eyes, Karlsson, it's right there, it's—"

But a further twenty yards dissolved the cabin details entirely. All the Wennbergs and Karlssons of the world could have put wish to it at once and still the profile would have been only what it was emerging as. The green roof roughening into growth of bush. The weather-silvered curve of wood, high as the men, dropping pretense of gray cabin wall.

A huge butt of cedar drift log, nursery of salal atop it. Mammoth chip from this coast of wood, undercut by some patient stream or other and carried in here, years since, by the tide.

Karlsson swallowed, felt an ache sharpen itself behind his eyes.

Wennberg stood and shook his head like an ox discouraging flies. "Why couldn't it've been—"

The way one plods the distances of a dream, both of them slogged on to the huge log. Wennberg slumped against it, sagged until he sat with his back to the silvered wood. His knees came up and his head went down to them.

Karlsson leaned against the inland edge of the log, propped his weariness there. A rust was spreading in him. Judgment, movement, both now seemed so tedious that he had to force his mind to them.

. . . Done it all this far. Done the work of the world. Can't end here. Oughtn't. Need to see how . . .

Karlsson made his feet turn until he was viewing north along the bay edge.

. . . Bay and bay and more of it. Got to be a mouth there somewhere. Over those dunes. Find it, figure . . .

"Wennberg. Wennberg, we need go for a look. Just over there. Find how to get the canoe out of here."

"No use to it." The blacksmith's tone was muffled, head still to his knees. "No use," he droned. "Just more muck."

"The bay mouth. Need to see what it's like."

"No."

"It's our only way out of here."

Wennberg did not answer.

"You'll stay here to the log, then." Karlsson tried to focus instruction. "Just where you are."

. . . He goes off into the mire and tide catches him, there'll be his end. Ironhead he is, but not that. Doesn't deserve that. . . .

"Wennberg! Wennberg, hear me! You'll stay to the log. Aye?"

"Stay—" agreed the muffled voice.

Karlsson aimed inland, off the mud of the tideflat. When he reached sand and made his turn north, now he was wallowing through dune grass high as his waist.

. . . Maps, we'd know. Could see to the place Astoria, on them. But we'd still be in here. . . .

He pushed the grass aside as he trudged, until he felt its sharpnesses biting at his hands. To stop the stabs he brought his hands up and in, put his elbows out, woodsman's habit against brush.

. . . Step it off. Like pacing where the tree'll fall. . . .

The whetted grass was on all sides of him now, color of a faded rye field, lines of these sown dunes rolling parallel with the bay.

. . . Guts are out of Wennberg. Someway get him on his feet, get us out. . . .

Whiteness stroked up into the sky, in a slow strong swim passed before Karlsson. Two yellow eyes estimated him harshly.

The snowy owl flapped far into the dunes before perching again.

Karlsson tramped on north until it came through to him that the footing was wavering, creeping in front of him. A slow crawl like tan snakes: sand blowing in ropy slinking patterns. He was out of the dune grass. Water lay a meadow's width in front of him.

Now at water edge. Beautiful blue.

Peering out into the bay entrance which the fog had poured them through.

Squinted to be sure of what he was seeing.

Instead of surf stacking against the shore three and four and five deep as had been happening all along this coast, here the waves flowed and flowed, breaking into the bay as if in stampede. They flashed, right, left, and before, across the entire neck of entrance. A mile-breadth of whitecaps.

Karlsson stared long at the breakers, willing against what he knew to be the truth written white in them. Even could he persuade Wennberg back to the canoe and they someway summoned muscle to launch into the mud bay, against such flow as this the two of them were too weary to paddle through to ocean. Never in this lifetime. Whatever candle end of it was left to them.

. . . Melander. Then Braaf. Oughtn't happened, either time. They were keeping in life, bending themselves to our voyage. So why . . .

The dune grass was attacking the backs of Karlsson's hands again.

. . . Hadn't been for the last storm and the fog we'd maybe done it. Be at Astoria now, wherever place it is. Wherever . . .

Whatever figure it took in his mind at any moment, one constant mood was within Karlsson now. Anger at how it was all turning out. The way their lives had been, these vast weeks of dare since New Archangel; and tall clever Melander gone, and deft skylark Braaf; and Wennberg, even Wennberg had earned survival, broken that Kolosh canoe and provided more than his share of paddle strokes, paid out what endurance he had. Not right, that it all dwindled to this. This jinxed goddamn day. Karlsson despised the injustice of it. Whetted his resentment on its minutes. Aimed his aggrievedness to the sand defying his feet.

After long, the surface under him changed. Slogging on the tidal mud again now. The gray log with its wig of green was ahead.

Wennberg was against the log as he had left him.

Karlsson reached down, gripped a wide shoulder. Wennberg was shivering again and when he lifted his head, his eyes were indifferent.

Karlsson sought anything to say. Everything now seemed too major for words.

Wennberg mumbled something, and lapsed off again.

. . . Finish me, Wennberg made me the promise once. At least we've jumped that. No need, coast'll do it for him. . . .

The cost of air is mortality. This principle Karlsson now knew in every inch of himself.

. . . Not yet though. Not just damn yet. Takes God and his brother to kill a Smålander. . . .

Karlsson put his back against the high drift log, could feel the cedar grain beneath his fingers. Against every urge of the fatigue all through him, did not let himself sit but stayed propped there, looking across the tideflat to the shore forest. To the blue spread of bay. To the four marking sticks, tall and thin and stark, striking their reflections crooked across the tidewater. To a lone dark stretched form between the mud and the timber which, his mind slowly managed to register, was the canoe.

SEVEN

THE dark-bearded man carried a lamp to the table, trimmed the wick, lent flame to it from a kindling splinter lit at the fireplace; established the lamp at the farthest side from the draft seeping in under the cabin door, then sat to the pool of yellow light.

Across the next minute or so he fussed at the materials that awaited on the table. Unusual, but he was a trifle uneasy with himself. It being Sunday night, he was going to need to trim scruple next. Keeping the Sabbath ought be like a second backbone in any New England man, even one away here as far west from Vermont as you could venture and not fall off America. But in the morning Winant's schooner *Mary Taylor* would sail from the bay and packet the mail out with it, possibly three weeks, a month, intervening before the next postal opportunity. Too, there was the consideration that Waterman paid coin for worthwhile report, and the clink of specie was rare sound at this back corner of frontier. . . .

He slid the paper to him, dipped the goosefeather pen to the ink, and began.

Shoalwater Bay
March 20ᵗʰ 1853

Mr. John Orvis Waterman
Editor, Oregon Weekly Times

Dʳ Sir—On Monday last, as I was riding with my son Jared to examine our oyster bed at a tideflat north of our land claim, our attention was taken by a column of smoke. Knowing that no settler dwelt in that vicinity, we thought to investigate, a vessel perhaps having run aground near the bay mouth there.

Much was our astonishment to find, beside a big tidal log, two men, much emaciated and looking the perfect pictures of misery and hardship. One of the poor fellows could only utter again and again '*Merica*, '*Merica*, so fixed was his mind on their arrival to this portion of America. The other man, a slender sort worn thin to the extreme by their ordeal, we could speak with, but could not make ourselves understood. *Astoria* was his oftenest word, and by trying our utmost, we at last conveyed to him that that locality lay just beyond the southern reach of the bay, on the opposite bank of the Columbia River.

We cooked a rough stew of some venison jerky we had with us, the pair eating as though they never could be sated. We then contrived to lift them onto our horses and after taking them to our house, summoned some of the other settlers from around. Among us since the grounding of the *Willimantic* in Gray's Harbor has been a Dane, dwelling at Chinook, who was steward of that vessel, and through his endeavors we succeeded in conversing with the hard-used pair. Their history is as follows:

In 1850 they engaged to work for the Russian Fur Company seven years, and accordingly embarked, in company with eighteen others, for the northwestern coast, bound for New Archangel. After a residence of nearly two years, they found they could not bear the ill usage which they were receiving, and determined to make their escape. They were four, who determined on that leave-taking. At a place beyond Vancouver Island, one of their number was slain by the Indians. A second unfortunate was drowned in the descent of the coast between the Strait of Fuca and here.

When found, the two who have survived had been in this bay for a span of time they did not know. They mistook the large drift stump for a cabin and were very nearly done up by their exertions to reach it. The more slight of the pair, and thus better fitted to tread his way atop the tideflat, returned to their canoe—a craft about twenty feet in length by three in width, sprightly built;

and with this they have made a winter voyage of over a thousand miles on one of the worst parts of the coast! —and from there fetched a cylinder of maps enwrapped in waterproofing. With these large sheets, and flint and steel, and branches and driftwood got from around, he was able to construct atop the log the smudge fire which signaled us to their aid.

They are well cared for by the citizens here, and at present are comfortably situated at Chinook, whence they will be taken across the river to Astoria when their strength is sufficient.

Their names are Nils Karlsson and Anders Wennberg, and they are of Sweden.

Yours &c
Jonathan E. Cotter

The End

AUTHOR'S NOTE

IN THE WORDS of an admired friend, the novelist
Mildred Walker, my sea runners "have lived only in
the world of this book." But their life in these pages
does draw breath from actuality. According to a contemporary letter-to-the-editor in the *Oregon Weekly
Times*, during the winter of 1852–53 oystermen at
Shoalwater Bay (modernly renamed Willapa Bay)
north of the mouth of the Columbia River came upon
three men, "the perfect pictures of misery and de-
spair," who had achieved a canoe voyage down the
Northwest coast from indentureship at New Archangel. Their names were reported as Karl Gronland, An-

dreas Lyndfast, and Karl Wasterholm; a fourth man, whose name was not reported, was killed by Indians along the way. Their great and terrible journey is not known in detail. I would hope that Melander, Karlsson, Wennberg, and Braaf are in the spirit of those actual voyagers.

Naval Captain of Second Rank Nikolai Yakovlevich Rosenberg and the Lutheran pastor, and Whalaltl Asabuy and the Astoria collector of customs, did exist but their conversations herein are imaginary.

To cut down on complication, I've employed present-day usages in the following instances: Alaska as synonymous with Russian America; Baranof as the name of the island which in 1853 was still called Sitka Island; and governor for the personage whose title in Russian is more accurately "chief manager."

The term "pood" is a Russian unit of weight equivalent to 36.11 pounds.

Kaigani Strait herein is not the modern-day passage between the Alaskan islands of Dall and Long, but the contemporary Russian designation of Dixon Entrance.

Arisankhana Island is a composite of the Northwest coastal islands from whose names I made it up.